The MAIDENSTONE LIGHTHOUSE

Books by Sally Smith O'Rourke

THE MAN WHO LOVED JANE AUSTEN

THE MAIDENSTONE LIGHTHOUSE

Published by Kensington Publishing Corporation

The MAIDENSTONE LIGHTHOUSE

SALLY SMITH O'ROURKE

KENSINGTON BOOKS
http://www.kensingtonbooks.com

KENSINGTON BOOKS are published by

Kensington Publishing Corp.
850 Third Avenue
New York, NY 10022

All Kensington titles, imprints and distributed lines are available at special quantity discounts for bulk purchases for sales promotion, premiums, fund raising, educational or institutional use.

Special book excerpts or customized printings can also be created to fit specific needs. For details, write or phone the office of the Kensington Special Sales Manager: Kensington Publishing Corp., 850 Third Avenue, New York, NY 10022. Attn. Special Sales Department. Phone: 1-800-221-2647.

ISBN-13: 978-0-7582-2064-6
ISBN-10: 0-7582-2064-2

First Kensington Trade Paperback Printing: September 2007
10 9 8 7 6 5 4 3 2 1

Printed in the United States of America

For Michael

From ghoulies and ghosties
And long-legged beasties,
And things that go bump in the night
Good Lord deliver us.

—Scottish prayer

Chapter 1

In October I came to Freedman's Cove.

Though more than three months had passed since I'd lost Bobby, I had not yet regained the ability to cope with the everyday demands of my life in the city: I was still searching the faces of strangers glimpsed through the rain-streaked windows of passing cabs. Still hoping against desperate hope that the next tallish, fair-haired man I spotted coming toward me on the street would turn out to be my Bobby. Still forgetting for minutes on end that he was truly gone.

I suppose I was more than half-convinced then that he was suddenly going to appear around the next corner and rush to embrace me, explaining between urgent, tearful kisses where he had been for so long. Explaining why he had never called to tell me he hadn't died after all.

Denial is the clinical term for the way I dealt with the news of Bobby's death. Which is to say that I did not deal with it at all. Perhaps I clung so doggedly to my forlorn hope of finding him again in some familiar place because that was exactly the sort of thing that might have happened when he was alive.

And then there were my daydreams.

In my favorite waking fantasy, Bobby had come home

again at last. Though I was terribly angry with him over the agonies I had suffered through a hundred lonely nights of bitter tears, the pain always melted away like springtime snow at the first brush of his lips against mine. And our renewed lovemaking was possessed of an intensity that transcended mere passion.

Afterward, naked beneath our warmest down comforter, we'd cling desperately to one another in front of a fire in the smoky old fireplace he'd kept promising to fix but never had. And after we'd ordered take-out from the little Greek place down the block, flushed from hours of lovemaking and too much of the blood-red Cape wine he'd brought from a trip to Africa, I'd listen dreamily to the details of Bobby's miraculous escape from certain death.

For, despite what the Royal Australian Navy had reported, it would turn out that his plane hadn't really gone down in the shark-infested vastness of the Indian Ocean after all. Instead, blown far off course by a sudden storm, and with all its radios out, the damaged aircraft had crash-landed on a tiny island, an uninhabited speck of land the searchers had overlooked because it was so far off the plane's planned route of flight.

As he related the incredible story of his survival to me, Bobby's mischievous blue eyes would sparkle in the firelight, and he'd somehow manage to make the entire incident seem funny and not even very dangerous. So that by the time he was describing how he had built a clumsy bamboo hut on the beach and tried unsuccessfully to catch fish while he waited for a passing ship to rescue him, there'd be tears of uncontrollable laughter rolling down my cheeks.

But that was all just in my lovely fantasy.

Because, in real life at least, six-hundred-mile-per-hour business jets like the one that Bobby had been piloting when he disappeared last July do not make forced landings on uninhabited tropical islands. And, even if they did, everyone onboard would almost certainly be killed in the fiery crash that an off-airport landing in a crippled jetliner virtually guarantees.

Grim reality is the proper term for that.

So absolutely nothing about my waking dreams of Bobby's return was real.

Nothing but my tears at the end.

Laura, the svelte, softly tailored Park Avenue shrink I visited a few times after I realized I was slipping deeper and deeper into my fantasies, says that delusions like mine are quite common following the death of someone very dear to one's heart, especially when there is no physical proof to confirm the awful finality of the loss.

Physical proof, of course, was Laura's delicate way of referring to Bobby's absent corpse. For, as she had carefully explained on my first visit, without a cold dead body to see and weep over, a funeral to grieve at or a gravesite to visit, the dearly departed tend to remain forever vibrantly alive in the memories of their loved ones.

In such cases, Laura professed, it is often death itself that seems like the delusion.

I knew exactly what she meant.

Bobby dead at thirty-two! *My* Bobby, who had survived half a dozen near catastrophes in his career, first as a daring young navy carrier pilot, then, later, flying tiny geological research planes into the teeth of Arctic blizzards for a North Slope oil outfit. Bobby dead! The very idea was incomprehensible to me.

Because while I was painfully aware that my handsome

love had spent most of his brief adult life deliberately taunting the Grim Reaper in the sky, hadn't I also nagged, threatened and browbeat him into quitting that dangerous game?

I can still remember the words of heartfelt thanks I whispered to Heaven on the day he finally gave in to my desperate pleas. Because I knew it was for me alone that Bobby had traded his exciting, high-risk North Slope job for the dull, blessed tedium of piloting executives around the world in the oil company's shiny new Gulfstream 550 corporate jet.

"I look like a damn bus driver."

That had been his joking complaint as he stood before the bedroom mirror adjusting his uniform tie early on the morning of the first day he was scheduled to fly the Gulfstream on a trip. At first I couldn't tell whether he was truly annoyed or just having fun with me.

Reaching around to help him with the tie, I had stopped to stare at his reflection in the mirror. I'd grown so used to seeing him off to the airport in his beat-up old navy flight jacket and jeans that the effect created by the dark blue captain's uniform required for his new corporate job had taken me completely by surprise.

Standing there that morning, all sharply creased and clean-shaven, and with the pink light of dawn glinting on the silver wings above his left breast pocket, he had looked like nothing so much as a heroic young Brad Pitt on his way to some exotic destination where he would, doubtless, save the world.

"Some bus driver," I'd breathed, slipping my fingers lovingly inside the jacket and caressing the snowy fabric of his crisply starched shirt.

"Well, this corporate job is going to be just *like* driving a bus, but without the element of danger."

Bobby had laughed then, turning to flash me that devastating movie-hero smile before gently kissing my lips. "Sweet Sue," he whispered, using the silly pet name he knew I loathed, "I hope you're happy now that you've thoroughly domesticated me."

"Mmmm, yes," I sighed, moving as close as I dared without rumpling the beautiful new uniform, and feeling in the warmth of that wonderful possessive kiss that he was only pretending to be upset with me over the boring new assignment.

But happy was not the word I would have chosen to describe the secret emotions I was experiencing at that moment. In truth, I was positively ecstatic, because I was so sure that I had done the right thing by forcing him to change jobs.

It's funny how decisions that we think at the time we're making for all the right reasons can seem so foolish in retrospect. For I can clearly see now that I had only been acting selfishly then—because I was so much in love with Bobby that I couldn't bear the thought of ever losing him.

But, of course, I lost him anyway. And, irony of ironies, it was the "safe" plane, the thirty-million-dollar high-tech corporate jet that I had so calculatedly pushed him into flying that had carried him to his death.

If . . . if he really was dead.

If . . .

That was invariably the first word that ran through my mind every time I thought of Bobby dying. Because it just didn't seem possible that he could have kissed me goodbye on that last glorious morning in July and then simply flown out of my life forever!

But that was exactly the way it happened.

Weeks passed after I got the news, then months, the initial shock and numbness of my freshly minted grief slowly turning to doubt and, finally, conviction that Bobby might somehow have survived. Until no matter how I tried I could not put away the feeling that there had to be some grotesque mistake, that he could not be gone.

And even knowing to a logical certainty that there was no possibility of a mistake did nothing to alleviate my guilt and pain.

I began imagining that I had caught fleeting glimpses of Bobby, speeding by me in a passing subway train, ducking into a doorway across a traffic-filled street. That was when my giddy daydreams of his safe return began to haunt me, in the end making me fear for my own sanity.

Predictably, Laura the shrink had assured me in her best clinical manner that there was absolutely nothing at all wrong with my mind. Nothing that time and modern pharmacology would not eventually heal. So she prescribed an antidepressant and had me join a grief-management group comprised of other miserable souls who, like me, had recently lost loved ones of their own.

I went to one group meeting where I wept uncontrollably for a distraught young mother whose beautiful five-year-old son had darted out in front of a midtown bus in pursuit of a wayward kitten and had been instantly killed. I left feeling even worse than I had before.

"Well, group doesn't always work for everyone." With that remark and a small wave of a perfectly manicured hand Laura casually dismissed her first shot at ending my anguish. She had then prescribed a new and even stronger antidepressant and suggested that I go away for a while, preferably to a place where I had spent little or no time with Bobby. A place that was essentially free of his memory.

Praying that she was right, for I had no wish to spend

my life in perpetual mourning, I threw away Laura's new prescription and went to see Damon, my partner in the antiques appraisal and authentication business that we had founded together half a dozen years earlier, when we had both been penniless art students.

Chapter 2

How can I possibly explain Damon if you have never known him? After nearly a decade of friendship I still find it difficult to accurately describe my odd and funny little partner in any terms that don't seem hopelessly clichéd.

Oh, his physical description is easy enough. Imagine if you can, a wild tangle of untamed dreadlocks surrounding a shiny, round ebony smiley face. Place that silly head atop a short, comical figure that seems precisely as wide as it is tall. Now, drape the whole lopsided creation in a wardrobe tending toward the sort of shiny tights and billowing sleeves you might find in a bad high school production of *The Pirates of Penzance* and you'll have an approximate snapshot of Damon.

Not too surprisingly my strange friend's manner closely matches his clothes. For he is always flamboyant, often outrageous and, sometimes, thoroughly ridiculous. Bobby once jokingly remarked that Damon reminded him of the rubber Michelin Man on uppers.

Damon is nothing short of brilliant with an eye that can spot from a hundred paces the slightly improper curve of 19th-century feet that have been cleverly "married" to a 17th-century French Provincial sideboard, with the devious intent of elevating its value by some tens of thousands of dollars. Let him poke around removing drawers and examining the piece for a few minutes and he'll identify the wood by its grain and color alone, and name its precise region of origin. Given a few more minutes, Damon will probably come up with the exact year of manufacture, the cabinetmaker's name, and then go on to inform you that it was actually the man's youngest son, a deaf-mute, who added that tiny, exquisitely carved floral relief to the drawer fronts.

In the highly competitive world of high-end antiques, Damon St. Claire is more than conventionally brilliant. He is legendary.

When we were at NYU together Damon frequently skipped classes in order to haunt the museums, junk shops and galleries of the city, in search of beautiful furniture. And while I often went along on his excursions for fun, I was generally content to merely observe and admire the rare and valuable objects that he invariably discovered.

But not Damon.

Damon had to lay hands upon the satiny woods, sniff the scents of the centuries-old glues and lacquers, trace with his short, stubby fingers each cunningly wrought curve and plane of the exquisite Italianate chair found tucked away in a forgotten corner of the Met, or the dusty Georgian settee discovered in some Village pawnbroker's dusty storeroom, as if by so doing he was able to somehow read the secret history hidden at the heart of each lovingly wrought masterpiece.

Visiting a museum with Damon was like participating in a terrorist raid. And many's the time I served as his lookout—me, the demure young college girl lurking in a doorway, pretending to be studying an exhibit brochure—while my dwarfish accomplice was behind the velvet ropes in the next room, mumbling like a demented witch doctor over some priceless artifact or other.

Despite the fact that we actually lived together for more than a year—if sharing two drafty rooms in a SoHo walk-up could actually be called living—everyone who knew us then was absolutely certain that Damon was gay. And perhaps he is, though I have never heard him utter so much as a single word expressing lust or longing for another living soul of either gender.

As far as I know, Damon's passion is and always has been reserved exclusively for the fabulous objects of earlier times.

When we were living together our small circle of artist friends considered Damon's obsession with furniture to be nearly as hilarious as his appearance. At least that was how they felt until the incident that later came to be known as The Armoire Affair.

It all began with the news that an extremely rare and beautiful Louis XV armoire was to be sold at auction. Damon, who even when we were starving, always managed to obtain the elaborate and glossy catalogs that exclusive auction houses send out to carefully preselected buyers, usually at a cost of several hundred dollars per copy, had merely glanced at the full-page color photo and accompanying description of the fabled French armoire.

Then he pronounced it a fake.

Because he claims to loathe writing, he drafted me to compose a brief note to Christie's, the auction house that was handling the sale of the armoire. In the letter I carefully explained why the alleged masterpiece could not possibly be genuine.

Not surprisingly, Christie's was underwhelmed by our brash analysis of the Fabulous Object. In fact, they did not even bother replying to our letter. Three days later, we read that the French armoire had been sold for $450,000, at the time a near-record price for a piece of 18th-century European furniture.

So you can imagine our astonishment when, several months after the auction had taken place, we received a mysterious luncheon invitation from Sir Edward North, Christie's senior curator of European decorative arts.

Sir Edward, a scholarly Englishman who looks as if he belongs in an Oxford lecture hall, apologetically informed us that our letter had been misplaced until long after the sale of the French armoire. But when he had finally gotten around to reading it, the prim curator confessed, he had instantly realized that he and his firm had been embarrassingly duped by an antiques forger.

A forger who was clever, but not as clever as Damon.

What had impressed Sir Edward most, he continued during the course of that extraordinary luncheon, was not the fact that Damon had detected a subtle inconsistency that exposed the fraud—an exotic hardwood mentioned in the catalog as part of the armoire's inlaid marquetry was a rare mahogany found only in the Brazilian rain forest, a section of the world not explored by Europeans until well *after* the reign of Louis XV—but that he had done it without ever having seen the armoire itself.

The persistent curator had then offered Damon a staff position at Christie's that seemed like exactly the kind of job my eccentric friend might have spent his whole life dreaming of.

But, to my utter amazement, Damon had flatly refused, explaining that he wouldn't consider any job that required him to remain in one place every day, much less one that involved the writing of long and dreary appraisals. He had to be free, he said, free to wander his beloved museums, galleries, junk shops and libraries, as his whims, appetites and hunches dictated.

Desperate to have the mad genius at his disposal under any terms, Sir Edward had immediately countered by offering Damon a position as a consultant with a generous monthly retainer. At that point, Damon had looked over at me and asked if I would be willing to write up his appraisals and handle the finances of such an arrangement.

Thus was born our little company, St. Claire & Marks, official consultants and appraisers to Christie's. A long list of prestigious dealers, insurance companies and private collectors had quickly followed suit, all in time becoming loyal clients.

In the six years that we had been in business together, I had never once asked Damon to write an appraisal or even to make regular appearances at our small midtown office.

But now I had no choice.

Because of my growing inability to deal with Bobby's disappearance, I absolutely had to get away from New York for a while. Perhaps a very long while.

And though I knew Damon loved me like a sister, I was not at all certain how my free-spirited partner was going to react to my urgent request that he take over the daily running of the business while I was gone.

I should have known better than to worry.

"Of course you need to get away, Susan. Isn't that *exactly* what I told you *ages* ago?" Damon fumed in the soft Louisiana drawl that ten years in deepest Manhattan had failed to appreciably alter. He spent a few more minutes lecturing me like a naughty child, mostly for having wasted $150 an hour to have "some god-awful pill-pushing headshrinker" give me the same advice that he had so wisely dispensed for free.

Then, with tears running down his shiny ebony cheeks and splashing onto the floppy collar of his striped magenta shirtfront, he enfolded me in his arms and assured me he could run the company single-handed for however long I needed to be away.

"Just you go off and heal yourself, girl," he whispered throatily. "That's the only thing that's important now."

Of course, I had suggested to him that he might want to think about what he was getting himself into before committing. And I reminded him of his professed need for absolute freedom and of the difficulty he had always had in putting his thoughts on paper.

At that Damon's round Buddha features had contorted into a sly, puckish grin. "Sue, honey," he laughed, "it's not that I *can't* do all of that boring bullshit that you're so wonderful at organizing and keeping track of, it's just that I *won't*. Not without a very good reason."

Then he stood up on his tiptoes and softly kissed my cheek. "And you are the very best reason I can think of," he sniffed. "Now, get out of here before I come to my senses and change my mind."

Chapter 3

At home came one final daunting task: packing up Bobby's things. I'd left everything just as it had been the morning he kissed me good-bye and then vanished. The dream that he would come sauntering through the door and back into my life was fading along with my sanity.

His clothes and shoes went into boxes for the Goodwill and so did most of his sports equipment. I stacked the boxes near the front door and returned to the living room for the part that would be the hardest. It was these smaller, more personal things that brought on my tears. Holding his battered flight jacket to my face caused yet another rush of memories. How many times had my cheek crushed the butter-soft leather when he held me in his strong arms? I laid it gently in the box as the tears continued.

The dust-covered ski trophy had been a particular source of pride for Bobby and was a warm memory of our first romantic trip together. "Romantic? Are you nuts? You were alone most of the time," my rational mind—I call her Miss Practical—chided me.

My romantic side, often at odds with Miss Practical, dredged up the memory of that Saturday when a storm had kept the skiers off the slopes—Bobby and I had spent the entire day in front of the fire making wonderful, languid love.

Miss Practical snapped me out of my reverie with a reminder that it had been the *only* trip we took together, not the *first*. She was right: like so many of Bobby's big plans, none of the vacations we had meticulously planned had ever materialized. I tossed the trophy into the box.

This was the box I had intended to keep, mementoes of my life with him, our life together. But it really was just more of his stuff. None of it represented us. I finally decided that it should go with the others and set it atop the stack to be disposed of by Damon as he saw fit. A gesture I greatly appreciated since Damon and Bobby had, in reality, hated each other.

It always saddened me that the two most important men in my life could barely tolerate being in the same room together.

From the beginning Damon had insisted that "there was something not right about Bobby." He said he was smarmy and insincere. Damon had even gone so far as to claim that he'd seen something evil in Bobby's eyes. Bobby had convinced me that Damon was simply jealous of the time I spent away from him.

That seemingly logical explanation didn't stop Bobby from defaming my eccentric business partner and friend for the way he looked and acted. Bobby even said Damon had an arrogance that made him nothing more than an uppity N—I was shocked at Bobby's use of the "N" word and he apologized profusely with multiple mea culpas, convincing me, as he so easily could, that it had been a simple slip of the tongue and he was heartily ashamed.

But the truth of it all was that the only time Bobby and I really fought was over Damon. And while I was angry at both of them for making things so uncomfortable I dealt with it the only way I could. Never discussing home with Damon even when there had been times when I could have used the ear of a good friend; for there were times I wondered if Bobby really loved me. At home I no longer discussed work, no matter how exciting a particular estate or single piece that we had been called on to appraise.

Occasionally my resentment and frustration of the enforced silence would get the better of me. A snide remark from Damon or an inflammatory comment by Bobby would send me out into the night. I would walk the city streets alone. Angry that it was necessary to be away from them.

Shutting out the memories I stood in the entryway after depositing the small box with the others and just stared at the door. No, he would never come through that door again. Bobby was gone and I didn't need to walk on eggshells anymore.

I went to bed tired from the effort and emotions.

The next morning I threw some favorite research books, a battered case of drawing materials from my art school days, an overnight bag and some casual clothes into the back of my blue Volvo. Thus prepared for travel, and without a backward glance, I abandoned the city and the lonely loft apartment with its overflowing trove of bittersweet memories.

Where do you go when there's nowhere else to go? When you don't want to see anyone to whom you might have to explain why you may suddenly burst into tears at odd moments. When you wish to be alone with the tattered remains of your once happy life.

I couldn't think of anywhere better suited to those particular needs than Freedman's Cove, Rhode Island.

Tucked into a tiny indentation along the rocky Atlantic coastline north of Newport, the village of Freedman's Cove is known locally for its succulent lobsters, a postcard-pretty waterfront and the scores of extravagantly overdone Victorian summer houses that line the surrounding shore.

The Freedman's Cove Victorians, as they are often referred to in New England travel brochures, were built in the late 1800s, a time when America's super-rich were sparing no expense in attempting to outdo one another with their palatial retreats along the beaches of Newport, a few miles to the south.

When it comes to money and fashion some things never change. And, as is still the case today, wherever the truly rich congregate, the near-rich and the wannabe rich are sure to be close at hand.

So, around 1885, when Rhode Island became *the* fashionable place for the very rich to summer, plenty of well-off families with slightly lesser means than the Whitneys and the Vanderbilts were more than happy to build mini-mansions of their own, just up the strand from their financial and social betters. And so, during the hot months of the year the wives and children of prosperous Eastern bankers, factory owners and investors fled the teeming and unhealthful cities for the pleasant seaside community of Freedman's Cove. There, attended by a favorite family servant or two, they resided from June until September, bathing, sailing, picnicking and calling upon one another in idyllic Victorian splendor.

Their industrious menfolk, meanwhile, remained hard at work in the steamy, malodorous canyons of Boston, New York and Philadelphia, commuting up by rail on weekends to join their pampered dependents by the sea.

More than a century later the pattern of summer living in Freedman's Cove has changed only slightly. Entire families of prosperous city folk still escape the heat and humidity by flocking to that pleasant northern shore. But now they generally arrive together—Mom, Dad and the kids renting one of the charming old Victorians with a seaside view for a week or so at a time, then returning as a unit to their modern air-conditioned homes and condos in the cities.

And, nowadays, thanks to easy highway access and ample facilities for dining and lodging, Freedman's Cove also plays host to a new breed of short-term visitors. These are the day-trippers, in town for an afternoon. Or the lovers who come for long, romantic weekends.

However you wish to classify them, from the first of June until Labor Day, hordes of sunburned tourists wander Harbor Street, licking triple-scoop ice-cream cones served up at the magnificent marble counter in Brewster's Ice Cream Parlour & Confectionary or squinting through the wavy mullioned windows of The Ancient Mariner Nautical Emporium. They all stop in at Cora's Olde Tyme Fudge Shoppe and pause to finger the Taiwanese Hummel figurines at Shelly's Victorian Gifts. And most wander down to the old commercial pier to see the lobster boats, or rent bicycles to ride along the shaded streets of brightly painted Victorians on their way out to the historic lighthouse on Maidenstone Island.

Or sometimes they simply drive in to dine at Krabb's Seafood House on the wharf.

But no matter how the tourists have changed over the course of the past hundred years, one aspect of Freedman's Cove remains completely unaltered by time: when summer ends the city people still go home again, leaving the village to face the coming storms of winter on its own.

The day after Labor Day the sounds of clattering hammers echo along the deserted streets, as the tourist shops and B&Bs along Commodore Milton Lane are snugly shuttered and battened down. And when the work is finally done and the beach floats and umbrellas have all been folded and stored for another season, the few hundred full-time residents of Freedman's Cove settle in to enjoy the brief peace of autumn and brace themselves for another harsh New England winter.

By mid-October, chilly breezes are already sweeping south from the Canadian Maritimes. Bulky Fisherman's Sweaters have replaced T-shirts as the favored garment for outdoor wear. The long lines of strangers clogging the checkout counters in the Food Mart with their baskets of beer, suntan lotion and picnic supplies are merely a fading memory. And there are once again plenty of parking spaces out in front of Krabb's, the only restaurant in town that remains open year-round.

Within another week or so the last of the sailboats down at Maury's Marina have been hauled out and had their bottoms scraped and painted for next year. The magnificent old maples in the square are already beginning to shed their colorful autumn foliage. And before the month has fully gone, Freedman's Cove, Rhode Island, has once more become an excellent place to be alone with your thoughts.

My decision to flee Manhattan for this strange little summer tourist destination was hardly accidental. But neither was it based on any particular research or some Manhattan travel agent's slick brochures of quaint New England retreats.

Freedman's Cove was simply the easiest choice. A no-brainer, if you will. Because my great-aunt Ellen had lived most of her long life in one of the town's famed old Victorians. And though it is a place that Bobby once visited with me, the two of us had remained there for only part of one very brief and unhappy weekend.

Chapter 4

Our trip to Freedman's Cove three years ago was supposed to have been a glad occasion. Ellen was my father's aunt, making her my great-aunt but for a small child Great-Aunt Ellen had been a mouthful so for the rest of my life she was simply Aunt Ellen, my favorite relative. I spent every summer of my childhood in her big yellow and green Victorian by the sea. So the old place held many happy memories for me, memories that I had wanted to share with Bobby.

But on that spring weekend when we drove up to see her, Aunt Ellen, who was well into her eighties at the time, made no effort whatsoever to disguise her instant dislike for my dashing young pilot.

Bobby and I had arrived late on a Friday night. And the old lady's cranky hostility had been evident from the moment we stepped through the front door. To his everlasting credit, Bobby had handled the unexpectedly awkward situation with grace and understanding—which is far more than I can say for my own behavior that weekend.

But even now I can't help smiling as I recall the gallant wink he gave me as Aunt Ellen, all of five feet tall in her tiny bare feet, her long white hair coiled in a giant, untidy braid atop her head, abruptly announced that she had prepared a nice cot for him out on the sunporch at the rear of the house.

Naturally, I was mortified . . . and angry.

For though the crafty old girl knew damn well that Bobby and I had been living together for more than six months, and had never once voiced a word of disapproval in her frequent letters to me, that night she'd seemed hell-bent on preserving the illusion of my chastity by pointedly consigning Bobby and me to sleeping quarters at the farthest possible distance from one another.

I hadn't known what to say.

During the whole of the long drive up from New York I had been describing to him in exquisite detail my sweet old auntie and her wonderful house. And I had been especially enthusiastic about the splendid bedroom high up in the turret facing the sea, the room that had always been mine.

From the lovely Italian marble washstand with its painted china bowl and pitcher to the delicate lace curtains that on soft summer nights fluttered like the wings of butterflies in breezes from the bay, I had not left out a single detail of that marvelous room with its breathtaking view of rocky Maidenstone Island, the picturesque Maidenstone Lighthouse and the Atlantic beyond.

Thoughtlessly, I now freely admit, I had assumed that Bobby and I would be sleeping together in that lovely chamber where, by the flickering glow of a tiny blue art glass fairy lamp, I had woven a thousand girlish dreams.

And though I was completely at fault for having failed to take into account Aunt Ellen's Victorian-era sensibilities regarding the matter of cohabitation by unmarried lovers, my embarrassment at her rude and tactless behavior that Friday night had prompted my usually restrained temper to flare.

Fortunately, Bobby had seen the warning glint of fire in my eyes. Before I could open my mouth to complain, he'd yawned theatrically and told Aunt Ellen he was positively desperate for a little shut-eye after the long, long drive from Manhattan, embroidering his huge lie—because he had actually spent the previous hour in the car describing in lurid detail all the wicked and depraved things he was going to do to me the moment he got me alone—by assuring her how much he loved sleeping out in the fresh air.

Great-Aunt Ellen had simply grunted suspiciously and led my poor, deprived lover away through the kitchen to his lumpy cot on the sunporch.

I'm sure she would have had a heart attack on the spot if she'd known what happened after she limped upstairs to her lonely spinster's bed that night. For, less than an hour later, when I was sure from the buzz saw drone of the snoring from her room that she was fast asleep, I crept down from my virginal chamber and went to Bobby on the sunporch.

At the foot of the deep backyard there is a little curve of sandy beach hidden from view by a thick screen of wild rose and oleander. Taking my smiling lover by the hand, I had boldly led him to the water's edge. And there under the stars, on the very spot where once I had built elaborate fairy castles in the sand, we peeled off our clothes and made love until dawn. Then, giggling like the naughty children that Aunt Ellen obviously knew we were, we had crept back to the house and our separate beds.

Needless to say, the planned weekend in Freedman's Cove turned out to be more than a little awkward for all of us. As a result, Bobby had spent virtually no time at all in the house. We had a late breakfast on Saturday. And as soon as it was over he had volunteered to take a long hike across the stone causeway to the lighthouse on Maidenstone Island, so that Aunt Ellen and I could "visit."

So, after we silently cleared away the breakfast things, the old lady and I had sipped herbal tea dispensed from the solid coin silver Shreve & Co. tea service in her claustrophobic front parlor, with its funereal wine-colored draperies, heavy claw-foot furniture and drooping rubber plants.

As was always required on such occasions at Aunt Ellen's, I dutifully pretended to be interested while examining her faded albums of long-dead ancestors by the feeble glow of a prized Tiffany lamp, and listened for the hundredth time to her rambling recitations of who had married whom, who their children and grandchildren were, how they were related and what had become of them all.

Then, after a while, something unusual had happened. Aunt Ellen had casually uncovered a photograph of a pretty, dark-haired young woman in a high-collared turn-of-the-century gown. My anger momentarily forgotten, I had immediately picked up the photo, remarking on the loveliness of the girl and asking who in the world she was. For hers was a face that I could not remember having ever before seen in the familiar ancestral gallery.

The old woman had scowled and her teacup trembled slightly in her frail hand. "Now, that one up and went off to New York years before I was born. Around about 1910 or thereabouts," she had muttered darkly. Then her thin, creaky voice dropped to a mere whisper, forcing me to lean forward to hear.

"They say she was carrying on with a *man* down there," she'd continued, pointedly fixing me in her watery, gray-eyed gaze. "A Bohemian artist who painted pictures of naked women . . ."

. . . I laughed, suddenly understanding that the mysterious photo was intended to warn me against my current romantic folly. "Bobby is a wonderful man and I am not 'carrying on' with him, as you so charmingly put it. We're both deeply in love and we are probably going to be married soon—"

"That's what that Bohemian painter promised *her,* but I can assure you that men like that do not marry," she said, casting a knowing glance out the window toward the island. There had next followed a long silence as Aunt Ellen sadly shook her head and gazed down at the pretty, unsmiling face looking out at us from the sepia background of the ancient studio photo.

"Her father, that would be my mother's uncle George, went all the way down to New York on the train and pleaded with her to come back home," she finally went on, "for the sake of common decency and the family name." Aunt Ellen had gazed at the old photo again and then abruptly snatched it from my hand.

"What happened to her?" I asked, by then genuinely intrigued. For the scandalous story, and even the existence of the anonymous young woman in the picture, had obviously remained a closely guarded family secret for generations.

"She came to a no-good end. And that's all I'm going to say about it," the old lady stubbornly concluded, the somber finality of her tone making it clear that some unspeakable fate had befallen the wayward girl.

Then, as if a lightbulb had been switched on, Aunt Ellen's bloodless lips had suddenly stretched into a semblance of a smile, unappetizingly exposing the pink plastic gums of her dentures. "Now then," she had said, slipping the scandalous photo into the back of the album from which she had taken it, "I suppose that whatshisname feller you brought up here with you will be expecting me to fix him some kind of a big shore supper."

"Aunt Ellen," I said sharply, "since you deliberately trotted out that old photo in order to justify your antiquated and prudish view of Bobby and me sleeping together, the very least you can do is tell me who the girl was and what became of her."

Her dignity visibly shaken by the harshness of my accusation, the old woman had set her fragile china cup on the magnificent silver tray and rose slowly to her feet. "Why, Miss Susan Marks, I cannot imagine what you are going on about," she proclaimed innocently. "And you have no call to raise your voice to me, young woman."

"The name, Aunt Ellen. What was the damn girl's name?" I shouted at her in frustration.

The blood rose to her face then, centering in two bright spots on her heavily powdered cheeks. "That person's vile name has not been spoken in this house for more than eighty years," she hissed in reply. "And I do not intend to speak it now, or *ever*."

Then, without waiting for my reply, she had turned her hunched old back on me and hobbled out to her whitewashed kitchen, muttering to herself some inanity about the boiled lobster and parsnips she was planning for supper.

Bobby and I left Freedman's Cove shortly after he returned from his hike out to the lighthouse that afternoon. As I angrily tossed our belongings into the car, Aunt Ellen had stood on her front porch, stubbornly pretending not to comprehend what she had done or said to drive us away.

Anxiously wringing her gnarled old hands, she had at the last moment even partially swallowed her stiff-necked

New England pride by begging us to at least stay on until after supper.

She was still standing there in the chilly afternoon breeze as we drove away, a tiny, bent relic from a bygone age when the universally accepted wisdom of one's elders allowed and even encouraged them to lecture their foolish young folk when and as they pleased.

"You sure you don't want to go back and give the old girl another chance?" Bobby was looking at me with genuine concern as we drove slowly down the charming, sun-dappled street.

I turned then and glanced back at the frail, white-haired figure standing there small and alone on her big old-fashioned porch. I could feel the hot tears of frustration and anger welling up in my throat as I shook my head and fumbled in the bottom of my purse for a crumpled cigarette, even though I'd quit months earlier. "Oh, to hell with her," I sobbed, punching the lighter on the dashboard. "Just drive."

That was the last time I saw Aunt Ellen alive.

A few weeks later I received a call from the town constable, informing me that my aunt had suffered a massive stroke and passed away in her sleep. She had been discovered dead in her giant four-poster bed, by her cleaning lady.

When the news came, Bobby was somewhere far out in the North Sea on a mysterious, monthlong assignment for the oil company. So, overwhelmed with guilt at the horrible way that Aunt Ellen and I had parted, I drove up to Freedman's Cove alone and made the arrangements for her funeral.

Nobody else was at the gloomy service but the cleaning lady, a few other old people that I didn't know and my aunt's elderly lawyer. Following the burial in the little cemetery behind the stern whitewashed Unitarian Church, the lawyer took me aside and informed me that my Aunt Ellen had left me her entire estate, which consisted mainly of the house and all its contents.

Feeling absolutely rotten, for, despite our last ugly encounter, Aunt Ellen had for most of my life been like a mother to me, I had called and asked Damon to come up and stay with me while I dealt with the house. And though he loathed flying, my dear partner had bravely caught the first commuter flight to Newport.

Surprisingly, Tom Barnwell, the boyish real estate agent I had called, mostly because we'd dated for part of one breathless, hormone-charged summer right after high school, also immediately came to my rescue. Driving a new BMW convertible and looking far better in faded jeans and crewneck sweater than he had any right to, he had arrived at the house bright and early the next morning.

Touring the cluttered rooms with Damon and me, Tom had suggested I brighten up the old place, whether I wished to sell or turn it into a summer rental: Aunt Ellen's house, with its secluded private beach and spectacular sea views was the last of the Freedman's Cove Victorians that had not yet been converted to a summer rental. And, according to Tom, it would command a handsome weekly rate.

Later, as we lunched together in a window booth at Krabb's, Tom had offered to find reliable workmen to do the necessary remodeling, and said he'd personally take charge of the house after I returned to New York.

Initially I was baffled at the extraordinary attention Tom Barnwell was lavishing on a potential realty client. Then Damon had excused himself to go to the restroom and my old beau's motivation suddenly became clear.

"Sue, I've never forgotten that night we spent together on Dad's boat," he said huskily.

I felt myself flushing bright crimson as he suddenly leaned across the table and squeezed my hand.

"Well, Tom," I replied, patting his big, capable hand and injecting what I hoped was a carefree tone into my voice, "we were a couple of wild and crazy kids, weren't we?"

In fact, I had never forgotten that night, either. But then, I don't suppose many people do forget their first genuine sexual encounter. For that was what the night aboard his father's sleek new motorsailer had been for me. And, I suspected, it had been the first time for Tom as well.

Thankfully, Damon had returned quickly, ending the awkward moment. Tom had sheepishly gone back to discussing the lucrative summer-rental market in Freedman's Cove, sparing me the necessity of reminding him that he was married, or boring him with tales of my handsome and fabulous lover.

The next day we went to work on the house.

While I went through countless boxes, trunks and closets, deciding what to keep and what to dispose of, Damon took charge of the redecorating. Helped by Tom, he hired workmen to redo the place inside and out including a modest updating of the old-fashioned kitchen. Partly because of the clutter at the house, but mostly because of my unpleasant memories of my last visit with Aunt Ellen, we had both stayed at a pleasant little B&B a few blocks away.

Damon and I drove back to New York after five days, leaving Tom to see that the decorating was properly finished. We took with us only Aunt Ellen's silver tea service, the Tiffany lamp and a few other items that she had treasured. Everything else either had been left for the use of summer renters, given away to local charities or, in the case of Aunt Ellen's innumerable boxes of letters and old photos, locked in the still-unexplored attic, to be sorted out later.

I soon forgot all about the embarrassing incident with Tom . . .

Chapter 5

It was very late when I pulled into the narrow drive beside the house and switched off the Volvo's engine.

Stepping wearily out of the warm car I stretched my numbed shoulders and looked up at the proud old Victorian. While she was still alive, Aunt Ellen had always kept a light burning in the parlor at night, so the house would seem warm and inviting to visitors, she said. But now the windows were dark and the place looked inexpressibly sad and empty.

The beacon from the lighthouse on the point swept across the pale yellow clapboards, illuminating the tall, angular structure like a flash of lightning in a cheap horror movie. In that instant I had the fleeting impression that a face was peering down at me from the high window of the turret bedroom. Then the light moved on, plunging the house back into the darkness of the cold, moonless night.

I stood there a moment longer, staring up at the blank window thirty feet above and wondering if it was possible that the place could be occupied. For, though summer rentals of the property had far exceeded my most optimistic expectations, no one had ever taken the house after mid-September. And I hadn't even bothered calling Tom Barnwell before leaving the city to tell him I was coming up.

Anyway, I was almost certain that I had only imagined the face in the window.

A chilly blast of wind from the sea riffled my thin sweatshirt, sending a chill through my exhausted body and driving me back into the car for my keys and purse. From the cluttered rear seat I retrieved only a small overnight case and the bag of basic groceries I'd picked up at a minimart just off the interstate. Everything else, I decided, could wait until morning.

With my arms full I hurried to the front porch and climbed the broad steps. On the off chance that the face in the window had not been merely a trick of the light I pressed the old-fashioned doorbell and listened to the sound of chimes echoing through the house.

When after several seconds no light came on inside and I heard no footsteps on the stair I fumbled with the unfamiliar new lock that Tom had installed on the oak-framed glass door and let myself in. From memory I located the switch on the foyer wall. The glittering Austrian Crystal chandelier blazed to life at my touch, flooding the marbled entryway with light.

"Hello," I called out loudly, just to be absolutely certain that I wasn't stumbling in on some poor couple snuggled in for a romantic New England autumn weekend—something that Bobby and I had often talked about doing but had never quite gotten around to.

Somewhere above my head, in the vicinity of Aunt Ellen's old bedroom, I thought, a rafter groaned under the buffeting of the rising wind outside.

The house was otherwise silent.

Satisfied that I was alone, and feeling just a little foolish, I sighed heavily and dropped my overnight case onto the worn pine deacon's bench beside the front door. Then, switching on more lights as I went, I walked back toward the kitchen with my groceries.

As I passed through the parlor and the dining room a small smile of pleasure crossed my lips. When Damon and I had left Freedman's Cove three years before, the workmen were still finishing up the remodeling and the place had been a complete mess. Now, however, with my aunt's best furniture neatly rearranged and gleaming with lemon-scented polish and with the clutter of painter's drop cloths and ladders gone, I realized that Damon's hurried makeover had done absolute wonders for the Victorian.

Gone, along with Aunt Ellen's somber, densely patterned wallpaper and heavily swagged velvet draperies, were the horrid rubber plants and the grim portraits of my stern New England ancestors that had hung, late-1800s fashion, tilted away from the cheerless walls on braided cords. Now, those funereal trappings had been replaced by expanses of creamy white plaster, simple sea green curtains and a few good nautical prints, all of which perfectly accentuated the wonderfully molded floral copings below the high ceilings and showed the busy lines of the sturdy old period furnishings to best advantage.

Compared to their former melancholy atmosphere the big rooms now felt positively airy. And I imagined how pleasant they must be on bright summer days, with puffs of soft sea air wafting in through the tall cased windows.

In the kitchen, a similarly pleasing transformation had been accomplished with new cabinet facings, retiled countertops and parquet flooring. The removal of decades' worth of yellowing paint from the stamped tin ceiling, and the addition of plants along with modern appliances cleverly designed to replicate the antiques that they had replaced, had turned the room into a bright and cheerful space for work and living.

After peering briefly into cupboards and drawers stocked for the convenience of renters with adequate supplies of everyday utensils, I found some tea things. And while the kettle was coming to a boil I checked to be sure the gas and water were turned on and that the new refrigerator was working.

A few minutes later, with my little stock of groceries stashed in the fridge, and balancing a small tray in one hand and my overnight case in the other, I wearily climbed the narrow back stairs to the second floor.

Upstairs, Damon's pleasing handiwork was everywhere evident. Each of the three formerly cheerless guest bedrooms was now pleasant and welcoming, with brightly colored comforters on the beds and light, attractive wall coverings setting off the natural tones of lovingly polished woodwork.

But my pleased smile faded as I reached the end of the hall and paused in the open doorway of Aunt Ellen's room. For even the pleasant new floral wallpaper and the gaily colored patchwork coverlet could not disguise the massive four-poster bed in which the poor old dear had died so alone and lonely three years earlier.

As I stood there, tired and heartsick, I suddenly found the words that I had not been able to say at her funeral. "Thank you for all that you gave me, Auntie," I whispered to the empty room.

As if in reply to my heartfelt words a few spatters of freezing rain from the approaching storm rattled like grains of shot against the windows. So I turned out the light and proceeded down the hall to the short stairway leading up to the turret.

My old bedroom, half a story higher than the rest of the upstairs, looked just as it always had. When I was fourteen, Aunt Ellen had allowed me to redecorate the small round space to my own taste.

I'd spent most of that delightful summer choosing the colors and fabrics and the wallpaper with its delicate pink cabbage rose pattern, then laboriously painting and papering the entire room myself.

When Damon had taken charge of the latest remodeling the turret room was the one place in the house that I had absolutely forbidden him to change. But, ignoring me as usual, he had pointed out that the room's tiny closet was entirely inadequate for renters. And over my loud objections he had hauled up an old birdseye maple wardrobe from the basement where it had stood for decades gathering dust and old periodicals.

I had laughed out loud when I saw the huge piece of furniture he proposed moving into the small room. But to my great surprise the wardrobe had fit perfectly into a nook beside the windows. And, once relieved of its grime and gleaming with fresh beeswax, it looked as if it had always been there. So I had grudgingly allowed it to stay, secretly delighted to have the extra storage space.

The smile returned to my lips as I set the tea tray on the dresser and looked around my snug little space. The turret's three tall, closely spaced windows overlooked an unimpeded vista of Maidenstone Island and the sea beyond. So that, late at night, with the lighthouse beacon flashing in the distance and moonlight sparkling on the water, it is possible to lie in the elaborately carved, feather-soft bed—salvaged from the captain's cabin of a New Bedford whaler that had foundered off the point in 1889—and imagine that you are in the wheelhouse of a great tall ship.

At least that is what I used to do when I was a young girl, sailing away in my dreams to wildly romantic adventures in the East Indies, threading my way among the starlit islands of the Aegean or cruising the dangerous coasts of darkest Africa, always with a brave and handsome lover at my side.

I have never known such feelings of happiness and exhilaration as I experienced in those half-remembered girlhood dreams. And, deep inside, I suspect, by returning to Freedman's Cove I was hoping to ease my grief and longing for Bobby by recapturing a bit of that dimly recalled childhood magic.

So, on my first night back in the home of my summers, I walked slowly around the wonderful old room, touching familiar objects and happily ignoring the fearsome sounds of the wind and the sea raging just outside my windows.

After a few minutes I took the old electric space heater from the tiny closet, for the house's newly revamped central heating still does not include the turret room. I plugged in the heater and switched it to HIGH. And, as the glowing red coils drove the late-autumn chill from the air, I lifted my overnight case onto the bed.

Opening the lid, I took out the protective ball of underwear wedged between my hair dryer and shampoo bottles, and carefully unwrapped the soft package to expose the tiny, sky blue fairy lamp that I had brought back with me from New York. I placed the delicate antique object on my nightstand and touched a match to its slender wick. Then I turned out the room lights and stood back to admire the effect.

Just as I'd always remembered, a flickering azure glow suffused the circular room, magically transforming the swirling white textures of the domed plaster ceiling into a twilight sky alive with soft, cottony clouds that might have been painted by the hand of Maxfield Parrish.

Pleased with myself for having remembered to bring

along the treasured lamp, I yawned happily and traded my wrinkled jeans and sweatshirt for a thick terry robe. Then I slipped downstairs to try out the pièce de résistance of Damon's remodeling job.

Undoubtedly the biggest drawback to Aunt Ellen's house had always been the second-floor bathroom, a big, clammy, linoleum-floored chamber containing all of the necessities and none of the comforts of modern plumbing. The awful room's worst feature had been without question the great clawed iron bathtub that had dominated one corner like a medieval torture device.

Adding to its grim demeanor, patches of cold black metal showed through the ancient tub's yellowing porcelain finish. And the greenish copper taps had clanked and hissed menacingly before spewing out uncontrollable volumes of rust-tinged water whose only temperature variations were scalding and freezing.

When Damon, who values his creature comforts mightily, first saw the house he'd taken one look at the scabrous old bathroom and shuddered theatrically. "Positively barbaric," he'd drawled, scowling at the ancient tub, the cracked wooden toilet seat and the stained medicine cabinet mirror. "Sue, darling, no civilized person will even consider staying in this mausoleum once they've visited the loo," he'd announced, sweeping away my feeble protests about the unthinkable expense of remodeling the bathroom.

"If, as you've said," he reminded me, "the only way you can afford to keep this house is by renting it out to well-heeled summer tourists, then you can't afford not to fix the bathroom."

So once again he'd had his way, covering the glossy white walls in soft green fabric and wood and replacing the cracked linoleum with thickly luxurious carpeting a much darker shade of forest green. All of the hideous fixtures had been replaced with attractive new ones. And he'd added a bidet for good measure, a move that I'm sure would have sent poor Aunt Ellen into a swoon.

But finally, and best of all, Damon had junked the massive cast-iron bathtub, replacing it with a gorgeous sea green replica of the elegant claw-foot tub Queen Victoria herself had installed in Windsor Castle. Unlike Victoria's tub, however, the updated version came complete with a set of Jacuzzi jets and an infinitely controllable temperature dial.

Turning the gleaming taps full-on I sprinkled lavender salts into the rushing water. Then I slowly undressed and slipped into the blessed warmth of the fabulous new tub. As the glorious tingle of rushing bubbles massaged my aching spine, I reflected that Damon had been absolutely right, as usual.

I closed my eyes and blessed my business partner for his spot-on wisdom. Then I sank back into the soothing veils of steam. And as the scented water swirled around me I thanked Aunt Ellen for leaving me this lovely old house.

Once again I saw the scowl of disapproval as Bobby and I left that afternoon three years earlier. The sight of her tiny form on the porch as we drove away was a painful memory.

I pushed the guilt-ridden thought aside and instead went back to the very first visit I remembered.

At six I was something of a tomboy and my mother had long since given up trying to keep me in dresses playing with dolls. Aunt Ellen was horrified by my unlady-like antics and had made efforts to rein me in; but after several heated arguments with my mother she stoically refrained from further comment.

I chuckled to myself, remembering how much all my cousins feared her, but even at six I somehow saw through the gruff exterior and wouldn't let her dismiss me the way she did the others. I became her favorite. A fact she would have denied vehemently.

It was that summer the turret bedroom became mine.

In her best no-nonsense voice she told me that I was being consigned to the room farthest away from the living spaces because she wasn't used to having children in the house and wanted to retain as much peace as was possible with a rambunctious little girl around.

I smiled, remembering seeing the room for the first time, the curved walls and domed ceiling, the mullioned windows looking out on the raging sea. I'd become a princess in the highest tower in the castle. I was thrilled and threw my tiny arms around her legs. She'd gently disengaged me, saying I was wrinkling her dress, but I could see in her eyes that she was pleased.

Aunt Ellen. She didn't give hugs and kisses but I always knew she loved me. I hoped she knew how much I loved her.

I stretched and sank lower in the tub so the soothing jets could do their magic on my neck, stiff from the long drive.

When another drive swam into my thoughts. I still have nightmares where the truck crosses the center line and smashes into the side of the car. I cringed.

Even at ten Mother insisted I sit in the backseat buckled into the middle. She'd read somewhere that air bags were dangerous to children. So I was safe, not a scratch on me, but because the truck hit the side of the car Mother's air bag didn't save her.

My father and I were alone.

It was Aunt Ellen who was there for us, for me. I never

saw her cry but her strength helped my father and me through that first horrid year and after that I spent every summer here.

Starting to prune, I got out of the tub and went upstairs to bed.

Chapter 6

That night I dreamt of Bobby.

But my dream, for a change, was not one of the foolish longing fantasies with which I had been torturing myself ever since his disappearance.

Instead, that night, snug in my sturdy old sea captain's bed, with the October wind rattling the windows of my secure cocoon and the soothing glow of the fairy lamp fending off the freezing darkness outside, I dreamt of the day I had first met Bobby, and of the life we had shared together.

It was early on a bright autumn morning. Dressed in baggy sweats and bedraggled from an intense aerobic workout at my women's health club, I was coming out of a Seventh Avenue bakery, a bag of croissants in one hand, my open wallet carelessly clutched in the other.

Intoxicated by the delicious yeasty smell of the warm bread and squinting happily down the sun-splashed street, which looked fresh-scrubbed from a brief spring shower that had ended just seconds before, I could have been the poster girl for Mugging Victims Anonymous.

Suddenly, I heard the rapid slap of sneakers on the concrete behind me, and something hard and brutal—a fist, as it later turned out—landed squarely in the center of my back. I briefly glimpsed a pair of large, dirty running shoes as I fell face-forward onto the wet pavement and felt the wallet being ripped from my fingers.

Then the running footsteps were receding into the distance and someone was shouting in a deep, enraged voice.

I sat up groggily, clutching my bleeding nose and still only dimly aware of what had just happened to me. Slowly I realized that the angry shouting had not stopped. Looking down the glistening street, I saw that the noise was coming from a tall, blond-haired man in a worn leather jacket and jeans. He stood twenty yards from me, leaning over something in the rain-filled gutter.

Attracted by the shouts and my first startled scream, people were coming out of the bakery. I felt gentle hands helping me up. Concerned voices were asking if I was okay and debating with one another about whether or not to call the cops.

When I looked down the street again the blond giant was just stepping away from another man who was squatting by the curb, holding his ribs. The blond shouted a final threat and the other man staggered to his feet and weaved away, arms still wrapped tightly around his chest, his cruel, stubbled face pale as ashes.

Then, without warning my leather-jacketed hero was standing in front of me like some gorgeous avenging angel straight out of a Hollywood action film.

He held out my wallet and stooped slightly to peer closely at my damaged nose.

I tried smiling but it hurt too much. So I gave him sort of a lopsided grin and tilted my head like a wounded parakeet, trying to think of something appropriately grateful to say.

Meanwhile, content that I had been taken in hand, the small crowd of Manhattan sidewalk gawkers was drifting away.

"I think maybe you need to see a doctor," my handsome

savior said in a pleasingly basso voice that was edged with a crisp Midwestern twang.

I shook my pounding head vigorously. "I'm fine," I mumbled past my aching jaw. "Jus wanna go home now."

He must have seen me starting to sway, for I was suddenly overcome by a wave of dizziness. Before I had a chance to topple I felt his strong hand under my elbow. "Home it is, then," he said, effortlessly holding me upright with one hand while retrieving my miraculously undamaged bag of croissants with the other. "Is it close enough to walk, or should I call a cab?"

At my insistence, we had walked. Rather, he walked while I stumbled along, leaning heavily on him.

Ten minutes later I was seated at the chrome 50s dinette in my little apartment while he tenderly applied an ice-filled towel to my battered nose. I submitted to the soothing treatment like a broken marionette, gazing stupidly into the most devastating pair of ice-blue eyes I had ever seen, and marveling silently at the way the sunlight pouring in through the window at his back shone like gold on his wheat-colored hair.

The whole scene was so steeped in melodrama that I halfway expected violins to start playing an accompaniment to the ringing in my ears.

Of course, I was miserable to a degree far exceeding the superficial bumps and scrapes that had been dished out by my mugger. For I could only imagine what I must have looked like to my hero, all mud-stained and bloody, and with a jagged rip in one knee of my sweats.

And if my bedraggled appearance alone was not enough to send my kind new friend running for the hills, I had clearly demonstrated to him by my carelessness in having openly flashed my wallet on a busy Manhattan street that I was a complete moron, to boot.

So I kept waiting for the golden idol to finish up his obligatory first aid, make some hurried excuse and beat a hasty retreat.

Instead, he lavishly tended my mashed nose and scraped knee, then made hot tea for me. In the process, I learned that his name was Robert Jonathan Hayward—"but you can call me Bobby"—and that he was a commercial pilot. He said he was originally from Colorado. And when I asked about the Midwestern accent he confided to me that the laconic twang was something all professional pilots affect in the cockpit when talking on the radio, so that nobody on the ground will suspect how shit-scared they are most of the time, he added with a grin.

I had laughed then, which brought tears to my eyes, because my poor battered jaw really did hurt like hell.

Saturday morning slipped effortlessly into afternoon as I learned more about Bobby Hayward. He was an ex-navy fighter pilot, had lost both parents in a car crash when he was twelve, had no other family and did not generally make a habit of cracking the ribs of New York muggers, unless they ran head-on into him while making their escape, as mine apparently had.

Just before dark he finally left my apartment, explaining that he had to run out to LaGuardia to check on some repairs to a plane he was scheduled to fly to Greenland on Monday morning.

Coming from anyone else, such an outrageous macho claim would have sounded like pure Manhattan singles bar bullshit. At that point, however, I think that Bobby Hayward could have told me that he was blasting off to Mars for the weekend and I would have swallowed it whole.

So I had merely nodded meekly as he promised to return—just to be sure I was okay, he said—and threatened to take me somewhere for X-rays if the swelling in my jaw had not gone down appreciably in the interim.

The moment the door closed behind him I jumped into the shower, then found some clean clothes and tried to pull myself together. Afterward, I sat in the living room, staring at my scarred front door like a lovesick teenager and absolutely positive that I'd never lay eyes on him again.

Nevertheless, after a couple of hours, Bobby returned, bringing with him a huge container of steaming chicken and matzo ball soup—in honor of my injured jaw, he explained—and pastrami sandwiches from the corner deli. He also brought a bottle of delicious Chilean red wine and a bouquet of dewy spring flowers, which I ceremoniously enshrined in a priceless Steuben Crystal bowl that I was minding for an antique-dealer friend.

Later, we sat cross-legged on my authentic but sagging Duncan Phyfe sofa, eating the deli take-out and listening to classic country-western CDs while Bobby quizzed me about my life, my work and my dreams.

Sunday morning was just dawning as we slipped into the bedroom and made shy, gentle love for the first time.

Except for one brief foray to a neighborhood market for supplies, we remained together in the apartment all day Sunday, cooking, laughing and making love to the soothing sound of the gentle spring rain.

Early Monday morning, Bobby left on his trip, promising to call me when he arrived in Greenland.

I stayed home from work that day, nursing my jaw, which had gone from being grotesquely swollen to merely turning a hideous shade of purple. Too agitated to concentrate on a book or the stack of appraisals I had brought home to write up on my laptop over the weekend, I alternately dozed and watched a mindless parade of game shows, soaps and other trash TV as I attempted to assess what had happened to me.

Handsome and gentle, wild and adventurous, Bobby Hayward had swept into my life out of nowhere. Like the lead character in an idyllic, never-never land romance novel he had cared for me with the utmost concern and tenderness, talked with me for hours about books, music, life and philosophy. And, finally, perhaps more as the result of my desire than his own, for I certainly was no competition for Cindy Crawford and he was clearly fearful of further aggravating my injuries, he had made sweet, exquisitely thrilling love to me . . .

Then he had flown off to a faraway place that I hadn't previously imagined even had such normal, everyday things as people and airports and houses.

Expecting my romantic bubble to burst at any moment, I hovered by the phone at the appointed hour when he'd said he was scheduled to arrive in Greenland.

Miraculously, the phone rang and, sounding like he was across town and not in some distant, frozen land where the nights were six months long, Bobby confessed that he'd thought of me all the way across the North Atlantic. And I haltingly admitted that he had been on my mind as well. Then, suddenly, we were both talking and laughing like we'd known each other all our lives, and I had insisted on going out to the airport on Thursday to meet him.

God, it was all just so perfectly beautiful and exciting that it defies description. I never, ever wanted it to stop. And, except for the all-too-frequent times when Bobby was away on extended long-distance flying assignments, it didn't. Not really. For though we'd had problems—mostly having to do with his erratic, often dangerous work and the amount of time he was gone—the time we did have together was fantastic.

Bobby moved in with me the week after he returned from Greenland. Eighteen months later, we bought the loft on lower Broadway, which we were slowly remodeling. And we had been talking very seriously of late about getting married and having a baby . . . two or three babies, in fact.

Then, just as suddenly and unexpectedly as it had all begun, my life with Bobby had ended.

He'd been gone for over a week, flying three top executives of the oil company halfway around the world to conclude a merger with an Indonesian producer. And he was supposed to be coming home the next day, a Friday.

I'd happily planned a long, lazy New York summer weekend for us, a concert on Saturday, picnicking in the park on Sunday afternoon, with lots of lovemaking in between. I had been hanging around the office, waiting for his call—Bobby always called from his last stop, to tell me when he'd be "wheels down" at LaGuardia, where the company's planes were based.

But that last phone call never came.

Instead, late on Thursday afternoon, a somber-looking young company executive in an equally somber gray summer-weight suit had appeared at my office, where I was impatiently coaxing the final details of a large estate appraisal out of Damon.

I felt my whole life draining away as the nervous oil company emissary haltingly informed me that Bobby's plane was overdue and "presumed down somewhere in the Indian Ocean." The plane had only one passenger onboard, having dropped off the other two company executives for a short meeting before the long return flight to the United States.

The man had kept on talking, relating a bewildering array of technical details about bad weather in the area, the massive air-sea search that had already begun by several cooperating nations and the U.S. Navy destroyer that had been dispatched from the American base on the remote island of Diego Garcia. But I had absorbed little or none of it.

All I knew was that Bobby was gone . . .

I awoke with a start, bitter tears of anguish and regret streaming down my cheeks. The wonderful dream of Bobby had turned suddenly into a horrible nightmare.

And then I realized that I was not alone in the turret bedroom.

Chapter 7

Dressed all in white and shimmering with a faint fluorescent glow, she stood motionless beside the casement window farthest from my bed. Her back was turned to me and she was holding aside one of the sheer lace curtains, gazing intently through the rain-streaked glass into the black and forbidding night beyond.

At first I thought I was imagining her, the way children sometimes imagine they can see the figures of animals in the puffy white clouds of a summer's day.

Limned by the faint blue light of the fairy lamp and half-hidden by the shadow of Damon's wardrobe, she looked like a creature of pure imagination. The simple, flowing lines of her diaphanous gown merged seamlessly into the folds of the sheer floor-length curtain in her hand. And she stood as still and as silent as a sculpture of palest Carrera marble.

Stunned by the eerie sight before me, I felt my mouth go dry. The blood was pounding in my temples as I slowly sat up and stared, half-expecting her slender form to vanish among the deep, lurking shadows beside the wardrobe.

But she remained standing precisely where she was, one bare white arm raised nearly to her cheek, slender fingers clutching the transparent fabric of the intricately patterned lace curtain.

Despite the dim lighting, I seemed to see her with exceptional clarity. A luxuriant cascade of raven hair interwoven with narrow strands of pink satin ribbon fell down her back to below the waist. A chain of cunningly hand-sewn rosebuds decorating the bodice of her dress precisely matched the shade of the ribbon in her hair.

As I continued to stare at the apparition before me I realized that the garment she wore was not a dress at all but an elaborate nightgown, such as a new bride might wear to her wedding bed. And though her face was completely hidden from my view, I somehow knew that she was beautiful, and too young to have died.

Several more seconds passed and still she had not moved. I hardly dared to breathe as a frantic argument raged within my head. The logical part of my brain was insisting that there must be some perfectly rational explanation for what I was seeing. But my foolish emotional side—the part of me that regularly conjured up all of those impossible daydream fantasies of Bobby's miraculous return—said I was looking at a spirit.

I didn't know then whether I even believed in such things. But one can scarcely dabble in the antiques business for very long without being regaled with ghost stories.

I recalled having heard somewhere that the dead most often return to places where in life they underwent some profound emotional trauma. So it crossed my mind that the spectre at the window might possibly be my aunt Ellen. Though she had lived her life as a spinster, I knew she had once been engaged to marry. But her fiancé, a handsome local yachtsman, had died in a tragic sailing accident before they could be wed.

Had poor Aunt Ellen secretly watched and waited for her lost lover from this very room? In her grief and distraction over her loss had she donned her lovely bridal nightgown and crept up to this lonely turret room night after night? Stood by that very window, peering out into the darkness and longing to see his boat slipping safely into the harbor below?

And now that she was free at last from the prison of her time-ravaged Earthly flesh, had Aunt Ellen returned to resume her lonely nighttime vigil? Was she somehow trapped on this Earthly plane, unable to cross over to the other side until her long-lost lover sailed home to Freedman's Cove to claim her for his bride?

Even as those wildly romantic thoughts were racing through my mind, there was a soft swirl of motion at the window. And I found myself looking into the sad, luminous eyes of the lovely young woman in the long white gown.

But it was not Aunt Ellen.

I gasped and clapped a hand to my mouth at the sudden realization that I had seen her face before, the unforgettable face of the girl in the old photo album, my disgraced female ancestor whose name Aunt Ellen had refused to reveal to me three years before.

"Who . . . Who are you?" My voice was high and tremulous and I felt as if I might faint at any second.

The apparition at the window wavered like smoke and then she very slowly dissolved before my eyes. The soft oval of her face lingered before the window for just a moment longer than her body.

Then it too was gone.

I sat there for a very long time, staring at the spot where she had been. Then I switched on the bedside reading lamp, instantly filling the room with soft yellow light. I swung my feet out from under the covers and crossed the chilly floor to the window, just as the beacon from the lighthouse swept past.

Positioning myself where the ghostly figure had stood, I lifted the lacy curtain and peered out into the darkness, hoping to discover what had drawn her to that particular window. But there was nothing to be seen except the shadowy forms of the maples in the yard being stripped naked by the howling wind. That and the pale finger of the lighthouse on Maidenstone Island and the black sea beyond.

Returning to the snug comfort of my bed I turned off the bedside light and gazed at the window. As the soft blue glow of the fairy lamp once more suffused the room I lay propped against my pillows, trying to make some sense of what I had just seen. To my great surprise, I was more exhilarated than frightened by the eerie experience. Because, unless my eyes had deceived me and I really was losing my mind, I felt that the sad spectre at my window proved there was something beyond this Earthly life.

In my grief-stricken state that was a great source of comfort at that moment. It implied that Bobby, too, might still exist somewhere, in some peaceful afterlife that I could only dimly imagine. And I was filled with an overwhelming sense of hope that my lost love and I would be reunited again someday, somewhere.

With those soothing thoughts caressing my exhausted brain I fell into a deep, untroubled sleep, the first I had experienced without pills since the day the nervous young man from the oil company had stepped into my office with the news that my lover was gone.

I dreamed again of Bobby as he had looked on that very first day with the sunlight glowing in his golden hair. And I imagined I felt the gentle weight of his hard body on mine as we made love for the very first time.

Chapter 8

I awoke late, feeling better than I had in months. The storm had departed on the west wind and now the brassy ball of the autumn sun shone on a white-capped sea. I told myself I should get up and take care of getting the rest of my luggage in from the car and see about laying in a proper supply of groceries.

But I lingered in bed for a while instead, reluctant to leave the warmth of my snug refuge. Although the sky outside was bright and free of clouds I knew from long experience that the October sunlight on this stark New England coast is deceptive. It would be briskly cold outside and the whole house would be chilled until I went downstairs and figured out the controls on the newly installed central heating system.

So I just lay there, putting off the inevitable and thinking about my strange experience of the night before. Though I clearly remembered awakening and seeing the beautiful young woman at my window, in the harsh light of day I could not be absolutely certain that she had not been just another character in one of my frequent dreams.

After all, my practical side argued, I had once seen a picture of the same girl in Aunt Ellen's album. So it was probably entirely possible that my troubled mind had merely projected that melancholy face onto an imaginary figure in the shadows of my room.

At least I'm sure that would have been my shrink Laura's explanation for the strange experience.

"Well, to hell with Laura," my romantic self muttered aloud as I finally threw back the covers and got up to face the new day. "She's my ghost and I'm going to keep her."

I looked around with a start as a sudden gust of wind sighed through the eaves beneath the turret roof with a sound remarkably like feminine laughter. A tiny thrill ran up my spine as I contemplated the startling possibility that the sad apparition might really have been there at my window.

With that comforting thought in mind I briefly considered going straight up into the attic and digging out the old albums in an attempt to discover the true identity of my ghostly visitor. Then my practical side took control once more, arguing that if I was ever going to recover from my loss, steeping myself in ghost stories was probably not the best way to begin.

So I chalked up my vision of the lovely spirit to sheer exhaustion fired by my overly charged emotions and went downstairs in search of the thermostat.

It was nearly noon by the time I had breakfasted and transferred my clothes from the Volvo to the new-old wardrobe in the bedroom. But despite the fact that winter was just around the corner, once the morning chill had dissipated the air was warm and summery. So I walked back outside to survey the condition of the house—I was still having trouble thinking of it as *my* house—and grounds.

The front yard was littered with fallen leaves and badly in need of raking, but I noted with approval that the grass and flower beds showed signs of having been well tended.

The white wrought iron fence bordering the front walk had recently been given a coat of fresh paint and the house itself appeared to be in generally good repair as well.

Making a note to compliment Tom Barnwell on the excellent job his maintenance people had been doing in keeping up the property for me, I walked down the drive to the arched rose trellis that marked the entry to the backyard and the narrow strip of beach beyond.

The deeply shaded lawn behind the house had always been one of my favorite places when I was a child. And now as I passed beneath the trellis the familiar loamy smell of earth from Aunt Ellen's large garden plot filled my nostrils and a new wave of nostalgia swept over me.

Except for the bare trees in the yard, it seemed as if I had played there only yesterday.

The sturdy Adirondack furniture that graced the back lawn in summer had been put away for the season. But the white-painted bench where I had subjected several generations of overworked Barbies to countless "dream dates" and daring career choices still encircled the trunk of the enormous oak that dominates the yard. And I was thrilled to see the wide wooden swing still hanging from its stout chains beneath a sagging limb.

Brushing a scattering of bright leaves from the seat, I lowered myself into the creaking old swing, pushed off with both feet and closed my eyes. Suddenly I was twelve years old again and it was almost lunchtime. At that moment, I felt sure that if I opened my eyes and looked up at the house Aunt Ellen would come bustling out onto the big screened porch behind the kitchen, wiping her hands on her blue-checked apron and setting out tuna sandwiches and lemonade.

After a moment I did open my eyes. But the interior of the porch was obscured in silent shadows. Sadly, I would never again hear Aunt Ellen's voice chiding me to leave my silly dolls and come up to lunch before she fed my share of tuna to the cats who prowled the edges of the wood.

I was filled then with a profound sense of longing for the dear old soul who had, at a time in life when most women her age had long since finished with child-rearing, taken on the daunting task of mothering a willful and sometimes troublesome little girl every summer.

Fighting back a tear, I stood and walked down to the old carriage house beside the garden and peered in through a dusty side window. As I had suspected, the missing lawn furniture was neatly stacked inside. Behind the furniture stood a large, shapeless mound of bulky objects draped in tattered canvas tarps.

I was about to turn away when, at the lower edge of the nearest tarp, something glittered in a stray shaft of sunlight. I experienced a thrill of anticipation as I realized what might be hidden there. And then I was grinning and racing around to the front of the outbuilding, wondering if the most forbidden object of my teenage desire could actually have survived in storage for all of these years.

Larger than a modern double garage, the carriage house was never subjected to such pedestrian use during my lifetime. Aunt Ellen had not owned a car, which she contemptuously referred to as a "contraption," preferring either to walk or call the town's only taxi whenever she needed to go somewhere.

The carriage house had served only two functions: half of the dirt-floored space was reserved for odds and ends that were too good to throw away and too large to fit into the basement, the other serving as the potting shed for the considerable back garden that had kept us supplied with fresh squashes, wonderful tomatoes and crisp salad greens every summer.

As a child, I had always marveled at the mystical order of the carriage house. Because every spring the front half magically emptied of lawn furniture, porch rockers, window screens and awnings, just in time to provide exactly the right amount of space for Aunt Ellen's gardening needs. Then, in autumn, when the space was no longer needed for gardening, it somehow filled up again with all the unused trappings of summertime.

Now it was autumn and the interior was crowded. So I was forced to climb between the lawn furniture and a long, unpainted table littered with rusting hand tools, stacks of clay pots and glass jelly jars filled with seeds, in order to reach the items permanently stored under the tarps in back.

From my vantage point within the dimly lit room, the shiny surface I had glimpsed through the window was no longer visible. I stood uncertainly before a shrouded pile of discarded objects, trying to decide where to look first, and fighting off creepy visions of accidentally disturbing a nest of spiders.

Finally, my excitement overcoming my fear, I grabbed the edge of the nearest tarp and flung it aside, raising a huge cloud of dust and revealing the outline of a monstrously warped Edwardian china cabinet with a broken door.

Sneezing and flapping one hand at the cloud of sparkling motes that filled the air, I squeezed past the broken cabinet.

And there it was.

Except for two flat tires and a sprinkling of rust on the chrome spoked wheels, it was exactly as I had left it more than a decade earlier.

I cannot begin to describe the happy memories that came flooding into my mind as I stood there covered in grime and grinned down at that forlorn little machine. For it was a small miracle that my aunt had even kept the despised object after I had reached adulthood and gone away.

"Well-bred young ladies do not race about the shore on motorcycles!"

I can still see the two bright spots of color on Aunt Ellen's cheeks and hear the barely disguised horror in her voice as she stared down at the full-color brochure I had placed in her lap. It was the summer I had turned sixteen and the poor old dear was trapped, a prisoner in her favorite parlor chair with her left leg in a heavy cast as the result of a tumble down the cellar steps the week before.

"It is not a *motorcycle,* Auntie. It's a moped," I had argued with teenage fervor, determinedly keeping my cool and deliberately neglecting to mention that I had picked out the fastest machine of its type. For this particular moped, a Vespa capable of carrying a passenger behind the rider, had a far more powerful engine than many small motorcycles.

"Now that I have to do all of the shopping," I pointed out with what I was certain was devastating logic, "it'll save tons of money on cab fares. And we won't have to wait all day for Ed Griner's smelly old taxi to show up when we really need something fast, like your medicine."

Unimpressed by my pitch, Aunt Ellen thrust the glossy dealer's brochure back at me without even bothering to read about the moped's fantastic gas mileage, roomy saddlebags and optional shopping basket. "Out of the question!" she'd snapped, clamping her jaw firmly shut. "Besides, you have your bicycle."

"But this is practically the same thing as a bicycle," I countered, stubbornly pushing the brochure back at her. "See, it even has pedals. It's cheaper than a used car and I can pay for it myself and make extra college money by delivering prescriptions for Mr. Wall at the pharmacy."

Being the frugal maiden lady that she was Aunt Ellen had been unable to stop herself from actually looking at the brochure for the first time then, pursing her thin lips in disapproval while grudgingly conceding the irrefutable financial point. And, in truth, except for its gaudy chrome muffler and fat, knobby tires, the jaunty little Italian moped that I'd set my heart on did bear a passing resemblance to a bicycle, albeit a somewhat muscle-bound one.

"It's so hard pedaling up hills with groceries on my bike I can hardly carry anything at all." I had jumped seamlessly ahead to my next point, cheerfully disregarding the fact that most of Freedman's Cove is generally about as hilly as the Salt Flats of Utah.

"Well . . ." Aunt Ellen said, adjusting her little square spectacles to squint at the slickly printed photo on the brochure cover.

I could tell she was weakening so I moved in for the kill, raising my most powerful argument. "And I'll feel much safer on this than the bicycle, when I have to go out after dark," I said, stabbing my finger at a block of bold copy describing in detail the Vespa's bright magneto-powered headlight and lunch-box-sized taillight.

"You shall be absolutely *forbidden* to ride that awful motorized contraption after dark!" she had firmly declared, thumping her plaster-encased leg for emphasis. "Why I never even heard of such a thing!"

"Yes, Auntie," I had replied, meekly leaning over to kiss her pale cheek and trying to suppress my shriek of joy. For not only had I won, but she had caved in with far less persuading than I had expected.

"I suppose," Aunt Ellen had murmured in final defeat, "the young women are more liberated now than they were in my day." She emitted a long sigh and her thin fingers fretted with the pile of needlework in her lap.

"You know how I feel about motorized contraptions," her voice trailed away, and I knew she was thinking of my mother, "so promise me that you'll be careful, Susan," Aunt Ellen had whispered.

Of course I had promised.

And though I frequently did ride it after dark and was probably no more careful on the speedy little motorbike than any other sixteen-year-old experiencing her first intoxicating taste of genuine freedom, I was nevertheless careful enough to avoid ever wrecking the precious Vespa. And, except for the occasional skinned knee, I never did any serious damage to myself, either.

Chapter 9

The unexpected discovery of my beloved old moped in the carriage house sent all my other plans for the day straight out the window. Because, having been reminded of the delicious feel of the wind in my face and the freedom to roam wherever I chose, including remote spots that no car or even jeep could possibly go, I became determined to get the Vespa running again.

Of course, I'm now a responsible adult. So at first I very sensibly decided just to get the moped outside and clean it up a little. Then, perhaps in a few days or a week, I told myself, I would put it into the back of the Volvo and take it to a motorcycle dealer in Newport, who might be able to replace the ruined tires and restore the engine to running order.

As it turned out, though, the hardest part of getting the moped running again was extricating it from the carriage house. After an hour of shoving furniture around in the cramped space I finally managed to make a narrow pathway to the door. Then, with some difficulty I pushed the little bike into the sunshine on its flat tires and wiped it off with an old beach towel.

Outside in the daylight, the tires, though slightly worn, appeared to be free of cracks or splits. So I searched the carriage house for a pump but couldn't find one. Then I remembered the Fix-A-Flat can in the emergency kit that Bobby had bought for the Volvo, which I often drive to country auctions in out-of-the-way places.

In the trunk of the car I found the flat repair kit, which turned out to contain nothing more than a can of compressed air laced with some sticky substance. I shot a long blast into each of the moped's tires which, to my great surprise, both instantly fattened up and held.

Relieved of the dirt and cobwebs and with its tires inflated the bike looked almost as good as new. The gas tank, however, was empty. Then I vaguely recalled that each year before going away to school I had always drained the gas, along with the water from the cigarette-pack-sized battery. A few more minutes of rummaging in the carriage house produced half a can of the gas used for the lawn mower and a plastic bottle of oil. And the partially full bottle of mineral water that I'd left in the Volvo's front seat was more than enough to fill the tiny battery case to overflowing.

Having accomplished all of that, I stood back to admire my handiwork. My nails were split and greasy, my clothes were stained with sweat and my hair a dusty tangle. But it suddenly occurred to me that I was enjoying myself immensely. And I wondered if I could actually get the motor started.

Feeling more than a little foolish, for I was sure the old engine must need a complete overhaul after so many years in storage, I climbed aboard, switched on the gas and ignition and awkwardly pedaled down the drive for all I was worth.

To my utter delight and astonishment, after only a few yards the engine sputtered twice. That encouraged me to pedal even harder. Just as I reached the street the moped coughed once more and spat a cloud of viscous blue smoke from its little chrome tailpipe. Then, with a noise like a nest of vengeful killer bees, the motor surged instantly to life.

I laughed aloud, twisted the throttle hard and turned onto the street, heading out onto the stone causeway that connected Maidenstone Island to the mainland. With the fresh sea air whipping my hair into my eyes and filling my nostrils I suddenly felt wonderful. Still laughing, I brushed away the tangle and glanced down at the speedometer. It was hovering at thirty miles per hour—which on a moped feels more like sixty—and the engine was purring beneath my tingling bottom like a happy kitten.

I rode the two miles to the island without once slowing. Then it was a case of either stopping at the parking lot beside the lighthouse or plunging straight ahead into the chilly waters of the Atlantic.

So I stopped and just stood there, straddling the softly idling bike and drinking in the glorious view.

The Maidenstone Lighthouse—which is one of the few 19th-century coastal lights still in active service—is an old-fashioned structure that looks like an artist's idealized conception of a traditional New England lighthouse. The tall white tower poised on the huge gray rocks beside its quaint clapboard lightkeeper's cottage is possibly the most painted and photographed landmark in this part of the country.

As a result, during the summer tourist season the island is usually crawling with visitors. They walk down to the small rocky beach to photograph one another with the graceful white tower looming in the background, then line up by the dozen to make the daunting hundred-foot climb up a winding iron stairway to the tiny glass room on top. There they marvel at the gigantic hand-cast lenses that nightly beam lifesaving rays thirty miles out to sea, just as they did in the days when great sailing ships passed up and down this treacherous coast.

The visitors' fascination is easy to understand. For though those ships are no more and today's giant tankers and cargo carriers rely primarily on satellites and radar to warn them off the deadly rocks, the lighthouse carries on. Because satellite signals may be interrupted by solar flares and radar sets can break down, and frequently do. But the Maidenstone Light has never once failed in its entire one-hundred-and-sixty-year history. And though the beacon itself has been automated and the lightkeeper's cottage turned into a museum, the beauty and romance of the noble old lighthouse holds a special place in the hearts of all who have ever dreamed of faraway places and sailing ships and the sea.

Out on the island on this unseasonably warm October afternoon, however, the little museum was closed and there was not a single tourist in sight. Except for a battered Toyota pickup that looked as if it might have been abandoned by high school beer drinkers the night before, I was utterly alone.

I parked the Vespa on its stand in the shadow of the tower and sat down on one of the white-painted boulders that separate the parking area from the beach. Fumbling in the pocket of my jeans, I found a rubber band and gathered my hair into an untidy knot. Then I turned my face up to the sky and watched a pair of gulls gliding around the lighthouse.

It would be pleasant, I was thinking, to come out here, as I used to, with just a picnic lunch and my sketchbook. And that thought led back to Bobby. This was the place he had come so I could be alone with Aunt Ellen on that awful morning three years earlier. Now I feared that his memory of this beautiful spot had been spoiled when he'd returned to find me screeching at my poor auntie that day.

God how I missed them both, longed to see them for just one moment.

Grief, according to Laura, is not the most painful of human emotions. Regret has got it beat hands down.

I was pulled from my sad reverie by the sound of footsteps approaching close behind me. Jumping to my feet, I whirled to face the tall stranger who had just come up from the beach. The sun was at his back, lighting his light hair and casting his face into deep shadow. And my expectant heart jumped into my throat, as it had so many times in recent months.

"Nice view, huh?"

The sound of his voice broke the momentary spell and he looked up at the lighthouse, revealing a deeply tanned face that was, while handsome in its own way, nothing at all like Bobby's face.

"Yes," I stammered. "I haven't been out here in years, but it's just as beautiful as I remembered."

The stranger wore faded cutoffs and a paint-spattered T-shirt that was stretched tight over his heavily muscled chest and shoulders. He frowned at my words and I sensed a subdued air of menace about him that was accentuated by the dark tattoos that circled his biceps like two jagged chains. Suddenly I felt uneasy and very vulnerable in this isolated spot, so I casually began edging back toward the moped.

"I guess you know you're asking for trouble," he said, moving to block my way.

"I really have to go now," I breathed, deliberately stepping around him.

He shrugged harmlessly and let me pass. "Okay, but if Harvey Peabody catches you riding that thing around here without a helmet, you're going to get a ticket."

I turned around and stared at him. "Harvey Peabody is still the town cop? My God, he must be almost seventy by now."

All feelings of menace vanished as the stranger smiled, showing a line of strong white teeth. "Seventy-two, come next spring," he said. "Old Harvey is as permanent as the rocks on the breakwater. He busted me for skateboarding into Shelly's Victorian Gifts when I was in the seventh grade and he's still going strong. Most people around here just figure he'll last forever."

There was something vaguely familiar about the stranger, and I took a closer look at him.

"Danny!" I exclaimed. "You're Danny Freedman!"

"Guilty as charged," he replied. "Except that nobody calls me Danny anymore. Dan sounds better, don't you think?"

"I know that skateboard story," I cried delightedly. "You sped into Shelly's Victorian Gifts chasing another kid and crashed right into a big display of imported crystal or something—"

"It was a very small glass case of Lladro figurines," he corrected. "About $3,000 worth. Or at least that was what Shelly claimed at the time. She ended up settling for $1,200 after my dad made her show him her invoices. And I spent the next two summers working off the debt with a lawn mower and rake."

"You were thirteen and you had a bad reputation." I laughed. "I remember because I was only eleven and my aunt used to make me stay up on the porch when you came to cut the grass." I lowered my voice to a conspiratorial tone. "She said you smoked cigarettes."

"I'm afraid it was true," he admitted with a wry smile. "But then I was under a lot of pressure for a thirteen-year-old. It was never easy being the only juvenile delinquent in a town this size."

We both laughed and he sat down on one of the painted boulders and gazed at me for a long moment. Then he grinned and pointed a finger at me. "You're Susan Marks," he declared. "Summer Susan we called you because you didn't go to school here." He paused just a moment. "Everyone said you were stuck-up."

"That's not fair. I didn't really know very many people here."

"I suspect that's why they thought you were stuck-up."

Suddenly I found myself defending my childhood as I rushed to tell my story. "Aunt Ellen had very definite ideas about who my friends could be." Without taking a breath, I continued, "I wanted to go to school here but Daddy thought private school would give me a more proper education."

Dan Freedman rolled his eyes. "Proper education?"

I shrugged. "I don't think Daddy knew what to do with me so he sent me to an all-girls school. He thought that with Mom gone I needed female supervision and guidance. It's why I came here for the summers—he hoped Aunt Ellen's staid, upright attitudes would help make me more ladylike and keep me in check."

Dan smiled a sad smile and reached out, covering my hand with his. "I was sorry to hear of your aunt's passing. She was always kind and fair to me . . . despite my wild reputation."

I nodded thoughtfully. "Thanks."

Pulling his hand away he asked with a smile, "Why did you need to be kept in check? I don't remember you ever getting in trouble."

His sharp green eyes twinkled merrily and he regarded the moped parked nearby. "Wait! Unless memory fails me, you had a run-in of your own with old Harvey Peabody." He wrinkled his brow, pretending to think. "I seem to recall having heard a rumor about you driving that little putt-putt down Commodore Milton Lane buck-naked one night . . ."

I flushed bright red. "And that's all it was, a vicious, small-town rumor," I said ruefully. "Actually, I was wearing a T-shirt and shorts. But a slightly tipsy teenage boy had just thrown me off the town wharf and I was a little . . . damp. So I was trying to get home to change."

I suddenly found myself giggling like a teenager as I remembered that awful night. "Harvey did stop me in his police car," I explained. "But when he got a look at my, uh, wet T-shirt he was so flustered he just ordered me to go straight home. And whatever I did, he said, I was not to mention the incident to my aunt."

Dan laughed. "The poor old guy was probably afraid she'd have a stroke."

"She would have," I agreed. "And I would have been grounded for the rest of my natural life."

"Well, you seem to have turned out okay," he offered.

We sat quietly for a short time and watched a strange little pelican eat the remains of what, more than likely, had been a picnic for a group of teenagers who'd left French fries and hamburger buns on the beach.

We looked at each other and laughed. Then Dan asked, "So, are you back in Freedman's Cove for good, or just visiting? I seem to have heard somewhere that you'd made it very big on the antiques scene in New York."

My smile faded as I remembered the real reason I had returned to Freedman's Cove, and I immediately felt terribly guilty. Guilty for sitting there in the bright October sunshine, laughing with Dan Freedman. Guilty just for being alive on such a fine day.

Guilt is painful, too. In fact it ranks right up there on the pain charts with grief and regret.

More useless but expensive advice from Laura.

"I needed some time away from the city," I responded truthfully. "So I decided to come up here and do a few things to the old house," I lied. I didn't want to have to explain about Bobby or my near breakdown to Dan, or to anyone else, for that matter. Not now.

"Well," he said, getting to his feet and extending a callused hand to me, "I've got to go now, but it's been really good seeing you, Sue. Maybe we'll run into each other again while you're here."

"I hope so," I said, realizing that I sincerely meant it. I took his big hand in mine and gripped it tightly, not wanting to let go. Because Dan Freedman was the first human being in months with whom I'd managed to carry on a normal conversation. The normality felt damned good and I didn't want it to stop. But there was more to it than that.

I was also curious to know more about him.

When I was a teenager, Danny Freedman had been the older guy that all the younger girls whispered about and had secret crushes on. He drove a trashed red Mustang with illegal mufflers and dated flashy blonde Debbie Carver, who waited tables at Krabb's and was rumored to have had her first abortion at fifteen.

A small incident from my own woefully inexperienced fifteenth year flashed into my mind. I felt my neck growing hot as I recalled the way I had regarded Danny Freedman then: It was a warm night in July and I had been sitting out on the front porch when Danny's Mustang had rolled slowly down our street. There were two figures in the car and sensual music from the stereo pulsed in time to the deep throbbing of the Mustang's exhausts.

Of course, I knew why Danny and Debbie Carver were taking the long, narrow causeway to the deserted island. Because Maidenstone was the one place teen lovers could be sure that Harvey Peabody couldn't sneak up on them.

So I had watched them go. And whether it was the sultry air, the sensual music or only a sudden, painful awareness of my own awakening sexuality, I was intrigued.

Running upstairs to my room, I had watched the taillights on Danny Freedman's Mustang dwindle to glittering ruby specks, then vanish in the velvety darkness.

I sat by my window, staring at the spot where the lights had been. After a long while, I locked my door and stepped out of my denim shorts and cotton panties and pulled off my halter top. Then, lying naked on my bed with a soft breeze through the open windows caressing my feverish skin, I shut my eyes and fantasized that I was the one out there on Maidenstone Island with Danny Freedman.

Though the details are lost in time, I remember how desperately I had wanted to share the velvet darkness with him that night. To hear his voice whispering in my ear and feel his hands touching me.

Fortunately—or perhaps unfortunately, considering the dire consequences that might have ensued—by the time I was old enough to pursue my fantasy, Danny Freedman had left town. Someone said he had joined the marines, which had sounded about right at the time.

"You haven't told me what you're doing these days," I said, pushing away the embarrassing memory and finally releasing my grip on Dan.

"Oh, I do some work . . . painting, exteriors mostly," he replied, still looking down at my hand.

"Ah," I replied brightly. "Well, I guess this is the season for painting around here. You must be very busy right now."

Dan raised his eyes and gave me an odd look as we began walking toward the old Toyota. "Well, I find that one time's generally as good as another," he answered, "unless it rains."

I nodded vigorously to show that I was really interested. "I can just imagine what a problem that could be," I said.

"What do you do if it starts raining when you only have a house partially finished?"

He opened the creaky door of the truck and climbed in. "Oh, I usually just go have a few beers and then come back again when it stops." He laughed as he started the engine. "Well, so long now, Sue. And welcome back to Freedman's Cove."

"So long, Dan. It was great seeing you." I stepped away from the truck and waved as he drove off. He tooted the horn and waved back at me.

I watched as his battered truck got farther and farther away, from the lighthouse and me. The guilt that had surfaced earlier returned with the realization that I hadn't wanted him to leave at all.

How was that possible? How could I be this attracted to someone else when I was madly in love with Bobby and was here only to come to grips with the grief and reality of his loss?

An unsettling thought caused me to shiver as I got on my moped. Damon had once said that I was only in love with the idea of being in love and not with Bobby at all. Of course I'd screamed that he was insane, that Bobby was my life. And for the first time Damon didn't argue with me about it, he just patted my cheek and said, "Yes, dear," never mentioning it again.

As I pumped vigorously to push the little bike into action I had to wonder if he hadn't been right.

Chapter 10

The sun was nearly touching the horizon by the time I got back to the house. The summery breeze had turned positively cold on my return ride and I was shivering uncontrollably as I rolled the moped into the carriage house and shut the door.

Running into the house I stopped just long enough to turn up the thermostat before heading to the bathroom. Steaming water cascaded into the glorious new tub as I stripped off my filthy clothes and glimpsed myself in the long mirror by the door. My wind-burnt features gazed back at me in surprise. There was a long smudge of motorcycle grease across my nose and my dusty, knotted hair was beyond description.

I let out a groan, realizing that was exactly how I must have looked to Dan Freedman. And I wondered how he had managed to keep a straight face during our conversation. Not, I quickly assured myself, that it made any real difference what Dan had thought. After all, he barely even qualified as an old friend. Nor was I likely to run into him again.

On the other hand, I don't usually go around with black grease on my nose. So I made a face at the mirror, imagining how Aunt Ellen would have used my unsightly condition as an excuse to deliver one of her little lessons on feminine decorum.

"Really, Susan," I could almost hear her chiding me in the prim, disapproving voice she reserved for times like this, "no *proper* young lady ever goes out in public with cobwebs in her hair. You must take more care with your appearance."

"Tomorrow, Auntie," I murmured, gratefully lowering my body into the tub and punching the bubbler controls to HIGH with my foot. "Today was sort of like the first day of school," I added, just in case she really was listening. "It doesn't really count. Tomorrow I'll get my act together."

Then the soothing bubbles surged up around me and I lay there like a lobster in a cauldron, sorting lazily through my jumbled thoughts.

My first day back in Freedman's Cove had not gone at all as planned.

An hour later, bathed, combed and with most of the alien substances removed from my fingers—except for the sticky stuff from the Fix-A-Flat can, which refused to come off—I went down to the kitchen in my robe and slippers to see about dinner. For though it was still early I was absolutely famished.

The meager store of groceries I'd purchased at the minimart the night before formed a tiny, unappetizing island in the vastness of the nearly empty fridge. I contemplated the alternative choices of scrambled eggs with toast or poached eggs without toast, then considered driving to the Food Mart, a chore I'd originally had scheduled for the afternoon.

But going shopping and then returning home to fix something would take hours.

"Dammit!" I complained to no one in particular, "I'm hungry now."

Grumbling angrily at myself for having let the entire day slip away, I trudged back upstairs and changed into fresh jeans and my warmest sweater. First, I decided, I would drive down to Krabb's for one of their famous lobster dinners. Afterward I would hit the Food Mart with my grocery list.

I was pulling into the parking lot at Krabb's when it struck me that I couldn't remember the last time I had given any serious thought to food of any kind.

I parked the car beneath the restaurant's flashing neon crab sign and sat there in the garish pink light examining my feelings. The familiar ache in the pit of my stomach was still present. But it was not the same as it had been just yesterday.

Yesterday the ache had seemed to define only the vast emptiness I felt inside.

This evening, I realized, the pain had eased ever so slightly. And at least part of my empty feeling could be attributed to hunger. In fact, I was actually looking forward to eating dinner.

And as my encounter with the eggs in the fridge had demonstrated, not just any food would do.

Yesterday the bland eggs would have sufficed.

Tonight I wanted something delicious.

But that wasn't all. Today I had enjoyed myself, tinkering with the moped and riding out to the island. Today I had held a normal conversation with an old acquaintance. And though my thoughts had never strayed far from Bobby, not once had I burst into tears. In fact several times thoughts of Dan had displaced those of Bobby.

Perhaps, I reflected, Laura had been right for a change. But then I remembered that getting away from Manhattan had been Damon's idea first. So Laura was still batting zero.

The important thing, I decided, was that I seemed to be doing far better in Freedman's Cove than I had back in the city.

And that was progress enough for one day.

Reminding myself to call Damon with the good news when I returned to the house, I got out of the car and went into Krabb's for dinner.

Krabb's Seafood House is a sprawling 50s-style restaurant with chrome-edged Formica tables. Pierced metal light fixtures shaped like missile nose cones shine down on comfortable booths padded in vinyl the exact shade of a cooked lobster. Whether the color of the booths was accidental or deliberate nobody can say for sure, because Mr. Krabb, the original founder of the place, died long ago without ever revealing the truth.

Fortunately, the restaurant's shockingly bad décor is canceled out by the spectacular harbor view from its huge plate glass windows. And the food is uniformly excellent, if generally American-diner plain.

Krabb's jumbo-sized, plastic-coated dinner menus contain, in addition to the obligatory crab, fish and lobster, deep-fried, baked, broiled or simmered in rich chowders, a standard array of steaks, chops and pastas. The fifty-item salad bar is pretty good, too.

And, if you're so inclined, you can order a mixed drink, draft beer or wine from the adjoining sports bar, from which the sounds of customers cheering a televised football game was blaring as I entered the restaurant.

So, when the chunky teenage hostess had escorted me to my table in the nearly empty dining room I said I'd like to start with a glass of wine.

She left me a menu, promising to send a cocktail waitress right out. Meanwhile, a busboy appeared with a large basket of crusty French bread and a tub of savory garlic butter. I was busily attacking the bread when the cocktail waitress emerged from the sports bar. She was wearing tight black pants and a sheer blouse that accentuated her large bust. And she looked familiar.

"What can I get for you?" she asked pleasantly.

"Just a glass of Chablis," I replied, covertly examining her features in the subdued light that is Krabb's only concession to those in search of a romantic dining experience. Though she had on an excess of cheap makeup and her shoulder-length hair was still a little too blonde, Debbie Carver was actually a lot prettier than I had remembered.

"One Chablis. No problem!" She scribbled the order on a pad, then took a closer look at me. "Hey, didn't you used to live around here?" she asked.

I smiled. "A long time ago."

She nodded and smiled back. "I thought I recognized you. You used to spend summers up in one of the Victorians with your grandmother . . ."

"Actually, she was my great-aunt," I said.

"Sure! You used to ride around on that cute little red motorbike." She stuck out her hand. "You probably don't remember me. I'm Debbie Olson. Used to be Debbie Carver."

I smiled. "Debbie, I'm Sue Marks. Of course I remember you. You went with Danny . . . Dan Freedman."

She gave me a rueful little grin. "The curse of living in a small town. Nobody ever forgets anything. Wow, Danny Freedman! Now that's really ancient history. Gosh, I had such a thing for Danny . . ." She gazed wistfully at the harbor lights beyond the plate glass, obviously reliving some cherished old memory. "Isn't it crazy about Danny?" she asked. "I mean, of all people, who would have ever thought he'd end up like he did."

I returned a blank stare.

"Making it so big, I mean," she explained.

I shook my head helplessly. "As a house painter?"

"A house painter!" Debbie's round breasts jiggled merrily beneath the sheer fabric of her blouse and she howled with laughter. "I guess you're right, though," she said when she had gotten herself under control again. "Danny Freedman *is* a house painter!"

She rubbed the corner of her eye with a knuckle, wiping away a mirthful tear that threatened to ruin her mascara. "Wait 'til the guys in the bar hear that one." She gurgled. "It'll crack them up for sure."

I sat there with my mouth hanging open as she flounced away and disappeared back into the bar. Within seconds a burst of explosive male laughter rocked the room. A few moments later, Debbie returned with my wine.

"Compliments of an old friend," she said, placing the glass before me. Seeing my look of puzzlement, Debbie leaned close and jerked her chin toward the entrance to the sports bar. "A real nice guy," she whispered. I looked up to see Tom Barnwell coming toward me. He was wearing a yellow golf sweater and there was a lopsided grin on his face and a glass in his hand.

"Watch that one in the clinches," Debbie advised, giving me a just-between-us-girls wink. "He's newly divorced and horny as a billy goat."

Then she was gone and Tom was standing over me. "Sue, why didn't you tell me you were coming up? I would have had the house aired and the linens changed. The place has been empty since last month."

Before I could answer Tom leaned over to peck me on the cheek and slipped into the booth across from me.

"It was a last-minute decision," I replied, disgusted by the reek of scotch on his breath.

"Well, it's damn good to see you, anyway," he said.

"Damn good!" His eyes were glittering with alcohol-induced fervor and he captured both my hands in his.

"Y'know, Sue, I really made an ass of myself the last time you were up here," he confessed, breathing hard. "I don't know what got into me that day, bringing up our night together on the boat . . ."

I could see where this was going and I wasn't really in the mood to fend him off politely. Freeing my hands, I picked up my menu, hoping he would take the hint and shut up. I'd been doing just fine so far today and I didn't want it spoiled.

"I just wanted to apologize," he muttered, managing to look hurt. "Hell, I was still married to Becky back then . . . I didn't have any right at all."

"There's nothing to apologize for, Tom. No harm done," I said with as much civility as I could muster. "The house looks wonderful," I added, smoothly switching subjects. "You've done a really great job with it."

"Aw, do you really think so?" he asked, slurring his words slightly. "That makes me real happy, Sue. Y'know, I always give that old place my extra personal attention because, well . . . Because you and me go back so far," he said meaningfully.

I looked closely at him over the top of my menu, taking in his puffy eyes and the slightly drooping line of his jaw, which was going quickly to fat. Was that the reason for his divorce, or the result of it? I wondered. He looked like he was getting ready to say something even more personal, so I cut him off.

"I'm starving," I loudly announced, looking around for a waiter. Tom half-stood and gallantly snapped his fingers like a Latin playboy in an old Fred Astaire movie. In response to his summons, a middle-aged waitress sauntered resentfully over to the table and glared at us. I quickly gave her my order—broiled lobster and a green salad—and she went away.

Tom finally seemed to take the hint that I might possibly not be interested in having him watch me eat, because he started to get clumsily to his feet. "Well, I guess I'd better let you have your dinner," he said, waiting for me to insist that he stay.

"It's been nice seeing you, Tom." I reluctantly gave him my hand again.

"Call me when you get settled in," he said, giving it an overly familiar squeeze. "I'll take you somewhere really nice for dinner."

I forced myself to smile. "Maybe lunch would be better," I replied.

The surly waitress arrived with my salad, forcing him to move. I felt like giving her a big hug as he lumbered back toward the raucous sounds of the sports bar. My heart sank as he stopped halfway there and retraced his steps back to the table.

"I almost forgot," he said with a grin. "That was a good one you told Debbie."

My mouth was already full of salad and Krabb's delicious blue cheese dressing, so I raised my eyebrows theatrically, like a street mime.

"About Dan Freedman being a house painter," Tom reminded me.

I chewed faster, then swallowed and washed down the salad with a gulp of wine. "I don't get the joke," I said with a note of unconcealed annoyance creeping into my voice. "What is so funny about that?"

Now it was Tom's turn to look puzzled. "Christ! You really don't know, do you?"

"No, Tom, I really don't know. But I'm sure that you're

just about to enlighten me." If I had fangs they would have been dribbling poison.

Tom took another step toward me, then looked around, as if he feared someone might be listening in on the secret he was about to reveal. "Freedan!" he said in a low voice. "Danny Freedman is Freedan. That's why your remark about him being a house painter was so damned funny. Debbie thought you were making a joke."

"Oh!" I couldn't think of anything else to say.

"Don't forget now, call me!" Tom gave me a little wave and walked away.

I absently speared another Roquefort-drenched chunk of salad and watched him go back into the sports bar.

"Idiot!" I mumbled to myself, popping the dripping fork-ful of lettuce into my mouth. How could I have been such an idiot? Dan Freedman—Freedan to his adoring public—was perhaps the most successful commercial illustrator in the United States. His poster work appeared in magazines, movie promotions and national ad campaigns. His company, Freedan Studios, had a lock on a sizable percentage of the huge greeting card market. Limited-edition prints of his paintings sold for outrageous prices through a nation-wide chain of Freedan Gallery stores.

Danny Freedman *was* Freedan.

And Freedan's specialty, his most sought-after works, were marvelous, idyllic landscapes featuring Victorian-era houses and cottages. I buried my face in my hands and began to chuckle. Because it really was funny. "Danny Freedman is a house painter!"

"Pardon!"

I looked up to see the sour-faced waitress hovering over the table. She was balancing a lobster on a platter and squinting suspiciously at me.

"Danny Freedman is a house painter," I repeated.

The beginnings of a smile creased the corners of her thin, humorless lips. "*Ayeh!* That's a good one," she said and laughed, placing the steaming platter before me. "Enjoy your dinner now."

Chapter 11

"How are you feeling, darlin'?"

Damon's soft Louisiana drawl sounded far, far away. I pressed the cell phone closer to my ear, straining to hear him. "I'm fine, Damon. Can you speak a little louder? I haven't had the phone in the house hooked up yet, so I'm still on my mobile."

His voice came through a little stronger. "You sound different, girl. Better."

"I am," I agreed. "Coming up here to get away was really a wonderful idea, Damon."

"You should have gone weeks ago," he said.

And I was certain he was getting ready to launch into one of his rants about all the money I'd wasted going to see Laura.

"How is everything at the office?" I asked without much hope of distracting him from a lecture.

There was a long pause on the line.

"Damon?"

"Everything's fine, honey. Don't you worry about a thing. Damon's got it all under control."

Now, I can read Damon like a book. So I knew that three reassurances in a row from him meant trouble. "Oh, shit," I murmured. "What happened?"

"Nothing *happened,* Sue!" His voice had suddenly gone up an octave. Something was definitely wrong. "Nothing for you to worry about," he added, clearly trying to placate me.

I had been sitting propped up in bed with a teacup balanced on my knees. Now I was angrily pacing the confines of my small room, my euphoric mood of a few moments earlier shattered. "Damon, if you do not cut the bullshit and spit it out I'm getting dressed right now and driving back down there tonight!"

"Sue, calm down," he pleaded. "It's no big thing. I've already taken care of it."

"Taken care of what?" I shrieked. The first possibility that popped into my mind was that something had gone wrong with a complex estate appraisal we had just completed for a major insurer. The company was a first-time client, and a very important one. "Did we screw up on the Met job somehow?"

"Good God, no!" Damon laughed nervously. "The Metropolitan appraisal went fabulously. In fact, they're so pleased that they're putting us on a long-term retainer . . . It's something else. A minor annoyance, really."

I could hear Damon's breath coming in little gasps, a sure sign that he was working himself up into one of his stress-induced asthma attacks.

"Okay, I'm sorry I yelled at you, Damon," I apologized, speaking as slowly and calmly as I could. "Now, just tell me what happened, okay?"

"Your apartment was broken into," he confessed.

I sank back down onto the bed. Though I wouldn't class myself as well-off I do love beautiful things and the apartment was filled with antiques, many of them quite valuable.

"Sue, are you there?"

"I'm here."

"It's really not bad at all," he assured me. "A typical Manhattan junkie burglary. The morons went through all your drawers and closets, evidently looking for things like cash and cameras."

Damon emitted a high-pitched snort at the burglars' stupidity. "They took your third-rate Korean stereo but left the $20,000 Federal side table and the Tiffany sterling." Then he giggled. "Like I said, morons." He rushed ahead breathlessly, "Anyway, I've already made the police report, had new and much bigger locks installed and called a housecleaning service to tidy things up." He snorted again, then snickered nasally. "That tacky old stereo really did suck, Sue."

I finally laughed. "Okay," I said, taking a sip of my tea and managing to relax just a little. "If they didn't get anything of value I guess my coming back down there won't serve any purpose now."

"Precisely my thinking," Damon said. "Besides, you can't live in Manhattan without getting burglarized at least once. There's a city ordinance."

I must have been calming down because I even gave the weak joke more of a little ha ha than it deserved. Then I pressed him for the details. "When did this break-in happen?" I asked. "I've only been gone since yesterday morning."

"Last night, I guess," he replied uncertainly. "I was there last night to pick up Bobby's stuff . . ." His voice trailed off. "Anyway," he continued after a nervous pause, "when I came back this morning for the rest of it, the door was standing wide-open and the place had been ransacked."

"They didn't get any of Bobby's things!" I heard the panic rising in my voice again.

"I don't really know," Damon stammered guiltily, a sure

sign that he was lying. "I mean, dammit, Sue, they went through *everything*. So they might have taken some of Bobby's stuff. But I don't see what damned difference it makes. Half of it went to the dump and you told me to give the rest to the Goodwill, anyway."

"The bastards!" I dropped the phone and fell back onto the pillows, shattered by the thought of some slimy New York junkie walking around in Bobby's treasured leather flight jacket, or wearing his favorite running shoes. "The dirty, lousy bastards," I moaned through a sudden flood of tears.

I felt like killing somebody.

"For God's sake, girl, pull yourself together!" I was dimly aware of Damon's concerned voice shouting up at me from the fallen cell phone. "If I hadn't told you, you'd never even have known I didn't just take all that crap to the Goodwill," he yelled. "It was just a bunch of worthless personal junk and clothes, Sue!"

Something snapped inside of me.

"Damn you, Damon!" I screamed, scooping up the tiny phone and hurling it across the room. It bounced harmlessly off the wardrobe, skittered back across the polished hardwood floor and came to a stop at my feet. The tiny ON light beside the antenna pulsed like a malevolent green heartbeat.

Great, wracking sobs shook my body as I stared at the chunk of seemingly indestructible black plastic. "You were always jealous of Bobby!" I blubbered accusingly, though it's unlikely that Damon heard me.

Without bothering to pick up the phone I lurched out of the bed and ran to the bathroom where I felt like I would be violently ill. I leaned on the sink trying to regain control of myself.

Once the sobbing had subsided I questioned whether I

was feeling real pain for what I perceived as another of Damon's inflammatory stabs at Bobby or the newly discovered guilt causing what now seemed an overreaction.

I took in a stuttering breath. I could dimly hear the little phone ringing from the bedroom. It rang and rang and rang.

It was very late by the time I finally fell into a deep and troubled sleep, dreaming.

I was walking down the same New York street where Bobby and I had met. As it had been on our first day together, the sidewalk was wet with rain. But that had been a warm spring rain, full of hope and promise. This rain was cold and fell heavily, promising nothing but an endless succession of dreary winter days to come.

People kept coming toward me on the street, their faces hidden beneath big black umbrellas. In fact, everyone I saw had one.

Everyone but me.

My hair was drenched and my clothes were sodden with freezing moisture. I quickened my pace, anxious to get in out of the rain.

Then across the traffic-filled street I glimpsed a lone figure hurrying away from me. He was tall and blond, dressed in jeans and a familiar old leather flight jacket. And, like me, he had no umbrella.

I called out to him. He stopped and looked at me through the rushing traffic. Then he smiled and I saw that it was Bobby.

I started to run to him, splashing through the overflowing gutter and into the busy street. A truck blew its horn and swept past me, blocking my view of the opposite sidewalk and spraying me with foul black water.

When the way was clear again, Bobby had vanished.

I stood there in the rainy street calling his name. I could feel the hot, bitter tears of frustration coursing down my cheeks. But nobody saw my tears because the pouring rain continuously washed them away.

I moaned in anguish and cried out for Bobby.

Then I felt a cool, soft hand on my forehead and heard a soothing voice in my ear. "Hush now, dear," someone whispered. "Everything will be all right." I slowly opened my eyes, realizing that I was safe in bed and had only been dreaming again.

The lovely ghost was sitting at my side, smiling down on me with her sad, dark eyes.

"Oh, God!"

I sat up with a start as the room filled with an incandescent flare of white illumination from the passing lighthouse beacon. The figure before me vanished in the light. Then I was alone in the darkness once more.

"You were only dreaming," I murmured through chattering teeth. Though the coils of the old electric heater in the corner were glowing cherry red, the room was freezing. I turned my eyes to the windows.

The lace curtains were billowing gracefully around the antique maple wardrobe. For a moment I was certain my ghostly visitor was standing there in the shadows. But then I saw that the curtains were simply caught in a cold draft from a partially open window.

I got out of bed and scurried barefoot across the chilly floorboards, intending to close the window. As I drew closer I could hear a faint melodic voice drifting up from the lawn below. I looked outside, telling myself it must be the sound of the blowing wind, or perhaps one of the feral cats that Aunt Ellen used to feed. But the air outside was deathly still and nothing moved in the inky shadows around the house.

Then I heard the voice again, louder than before. My body shuddered with a chill that had nothing to do with the frigid air pouring in through the open window. Because it was unmistakably a woman's voice. Somewhere in the darkness below she was singing a sweet, sad melody.

The lighthouse beacon swept across the house again, illuminating her shimmering figure beside the wrought iron fence out front. She was dressed all in flowing white lace, as she had been the night before.

She did not look up at the sound of my astonished gasp. Instead, still softly singing words that I could not quite understand, she glided away in the direction of Maidenstone Island.

I stood in the window until the last faint traces of her voice were lost among the ordinary sounds of wavelets lapping against the nearby beach. With shaking hands I closed the window and went downstairs to make myself some tea.

I knew that I would not sleep again before morning.

When the tea was done I sat at the kitchen table, trying with little success to separate reality from imagination. For though I believed the beautiful spirit was real, I could not explain her appearances, which twice now had coincided with my vivid, unhappy dreams of Bobby.

Was it possible that she had heard me weeping and had come to comfort me in my grief?

But why? Who was she?

Desperate for an answer, I climbed the steep stairs to the large attic space above the main house. In the middle of the large expanse of the dark room I could see the white cord hanging from the bare lightbulb secured into one of the rafters high above me in the main peak of the roof. When I pulled it a yellow glow seemed to fill the room and I stood looking around.

In his zeal to finish the remodel Damon had deposited

here many of the things that had not been sold or discarded. Leaning against the far wall were the dreary family portraits that had hung in the parlor, hall and stairwell all of my life. But there was one I'd never seen before. I pulled it into the light and looked into Aunt Ellen's beautiful brown eyes. She must have been sixteen or so when this was painted—I had no idea she had been so beautiful—in a gown of white lace with a brilliant blue sash. By the time I remember her she was old and always wore black. I set the picture near the door; it belonged over the fireplace in her parlor.

I turned back to the room and found her folding rocking chair, the cushion a petit point rose design that I had done the summer I was fifteen. Aunt Ellen believed that ladies should know how to do handwork and so I had learned. I sat in her chair and could smell the violet fragrance that she loved so much. A tear came to my eye. I missed her.

In spite of my perceived rebellion as a young woman I had, in fact, enjoyed the cotillions, the afternoon teas, the special shopping trips that filled my dresser with gloves and hats because "ladies didn't leave the house without gloves and hats." Learning the ways of a Victorian lady had actually been one of the highlights of my girlhood.

I rubbed my eyes, back to the present. I found among the dusty relics of that vanished age Aunt Ellen's massive family Bible and her stack of carefully tended photo albums in a large leather trunk, exactly where I had placed them after her death.

Hauling an armload of heavy books down to the kitchen, I made myself another pot of tea and began searching the albums for some clue to the identity of the beautiful young woman I had seen in my room.

The flyleaf of the old Bible seemed the best place to

start. Because, beginning in 1842, all the marriages, births and deaths of five generations of Marks family members had been meticulously recorded there. Near the bottom of the list I found my own name, penned in Aunt Ellen's prim, no-nonsense style. Above it, written in by other hands, were the names of my father, my mother, grandparents, uncles, aunts and cousins.

On the day she had showed me the old picture, Aunt Ellen had indicated that her mother's uncle George, who was presumably the disgraced girl's father, had gone to New York to plead for her to return home. So I backtracked through the years until I found the names of George Hector Marks, Aunt Ellen's great-uncle, and his wife, Emily.

According to the Bible entries, George Marks was born in 1861, married in 1884 and had three children. The eldest, born in July of 1885 was a girl named Aimee. Two boys, Harold and Thomas, had followed in 1889 and 1890.

But there the paper trail ended.

The marriages and deaths of the two boys were duly recorded—Harold died young in France during the Great War in 1917, Thomas as an old man in Providence in 1969. But of Aimee Marks, who, if she was indeed my ghostly visitor, had looked in the photo I'd seen to be no older than twenty-five, no record had been made beyond her birth.

Frustrated, I put aside the Bible and tackled the old albums, searching the years between 1900 and 1910 for the studio photo of the girl that Aunt Ellen had briefly showed me but refused to name.

I had been at it for nearly an hour when the dark eyes and pretty face of my ghostly visitor jumped out at me from another old photograph. This was not a studio photo, but a group shot of several young people posing together on a beach.

Turning the picture over I discovered on the back a

faintly penciled inscription that read "Aimee's Sweet 16 party, July 1901."

"Yes!" Though the girl in the picture was younger than my ghost, she was definitely the one I had seen in my room. And if she was born in 1885 Aimee Marks would have turned sixteen in the summer of 1901.

Excited by my discovery, I pushed the album to one side and closely examined the sepia-toned photo. There were half a dozen teenagers in the picture, the girls all dressed in high-necked swim costumes, complete with dark stockings extending to their ankles, the boys in comical striped bathing suits and jaunty straw boaters. At the revelers' feet sat a wicker picnic hamper on a plaid blanket. And the familiar outline of the Maidenstone Lighthouse tower could be seen in the distance.

In the center of the photo Aimee was perched coquettishly atop an angular black bicycle, supported by two smiling boys, both of whom had their eyes fixed jealously on her. And despite the bulky, dark-colored swimming costume that clung damply to her slim, high-breasted figure, it was easy to understand the boys' transfixed expressions. Because, even at sweet sixteen, Aimee Marks had been an absolute knockout, with long, shapely legs that her prudish long stockings did little to conceal.

Though the whole party was stiffly posed for the picture—film exposures in that time being long, tedious affairs requiring many seconds of absolute stillness—there was something in Aimee's expression that set her apart from the other girls in the scene. Unlike the two captivated boys who seemed unable to take their eyes off of Aimee, the other girls were all squinting awkwardly into the camera—doubtless because the photographer had the sun at his back.

Aimee's eyes, however, were focused elsewhere. On

someone or something that lay just beyond the range of the lens.

Excited by my discovery, I worked my way through the rest of the albums for the time period, expecting at any moment to find another picture of the girl. I examined scores of fading family portraits, wedding shots and summer outings, until I determined from the gradually shifting trends in fashion, hairstyles and automobiles that I had reached the 1920s—far later, I believed, than my ghostly visitor had remained alive.

But I found no more photos of Aimee Marks. And, oddly, even the studio portrait that Aunt Ellen had showed me was nowhere to be found in the albums. In fact, not one of the hundreds of photos of the Marks family and friends that had been taken during the brief period when she had lived and died contained another image of Aimee Marks.

The first weak rays of the rising sun were lighting an ominous line of approaching clouds above a slate-gray sea as I closed the last thick volume.

Exhausted and vowing to more fully research Aimee's life as soon as I was fully settled into the house, I went back upstairs to bed and finally slept. Strangely, in my dreams, I was a teenager once more.

Danny Freedman was at the wheel of his old red Mustang and I was beside him. The sensual salsa rhythm was pounding in time to the beat of the gutted mufflers.

"Let's go out to the island and have a few beers," Danny suggested, slipping his arm around me and pulling me close.

"Well-bred young ladies do not drink beer with house painters," Aunt Ellen intoned from the tiny backseat of the Mustang. "It was one of his kind that ruined poor Aimee."

When I awoke, nearly eleven hours later, darkness was once again falling over Freedman's Cove and a high wind accompanied by hard, driving rain was shrieking around the house.

Chapter 12

Though I had hardly noticed at the time, the line of approaching clouds I'd seen that morning had heralded the arrival of the season's first big nor'easter. By late afternoon a frigid cyclonic storm roaring straight down from the Canadian Arctic was enveloping the rocky Rhode Island coastline in thundering surf accompanied by torrents of ice-laden rain.

Fortunately, after I'd left Krabb's the night before, I had forced myself to drive to the Food Mart. So I was well supplied with groceries and the other necessaries that one lays in before winter comes to Freedman's Cove. There were canned goods of every kind—in case there was no power to run the fridge. As an additional precaution against an electrical outage I had bought candles and boxes of big wooden matches for every room, along with extra batteries for the flashlights and a small portable radio for my nightstand.

The grilled cheese sandwich and canned tomato soup was comforting; a reminder of childhood lunches with Aunt Ellen. Of course she would have included sticks of celery and carrots because you had to have vegetables. I smiled at the memory. But with night closing in I hurriedly did the dishes and set about storing my supplies, checking the windows and shutters and generally battening down the place to withstand the unexpected bad weather.

Later, as the storm did its best to batter the sturdy old house, and with the distant boom of high surf crashing against the causeway, I phoned Damon to apologize for my unforgivable behavior of the previous night.

There was no answer at Damon's apartment, so I left a contrite message on his voice mail asking him to call me back when he got in.

As part of the remodeling before the house was put up as a rental property, Aunt Ellen's gloomy old formal parlor had been turned into a cozy sitting room. The idea—Damon's, of course—had been to create a cheerful space where summer vacationers might retreat on cold and rainy afternoons, not uncommon in Rhode Island, even in high summer. There they might enjoy a game of cards, a glass of wine or a film on DVD. And to that end the room had been furnished with comfortably cushioned wicker lounges and equipped with a nice reproduction Mission-style cabinet that hid a CD player, television and DVD player.

So, when my supplies were stashed and the windows all had been checked I went into the parlor and lit a fire in the cast-iron grate. I dashed outside and retrieved my laptop PC and a handful of favorite CDs from the Volvo, then brought a pot of hot chocolate from the kitchen and settled in to get organized.

Patsy Cline's heartrending "Crazy" was playing softly on the CD as I opened a new file and created a comprehensive list of chores still to be done around the house.

There was the phone to be turned on, of course. And if I was going to spend any substantial time up here during the approaching winter the heating oil tank in the basement would need to be checked and topped off, storm windows installed and a number of other basic but essential preparations made.

Boring though it was, I lost myself in the mundane details of the work, which was exactly the kind of structured activity—or so Damon had always claimed, anyway—that made me an asset to our antique appraisals business. Actually, I've always enjoyed the detail work. And that night in Aunt Ellen's house, with a good fire crackling at my feet and the pot of warm cocoa at my elbow, I felt positively snug and secure.

Might it be possible, I wondered, to move my work up here? After all, telecommuting was the in thing these days. Most of my duties in the city really involved nothing more than the writing of detailed reports and appraisals on the laptop. And that work was usually performed while I was at home listening to my favorite music.

As for the auctions and estate viewings that I was frequently required to attend on behalf of clients, as often as not I had to drive or fly to them in various locations, mostly in New England. But here I was in New England already. So why not adopt Freedman's Cove as my new base of operations? Certainly, I reasoned, anybody could answer the phone in the Manhattan office.

And by moving up here I could eliminate the fierce expense of my New York apartment, which, now that it had been ransacked and held only sad reminders of Bobby, I had little desire to return to, anyway.

I opened up my personal finance program and crunched a few numbers for rent, utilities and the like. The results were eye-opening. I saw that I could save almost $50,000 a year just by relocating to Freedman's Cove.

I was so excited by the whole concept that, even though it was nearly midnight, I decided to call Damon. I picked up my battered cell phone and punched in his number.

Strangely, I again got no answer.

Shutting down the computer and idly wondering where my unpredictable partner had gotten to, I went back out into the kitchen to warm up the last of my cocoa.

I was standing over the stove when a particularly hard blast of wind rattled the entire house. I peered out into the yard and saw the huge oak bending in the high gusts. Because the old house is very close to the sea, my concern was more for possible flooding than wind damage. So I returned to the parlor and turned on the TV, hoping to catch a late weather report.

CNN's Boston affiliate was just finishing up a story about the early winter storm. But before I could get any details, the reporter switched to a related story about a commuter plane crash that was being blamed on the bad weather. Since a plane crash of any kind was the last thing I needed to hear about, I turned off the TV and went up to bed.

My cell phone chirped as I was climbing the stairs. I switched it on, fully prepared for a tearful reunion with Damon. "Hello?" I answered. "Damon, is that you?"

Static crackled through the earpiece and a faint, garbled voice said my name. Then the connection went dead. I frowned at the phone, assuming that the storm had interfered with the reception. I was certain the caller had been Damon, because, except for Bobby, of course, he was the only person who had my private cell phone number. Grinning with relief, I immediately dialed Damon's apartment once more, but the static on the line was so severe that I heard only the first few words of his voice mail message.

"I'll call you tomorrow," I shouted, then switched off the phone and went into my room.

This would be my third night in my beloved turret bedroom. Twice before I had gone to sleep here, dreamed an awful dream about Bobby and then been visited by the sad ghost.

Such unsettling experiences would ordinarily have encouraged me to sleep on the sofa down in the parlor. But strangely I was not afraid.

In fact, I was almost hoping my gentle ghost would show herself again, though I could certainly do without the bad dreams. But I lit my blue fairy lamp anyway, then turned out the lights and climbed in under the covers.

I lay there in my snug sea captain's bed gazing up at the magical blue light tingeing the domed ceiling while the cold nor'easter howled outside my windows.

As I waited for the ghost I believed to be Aimee Marks to appear, I decided that I would attempt to communicate with her this time. For it seemed clear that she was aware of my presence. And, I believed, she had even spoken to me.

Sinking back onto my pillows I mentally composed a list of questions I wanted to ask her, beginning with why she haunted this room and this house. The wind in the eaves moaned and whistled. Pellets of freezing rain clattered against the windowpanes. The lighthouse beacon described endless circles of light and darkness across the leaping waves.

Slowly my eyelids grew heavy and I slept.

"Love me forever?" Bobby was whispering softly in my ear, his warm breath tickling the hairs on the back of my neck. "Mmmm," I sighed and snuggled down farther into the covers.

Chapter 13

It was still raining early the next morning when I awoke, though the wind seemed to have lost much of its force overnight.

Undeterred by the sloppy weather and anxious for some fresh air, I scarfed down a light breakfast of oatmeal and coffee. Then I dressed in warm clothes and an old yellow slicker I'd found in a closet and went out to the Volvo.

After trying unsuccessfully to reach Damon several more times, I spent the rest of the morning driving around in the rain—to the telephone company, the post office and the hardware store, checking off items on my long To Do list. By the time I had disposed of the most pressing items it was past noon and I was getting hungry again. So I drove down to Krabb's for lunch.

At that time of day the restaurant was bustling with locals, and I thought I recognized several faces among the fishermen and shopkeepers clustered around the pink Formica tables. Fortunately, though, no one seemed to take any notice of me, which was the way I preferred it.

I happily accepted a booth beside one of the plate glass windows overlooking the harbor. And, after consulting the simplified daytime menu, I ordered a fresh lobster salad and a bowl of fish chowder and busied myself buttering a cracker. The sky outside was growing lighter by the minute.

As I ate, several fishing boats chugged past my window, headed for the channel leading out to the open sea, a good indicator that the weather would soon be clearing.

"Nice view, huh?"

I looked up to see Dan Freedman standing at my table, watching a departing lobster boat.

"That's how you started our last conversation," I reminded him. "A conversation," I added, "that left me feeling like a complete idiot."

"That wasn't my intention at all," he said, looking not at all remorseful.

"Well, you did lead me to believe you were a house painter," I countered somewhat accusingly.

He shook his head and a mischievous grin creased his deeply tanned features. "No," he said, "you reached that conclusion all by yourself."

There was a long pause while a waitress delivered my salad. Then Dan leaned closer and said in a low voice, "Would you have considered our conversation any less satisfactory if you had thought I wasn't a house painter?"

"That's a trick question." I laughed.

"Well," he said, eyeing my plate, "I'll let you get on with your lunch."

"No, please sit down," I insisted, remembering how easily we had conversed that afternoon out on the island.

"Are you sure?"

I nodded enthusiastically. "I'm sure," I said, realizing that I really did want someone to talk to. Not someone like Tom Barnwell, but someone like Dan, who would not be particularly interested in the intimate details of my life, or in hustling me off to bed.

So Dan Freedman sat down and we had lunch together. He ordered a gigantic hamburger with fries and we joked about cholesterol levels and house painting, and generally had a great time just chatting.

By the time our coffee arrived I'd told him a little about the antiques business. And I had learned that he had indeed joined the marines after leaving Freedman's Cove, that he'd become interested in painting while serving as an embassy guard in Brussels, and that he'd gone to art school there following his military service.

"I'd always had a thing about the old lighthouse and the Victorians," he explained. "So after I finished school I came back here to spend a summer painting them before I went looking for a serious job." He shrugged. "That was seven years ago."

"And somewhere along the way you just happened to become rich and famous," I said with a hint of sarcasm.

"People liked my stuff," he admitted frankly. "First a couple of the local galleries started buying. Then a sharp business manager from New York took me on and talked an investment group into backing me." He smiled and a note of affection crept into his voice. "Her name is Heather," he said. "And she's really the one who's responsible for the success. Believe me, nobody was more surprised than yours truly." Dan grinned boyishly. "I just like to slap paint on canvas."

"And the name Freedan? Where did that come from?"

For the first time since he had sat down with me Dan looked slightly uncomfortable. "Well, that was sort of accidental," he replied. "See, I wasn't really all that convinced of my talent that first summer back here. And I didn't want to embarrass the family."

He swung his head to indicate a group of grizzled fishermen joking and drinking beer at a nearby table. The men waved and Dan waved back at them. "Those guys are my uncles and cousins," he confided. "Lobstermen, mostly. And a tougher bunch you're unlikely to meet anywhere.

"Anyway, I figured if I put my name on a bunch of what they would have regarded as fruity pictures of old houses, they'd take a lot of ribbing around town. So I started signing my work Freedan."

Dan shrugged and a flush of color tinged his cheeks. "By the time my pictures started selling and drawing some good reviews it was too late to change the name. So it just stuck."

He looked at me like a schoolboy who's just explained to the teacher that a bear ate his homework. "Pretty lame excuse, huh?"

I shook my head and laughed. "How do your cousins and uncles feel about your pictures now?" I asked. "Or have you let them in on your secret yet?"

"Those guys?" He grinned. "Naw, they all still think I'm a house painter."

We chatted for a while longer, enjoying the sight of the sun breaking out of the clouds and lighting up the harbor. Throughout the conversation we each carefully avoided probing too deeply into the other's life beyond our respective work. And though a few natural opportunities arose to bring them into the conversation, the names of Debbie Carver and my old beau Tom Barnwell were not mentioned.

All too quickly the coffee was gone, the check had arrived and lunch was clearly over. We got up to leave and went out together into the bright autumn sunshine. A few eager seagulls were wheeling and screeching overhead as we walked to my Volvo.

"Looks like the rain is gone for a while," Dan observed, squinting up at the clearing sky.

"Then I suppose that means you can start painting again," I said, intending it as a joke.

"Yeah, I was painting the old lightkeeper's cottage before the storm," he replied seriously. "So I guess I'll go on out to the island and finish up."

"When is the museum open?" I asked, thinking of Aimee Marks. Though I hadn't been inside the converted lightkeeper's cottage in years, I knew that it contained many newspapers and books about the town and the Victorians, as well as the history of the Maidenstone Light itself.

Dan looked interested so I explained. "I'm doing a little research on a couple of skeletons in the family closet," I said. "And I thought the museum might have some useful information."

"Well, after Labor Day the place is only open to the public on Saturday afternoons," he said, reading the disappointment in my face. Then he grinned. ". . . Unless you happen to have a key."

"Which, of course, you just happen to . . ."

He dug into his jeans and produced a ring of shiny brass keys. "What's the use of being a local celebrity if you don't have the keys to the town museum?" He laughed. "I'll be out there all afternoon, painting. Drop by anytime."

Chapter 14

By midafternoon the rain clouds had disappeared entirely. The heavy northeast winds had been replaced by a mild breeze that rippled the glassy surface of the sea with the little rough patches that old-time sailors refer to as cat's-paws. Since it was unlikely that I would have many opportunities to enjoy the moped once winter set in, I rolled it out of the carriage house and fired up the eager little engine. To my great satisfaction it caught on the very first try.

This time I was prepared for the breezy ride out to the island. I had found an old ski jacket to wear and with a bike helmet on my head and heavy sunglasses protecting my eyes, the trip was even more enjoyable than it had been the first time.

From a distance I saw Dan's Toyota beside the lightkeeper's cottage. So I rode into the parking area expecting to find him posed theatrically behind an easel. The sight that actually greeted me when I spotted him caused my jaw to drop.

Because Dan Freedman was standing at one corner of the old cottage, slapping thick white paint onto the weathered clapboards from a big plastic bucket. He turned at the sound of my approach and cheerfully waved his brush at me.

"I was wondering if you were going to show up," he called out over the buzz of my engine.

"You really are painting the lightkeeper's cottage." I laughed, not sure if he had arranged the whole thing as a joke for my benefit.

Dan raised his eyebrows mischievously and wiped his paint-soiled hands on a rag. "Well, that is what I said I was going to be doing, isn't it?"

I turned off the motor, parked the bike on its stand and pulled off my helmet and glasses. "That's what you said," I admitted.

"One of the duties of an honorary museum curator," he explained, "is helping to keep the old place shipshape. In fact, I suspect that's the only reason the town council gave me the job, though I've recently done a bit of redecorating on my own. Come on inside and I'll show you around."

He carefully replaced the lid on the paint bucket and led me around to the open front door of the cottage. "Welcome to the Maidenstone Island Maritime Museum and Lighthouse Tour," he said, ushering me into a cozy room with a large stone fireplace.

"Prior to full automation of the beacon in 1967, the cottage was the residence for a succession of lighthouse keepers and their families," Dan announced, sounding like a tour guide. "Based on old photographs and journals of the time, I've tried to restore this room to approximately what it would have been like in the late 1860s. At least," he added sheepishly, "this is my idea of how it might have looked."

"It's lovely," I said, looking around with an appraising eye. The small front room was filled with sturdy but comfortable country furniture of the period, and a gaily colored rag rug covered the polished oak floorboards. There was a blackened iron cooking pot on the hearth and a magnificent polished brass barometer on the mantel.

"Except for a few exhibits in dusty cases the cottage was practically empty when I took over as curator," Dan said as I walked around the room. "It was my idea to try to re-create the original feel of the place by furnishing it. I gathered up this stuff from antique shops around the area."

I smiled approvingly. Though the furnishings were authentic I was more impressed by the little touches that Dan had added to his re-creation of the lightkeeper's living space. Small items like a 19th-century child's reading primer lying open on the hearth and a half-finished wood carving beside a rack of well-chewed pipes gave the impression that the room's Victorian-era occupants had stepped out just a moment before.

"You've got an artist's eye for detail," I said, which brought a broad grin to his face.

When I had finished admiring the parlor, Dan led me into an adjoining room, which really did look like a museum. The whitewashed board walls were filled with photos of shipwrecks, storms at sea and portraits of generations of lightkeepers and their families.

Ranged beneath the pictures were glass cases containing small mementos, pieces of nautical gear and journals kept by the lightkeepers over the years.

"These are wonderful pieces," I said, leaning over to inspect a display of exquisite scrimshaw carvings beneath the glass.

"The lightkeeper's life was a pretty lonely one," Dan explained. "Before the raised causeway was constructed out here to the island in the 1940s the lighthouse was frequently cut off from the mainland by high seas. Creating handicrafts like that scrimshaw helped pass the long, stormy nights, and the objects produced were often sold in the village as a means of supplementing the lightkeeper's small salary."

"Too bad they didn't know what scrimshaw would be going for in today's collector's market," I commented. "All of their descendants could have been rich."

Dan halted and smiled ruefully. "My great-great-grandfather would have been very happy to hear that," he said, pointing to a picture of a white-bearded old salt standing before the cottage. "Old Ben Freedman there was the first keeper of the Maidenstone Light." Dan touched the photo affectionately. "Unfortunately, the poor old guy died nearly penniless."

Like every other child in Freedman's Cove I had heard the story of Ben Freedman many times while I was growing up. The town's name had been changed from Southport to Freedman's Cove to honor the lightkeeper after he had heroically risked his life rowing a tiny dinghy into murderous surf to rescue the victims of an 1875 shipwreck.

But I also recalled the whispered stories about the Freedmans, which Aunt Ellen had repeated often when rebellious young Danny had come to cut our lawn. Aunt Ellen had always said it was a disgrace that the town hero's descendants had turned out to be nothing more than a collection of poor drunks and lobstermen, and she hoped poor Danny wouldn't turn out the same way.

"Your ancestor must have been a remarkable man," I commented diplomatically while trying to read the flinty-eyed gaze of the grizzled old codger in the photo.

"Well, you won't find it in the official historical record," Dan replied, "but I'm afraid my luckless ancestor actually ended up as the town drunk."

I raised my eyebrows but said nothing, for that was exactly what I had heard.

"According to his journal," Dan continued, "Ben Freedman originally became a lighthouse keeper because he never could get along with people. So when the rescue turned him into an overnight celebrity he just couldn't handle it. Though he didn't write it down, Old Ben is reported to have once told my great-grandmother that he only took to the bottle because it made the people tolerable to him."

I nodded, not sure what to say.

Dan ended the awkward moment by taking my hand. "When was the last time you were up in the lighthouse?" he asked.

"When I was about twelve," I answered uneasily. I had gone into the tower on a dare and I vaguely recalled a long, dizzying climb up the winding iron stairway, followed by an even more dizzying view from the round glass cupola on top. I think I may have gotten nauseous afterward.

Generally I am not too fond of extreme heights.

We entered the damp, chilly interior of the lighthouse tower through a heavy steel door. An electric motor hummed softly somewhere high over our heads. The gloom of the place closed in on me almost immediately and I shuddered under the massive bulk of the black serpentine stairway that filled the tower and obscured most of the wan light filtering down from a hundred feet above.

Dan pulled the outer door shut with a loud clang that echoed through the enclosed space. "Well, how do you like it so far?" He grinned.

"It feels like a tomb," I replied, pulling my jacket tighter around me and trying to think of a good excuse to return to the cottage.

"Ah, but wait 'til you see that view again." He laughed, bounding away up the stairs and disappearing around the first twist before I could protest. "Come on. You'll love it."

I craned my neck helplessly, trying to catch a glimpse of him. But except for the hollow ring of his footsteps on the metal treads I might as well have been alone. So, wondering exactly how I had gotten myself into this fine predicament, I gripped the cold iron railing and started up after him.

Ten minutes later, huffing like an elderly asthmatic, I stepped into the small white chamber at the top of the tower.

"Your face is red," Dan observed with amusement. When I did not reply his smile faded and he reached out to touch my perspiring brow. "You okay?"

I nodded and unzipped my jacket, feeling the heat rise off my chest. "I'm afraid I've been neglecting the gym lately," I puffed, looking around the small space while I waited for my heart rate to slow to normal. The afternoon sun was streaming in through the circle of spotless glass panes that surrounded the room, casting dazzling reflections off the huge lenses suspended on polished brass fittings in the center.

"It really is a beautiful piece of work, isn't it?" I was gazing in fascination at the intricate clockwork mechanism of the old beacon.

He ran a hand fondly over the satiny finish of the massive gear wheel supporting the light. "We seldom give our ancestors enough credit for their technical accomplishments," he agreed. "This beacon weighs almost a thousand pounds. It projects a beam forty miles out to sea. And this same hand-machined gear has been turning it precisely once every forty-five seconds for over a hundred and sixty years without a single breakdown."

"Amazing," I said, stepping closer to examine the polished gears and counterweights suspending the mechanism.

"Makes you wonder how long your car would last if it had been made by the guys who built this thing, doesn't it?" Dan pointed to a spidery engraving on the metal wheel. "See here, the man who made this gear signed it. Arthur Thackeray, Greenwich, England, 1846."

"Pride of craftsmanship was everything in that time," I said, bending to peer at the inscription. "It's one of the things I love about working with antiques. You can feel the sheer joy that went into crafting something especially beautiful and enduring." I straightened and shook my head. "Nobody cares about things like that anymore."

"Oh, some of us still care deeply." Dan's voice was filled with fervor and I turned to look at him. Through the broad window at his back I could see the cold waters of the Atlantic that stretched endlessly to the horizon, their color in the sun exactly matching the shade of his clear green eyes.

The absolute perfection of the scene clutched at my heart. Suddenly I felt a wave of dizziness sweeping over me. I closed my eyes and reeled forward into his arms. He caught me effortlessly. "Sue, what's wrong?" he asked with concern.

"Nothing," I murmured, feeling extremely foolish. But I did not immediately open my eyes, savoring for just a moment the feeling of being held . . . the way that Bobby had once held me, I dimly realized.

No sooner had that thought come into my mind than I understood what was happening to me. I shook off the feeling and pulled free of his embrace, embarrassed.

"I'm afraid I have a little vertigo issue," I said, indicating the dazzling vista of sea and shore that lay beyond the windows.

"Why didn't you say so?" he asked, pulling a stool from a small desk containing nothing but a black emergency telephone. "I would have never brought you up here if I'd had any idea . . ."

I sat down, feeling the hot blood coloring my cheeks. "No, I wanted to come up here again," I insisted, forcing myself to look outside. Far away, at the base of the stone causeway, the line of stately Victorian homes dominated the shoreline. I could clearly see my bedroom turret above the outlines of the denuded trees.

"This is exactly the reverse of the view from my bedroom window," I observed, pointing.

Dan nodded absently. "I know," he replied.

I swung my head around and stared at him. Behind him the barrel of a large brass telescope gleamed in the sun. He followed my gaze to the instrument, which was pointed in the general direction of my house, and understanding slowly registered on his tanned features.

Dan raised his hands disarmingly. "Oh, no, Sue," he protested. "You don't think I've been sitting up here at night spying on you." He saw the shock in my eyes and realized that he had put into words exactly the first thought that had popped into my mind. "Good God, no," he spluttered. "Actually I was just remembering something I read about your house when I inventoried some of the museum's papers last year."

I gave him a blank stare.

"There's a series of entries in one of the old lightkeepers' journals," he hurried to explain. "They were all written around the time your ancestor fell to her death from this tower."

"My ancestor?" My voice was a hoarse whisper.

Dan nodded. "A young woman . . . Surely you heard the story from your family."

I shook my head slowly. "I never heard any story."

Dan paused, considering his next words carefully. "Well, maybe they wouldn't have told you. I mean, it wasn't exactly the kind of thing the Markses would have wanted spread around, especially back in 1910. I'm sure they probably preferred to forget the whole thing."

"What happened to her?" I asked, feeling my mouth go suddenly dry.

Chapter 15

Dan Freedman lifted a big canvas-bound book from a stack of similarly bound ledgers on my coffee table and placed it in his lap. "The journal of Amos Carter for 1909 and 1910."

It was dark outside and we were sitting before a roaring fire in Aunt Ellen's old parlor. Unable to recall all the details he had read more than a year earlier, Dan had not attempted to relate to me from memory alone the full story of Aimee Marks's death.

Instead, we had come down from the lighthouse and dug out the old journal from a huge cache of documents stored in the attic of the lightkeeper's cottage. Without telling me why, Dan had insisted on searching for three other journals as well. By the time we finally found them all the sun was going down. So we'd placed my moped in the back of his truck and returned to the house, where I had prepared an impromptu supper of canned soup and cold sandwiches.

Now, with our sandwiches eaten and mugs of freshly brewed coffee before us, Dan was ready to proceed.

"Amos Carter was the keeper of the Maidenstone Light from 1905 until 1913," he began, thumbing through the lined pages of the thick handwritten ledger. "And, like all lighthouse keepers of the time, he was required to keep records of everything that affected the light."

"Like a captain keeps a ship's log?" I asked with interest.

Dan nodded. "Exactly like a ship's log," he answered. "The idea was to put down important information concerning the operation of the light. But there were no hard rules about what had to be written, so journals might also include other information, such as daily weather reports, descriptions of shipwrecks along the coast and almost anything else you can imagine."

Dan found the entry he was seeking and looked up. "In many cases, depending on how detailed he wanted to get, a lightkeeper's journal might contain the only accurate historical record of local events. Of course," he added, "many lightkeepers entered only the absolute minimum information required."

He showed me a double page crammed with small, neat handwriting in faded blue ink. "But Amos Carter seemed to have spent a great deal of time working on his journal. In fact, it's a regular gossip column about life in turn-of-the-century Freedman's Cove." He took back the book and scanned it with distaste. "And it seems that Amos was also something of a Peeping Tom and self-appointed moral guardian," Dan said. "He describes several times in his journals how he kept his eye on the whole town through that big brass telescope up in the tower."

"Which is how you happened to know all about the view of my bedroom window," I interjected sheepishly.

He nodded. "Amos Carter had been watching your ancestor Aimee Marks for a long time and he wrote it all down."

I took a deep breath as Dan placed his finger on the page.

"For instance, here's an entry Amos wrote in July of 1909, more than a year before the girl's death:

> *"Weather unseasonably warm, sea dead calm. Saw young Aimee in the high turret window of the big Marks house again tonight. Figure if I can see her flaunting her naked bosoms before the whole town there must be others who see her as well. It is a disgrace to the community. The shameless girl stood for fully ten minutes brazenly gazing my way.*
>
> *"Will watch her closely each night now for further incidents and leave an anonymous note for her father when I row over there for supplies on the Saturday."*

"Dammit!" I angrily exclaimed. "Do you mean to say that this lecherous bastard was deliberately spying on her night after night without her knowledge?"

"All in the worthy interest of protecting public morals," Dan said sarcastically.

"That is such bullshit," I retorted. "It was a hot summer night and the girl came to her window, which does not, by the way, face the town. She was probably only hoping for a breath of cool air. Amos Carter was undoubtedly the only one who could even see her."

"Hey, I didn't write it, I'm just reading it," Dan replied defensively. He flipped through several more pages of Amos Carter's cramped handwriting. "But if you liked that," he said, "you're going to love this. Here's another entry, dated August of the same year:

> *"Spied the Marks girl on South Beach around dusk today with a stranger, some visiting New*

> *York dandy who claims to be an artist. Observed much unseemly touching before the two settled in behind the rocks, where they remained for an indecent interval of time. Something will have to be done. I shall write again to her father, and perhaps send a note to the town council and the church elders as well."*

"No wonder poor Aimee ran away to New York," I said, pitying the long-dead girl for the cruel injustice she had suffered at the hands of the sanctimonious lighthouse keeper.

"Life in Freedman's Cove must have become a sheer hell for her," Dan concurred, "with Amos secretly scrutinizing her every move and sending anonymous poison-pen letters to her family and God knows who else in town." He flipped to several more journal entries for August of 1909, all detailing Aimee's increasingly intimate liaisons on the beach with the same nameless artist.

Then, in mid-September, the stranger suddenly disappeared and Amos Carter had returned to spying on Aimee through her bedroom window. In a final entry, posted in early November, he wrote of observing "a fearful row" between the girl and her father, an argument that left Aimee alone and weeping in her room.

"My God," I whispered when Dan had finished reading, "the wicked bastard must have destroyed her reputation and forced her to leave town."

"Well, something happened," Dan agreed, "because there's no further mention of Aimee Marks in Carter's journal until late the following year, when she turns up dead here at the lighthouse."

He looked up from the book with a frown. "You say she went to New York?"

I quickly related the few sketchy details that I had gotten from Aunt Ellen about Aimee and the anonymous New York artist.

Dan listened thoughtfully. "So she ran off to New York to live with a painter," he marveled. "I can see how that would have scandalized your average straitlaced New England family of the time. Do you think this painter's interest in her was romantic or professional?"

I went to the bookcase and retrieved the group photo of the girl as a teenager. "You be the judge," I said. Dan regarded the picture for several moments.

"She was very beautiful," he said at last. "Not just conventionally pretty, but truly beautiful." His green eyes left the picture and met mine. "For a minute I was sure I'd seen that face before." He smiled. "Then I realized why she looked familiar. I suppose you know that you look a lot like her," he added softly.

I took the picture from his hand and stared at it, aware for the first time that there was indeed a strong family resemblance between me and the girl perched on the antique bicycle. "Well, I'll never see sixteen again," I said, trying to make a joke of it.

Dan's eyes hadn't left mine. "You're still the prettiest girl in Freedman's Cove," he said, reaching up to touch my cheek. "I remember wishing that you were a year or two older, back when we were teenagers . . ."

The touch of his fingers was electric on my skin and I recoiled in shock from the unexpected surge of emotions that suddenly welled up within me, emotions I hadn't experienced since . . . Bobby.

"Well, I probably couldn't have competed with Debbie Carver back when you two used to drive out to the island together," I quipped, in a poor attempt to cover my acute discomfort.

Almost before the cruel words had left my lips I regretted them, for Dan's face had turned suddenly dark.

"I'm sorry, Dan," I stammered. "I had no right to say that."

"It's okay," he said, picking up the journal and searching for another entry.

"No, it's not," I moaned. "You just paid me a lovely compliment and I repaid it by hurting your feelings. I feel like such a jerk."

Dan carefully set the book on the coffee table. "Sue, I know what people in this town always thought and said about Debbie and me," he said evenly. "And after all this time it doesn't really matter that none of it was true." His mouth curved into a wan smile. "Both of us have managed to survive."

I shook my head vigorously. "What I said was positively unforgivable," I insisted, thinking of the long-ago summer night when I had secretly watched his old Mustang driving slowly out to Maidenstone Island and wished I was the one with him. "As unforgivable as icky old Amos Carter spying through his telescope and spreading his poisonous rumors about Aimee Marks. I have absolutely no idea what kind of relationship you and Debbie Carver had," I concluded lamely. "Nor is it any of my damn business."

"Debbie and I were the best of friends," Dan said quietly, "two outcasts from the wrong side of the tracks who clung to one another when things got rough. Mostly we talked about escaping from Freedman's Cove . . . She wanted to be a singer, you know."

"Please, Dan," I pleaded, feeling even worse than before. "You don't have to explain anything to me—"

"Oh, but I want to," he whispered, taking my hand in his. "I really do want you to understand, Sue."

Then, without warning, our lips were touching and the

electricity had been turned back on. I felt it reaching down into my soul and let it carry me away, heedless of my guilty realization that Dan Freedman was not entirely to blame. For, like two magnets placed too close together, we had been irresistibly drawn together at the same instant.

An image of Bobby's smiling face flashed through my mind and I abruptly pulled away.

"I'm sorry. That was my fault—" Dan began.

I waved my hand, dismissing the apology. "No," I said, slightly breathless. "It happened and it was wonderful—"

"But?" He left the question hanging between us.

"This is just a very bad time for me," I said evasively. "It's complicated . . ."

"Let's just leave it there for a while, then," he said with a smile. "We'll just say it was a very nice kiss between friends—"

"No," I corrected, "it was a great kiss. And I hope we can have another one sometime soon."

Dan grinned at me, then took my hand and gave it a firm shake. "Deal," he said.

"Now," I resumed, clearing my throat to regain my composure. "What about my poor ancestor Aimee? Are you going to let me in on the rest of the details or not?"

Dan picked up the journal again and turned to a page he had already marked. "I thought it was important for you to understand everything that went on between Aimee and Amos Carter the previous year," he said. "Because this is the entry that Amos made on the night that she died:

November 6th, 1910. Light snow followed by clearing skies. Retired to bed at the end of the midnight watch. Was roused around two a.m. by the sound of a woman's scream. Went out to find Miss Aimee Marks of Freedman's Cove lying in the yard, having evidently fallen from the light tower. Checked for signs of life but she was beyond help. Commended her soul to the Almighty and covered the body with my coat. Rowed across at daylight to fetch the town constable."

Dan closed the journal and placed it back on the coffee table with the others.

"That's it?" My voice was a hoarse whisper.

"That's all he wrote," Dan confirmed. "Amos Carter never mentioned Aimee or the incident again. He stayed on as the keeper of the light until 1913 . . . when he leaped off the tower to his own death."

"Christ," I breathed.

"The strangeness of the incident intrigued me when I first ran across it last year," he said. "So the next time I went to the town hall to do research I checked the records for Aimee's death certificate. Her fall was ruled accidental."

"Accidental?" I snorted. "What on earth would she have been doing up in Amos Carter's lighthouse alone in the middle of the night in winter?"

Dan shrugged. "That remains a complete mystery. There was a short obituary in the local paper that simply reported Aimee had died from an accidental fall. Nothing more. So evidently the town authorities bought Amos's story, lock, stock and barrel. Possibly the fact that her reputation had already been ruined made her seem like a logical candidate for suicide. Or—"

"Or what?" I challenged. I was really extremely upset by the whole thing.

Dan shrugged. "Or perhaps she really did commit suicide. Maybe choosing the lighthouse as the place to kill herself was her way of getting back at Amos for what he'd done to her."

"Well, I'll tell you what I think happened," I exclaimed vehemently. "Aimee Marks went out there to the lighthouse to confront that son of a bitch about his spying and he killed her."

"That certainly seems like a good possibility," Dan conceded.

"A possibility?" I shouted, jumping to my feet and pacing the floor like a caged tiger. "It's the only answer that even makes any sense. Afterwards, that bastard Carter was obviously so overwhelmed by his own guilt that he ended up killing himself."

"Why is all of this so important to you?" Dan asked quietly.

The unexpected question caught me completely off guard. "Well, isn't it perfectly obvious that Amos Carter murdered Aimee Marks?" I spluttered.

"Maybe," said Dan. "But even if that's true, it happened almost one hundred years ago, Sue. Anyone who might have even known either of them when they were alive has been dead for several decades now."

I sat down and sipped cold coffee from my cup. "Well, of course," I murmured, reluctant to admit that I had in fact been visited by the ghost of Aimee Marks less than twenty-four hours earlier.

"You haven't by any chance seen her lately, have you?" Dan inquired casually.

My mouth fell open and I stared at him.

"That's what I figured," he said.

Chapter 16

I lay suspended among the surging bubbles in the Jacuzzi tub, trying to sort out everything that had happened during the day. It was very late and Dan had left only minutes before, after making me promise to call him if I wanted to talk further.

I feared I had already talked too much.

After my initial shocked reaction to his strange question about Aimee Marks, it had taken Dan nearly an hour to get me to admit that I had indeed seen her. But I had finally broken down and told him the whole story, hastening to qualify my ghostly sightings by explaining, somewhat tearfully, I'm afraid, about Bobby's death and the persistent dreams I had been having ever since.

Dan had listened quietly and attentively without commenting until I finished.

"So," I had finally concluded, sniffling miserably, "I guess you could say there's a very distinct possibility that I'm slightly crazy and I only imagined that Aimee Marks's spirit comes to my room at night. At least I'm sure that's what my shrink would tell you."

His response had not been what I was expecting.

"Your shrink," Dan had replied gently, "sounds to me like one of those smug, unpleasant people who revel in labeling themselves hard-nosed skeptics, and who feel unduly threatened by anything that can't be neatly wrapped in plastic."

I'd managed to laugh a little then, despite my tears, grateful that he at least didn't think I was totally nuts. "That's definitely Laura," I said. "But how can you be sure she's not right? Don't tell me you've seen Aimee's ghost, too?"

Dan shook his head. Then he dropped another bombshell. "Unfortunately, no," he replied. "But I'm pretty sure that many other people have. An apparition fitting your description of Aimee Marks has been seen many times on the road out to the point and up in the old lighthouse tower. In fact," he continued, "she was a famous attraction around Freedman's Cove for years. Most people had no idea who she was. But since she was young and seen so frequently around the Maidenstone Lighthouse, they took to calling her The Lightkeeper's Daughter."

Now it was my turn to be skeptical. "Dan, I practically grew up in this house," I countered. "If there's been a famous ghost wandering around here for all these years, how come I never heard anything about her?"

That was when he showed me the other journals that he had insisted on bringing along, journals written by lightkeepers who had held the job after Amos Carter's death.

As it turned out, The Lightkeeper's Daughter had been seen and described numerous times in the official lighthouse logs throughout the 1920s and 1930s.

So regular in fact were her appearances that several noted psychics and mediums had been attracted to Freedman's Cove from as far away as New York and Philadelphia, hoping to glimpse her.

Then, sometime in the early 1940s—around the same time the stone causeway was built—the apparitions had abruptly stopped and the ghost had been all but forgotten. Until now.

Considering that astonishing information, I reasoned, perhaps I wasn't really losing my mind after all. At least not to the extent of seeing things that weren't really there.

But the mere fact that others had witnessed my ghost in earlier times didn't completely let me off the hook. I was still worried that I might not be fully in control of my faculties. How could I be? Not only had I let Dan Freedman kiss me, I had wanted him to do it. In fact I had kissed him back and had enjoyed it, thoroughly.

The waters of the Jacuzzi swirled sensually about my body, conjuring up another quick, steamy remembrance of that long-ago summer night when I had laid naked before my open windows, fantasizing about Danny Freedman.

I pushed the carnal image from my mind, attempting to bring my thoughts back to an orderly assessment of my mental state. Still, if I truly wasn't crazy, I fretted, how could I have reveled so in the kiss of another man when I was so profoundly grief-stricken over losing Bobby?

I could not come up with a satisfactory explanation.

I stood at the casement window and watched the foam on the edges of the waves; it was almost fluorescent in the moonlight. As the beacon of Maidenstone Lighthouse cut through the night I thought of horrible Amos Carter spying on Aimee. My ire was replaced by an embarrassed blush at the thought that someone could have been watching me, too. I shuddered to think as the light fell across me.

Shaking it off, I went to bed and slept, anticipating more baleful dreams of Bobby's handsome face.

But instead of another melancholy rendezvous with my

lost love, I experienced a comical and perplexing encounter with Damon.

Funny even when he was at his most serious, my dear partner proved to be a howl that night. So much so that I could actually hear myself giggling at his antics in my sleep.

"Sue, darling, there's something we have simply got to discuss."

Damon was sitting behind his perpetually cluttered desk in our Manhattan offices. Gone were his flamboyant silk shirt and tight leather pants. In their place he wore a conservatively striped business suit, complete with a tastefully patterned silk tie. And his flyaway hair had actually been combed.

I remarked on his odd appearance, and Damon spluttered angrily and pointed a stubby finger at me. "I'm trying to be serious, so you'd better listen to me now, girl," he warned in his syrupy Southern accent. "'Cause I'm telling you this for your own good . . ."

I waited, giggling like a schoolgirl. Because, like Aunt Ellen before him, Damon was forever giving me practical advice and telling me things for my own good.

In my dream, Damon opened his mouth to speak and a cartoon bubble appeared over his head. The word BOBBY was printed there in shaky cartoon letters surrounded by little *POW!* marks and exclamation points.

My giggles turned to laughter. "I know, I know," I retorted, anticipating his next line. "If I'd had better locks on the apartment door, the junkies wouldn't have stolen Bobby's stuff. It's okay, I don't blame you, Damon. It was my own fault . . ."

Damon's round, moonlike features twisted angrily. He shook his head in frustration and rolled his eyes skyward to look at the silly cartoon balloon floating above him. "Sue, listen to me!" he demanded, his voice rising to a frantic squeal.

I bit my tongue, put on a straight face and listened.

"It makes me very sad to have to be the one . . ." he began. Big blue comic-book tears suddenly began to roll down Damon's fat, shiny cheeks.

I clutched my sides and howled at him, the sound of my laughter drowning out his feeble attempt to tell me whatever it was.

In the background, someone began tapping out a funny little tune on a jangling brass bell.

I awoke to the loud, persistent ring of the old-fashioned black telephone on my bedside table.

Struggling to come awake, I sat up and glanced sleepily at the travel clock beside the phone.

It was six-fifteen in the morning.

Gray light filtered in through the windows from a dull sky filled with threatening storm clouds.

The phone chimed again.

"Hello?"

The stranger's voice on the other end of the line was indistinct over the background clatter of a high-speed computer printer and I had to ask him to repeat his question.

"Yes," I replied when he finally made himself heard over the noise, "this is Susan Marks speaking."

I listened with growing bewilderment as he identified himself and rattled off a dispassionate message, followed by several disturbing questions that I could not answer. He then gave me a set of directions and asked if I had understood.

I nodded dumbly at the phone in my hand. "Yes," I replied dully. "I'll get there as soon as I can."

The line went dead and I sat there holding the receiver until it started to bleep annoyingly, prodding me to hang up. I replaced it in its cradle and listened to the silence closing in around me.

I didn't begin to cry immediately, that would come later. But I knew that I did not want to go through this alone.

Chapter 17

After I hung up from the early-morning phone call I hurriedly dressed and went outside in the rain to the Volvo. But one look at my trembling hands as I fumbled to get the key into the ignition convinced me that I was in no condition to drive. So, picking up my cell phone, I impulsively dialed Dan's number to ask if he could possibly go with me.

He asked me to give him twenty minutes to make a few calls—calls I suspected, that had involved scraping whatever other plans he might have had for the day. Feeling miserably inadequate, I waited for him in the Volvo, assuming it would be more reliable and comfortable on the long drive than his battered old truck.

In my agitated state I completely forgot that my unassuming new friend was the famous and successful artist Freedan. So I was momentarily surprised when he pulled into my driveway a short time later in a large and luxuriously appointed Mercedes sedan. Typical of Dan's low-key demeanor, he had casually described the Mercedes as his "other car." The old Toyota pickup, it seemed, was strictly for hauling around paint and the other frequently messy trappings of his work.

After I briefly explained the situation to him, we immediately started for Boston, pausing only long enough to pull into a nearby truck stop to fill the Mercedes' gas tank and pick up coffee and doughnuts.

Now we were speeding north, with Dan skillfully guiding the powerful car through clouds of blinding mist thrown up by lumbering tractor trailer rigs and around lines of slower traffic.

"So this guy who called you was from the FAA?" Dan Freedman took his eyes from the rain-swept interstate access ramp and glanced across the car at me.

"No." I wearily shook my head. "He said he was from the National Transportation Safety Board . . . NTSB. That's the branch of the FAA that investigates all crashes of U.S.-registered aircraft."

I had learned the distinction between the federal aviation authorities the hard way, following the disappearance of Bobby's plane. After all fatal aviation accidents the NTSB routinely interviews the friends and families of flight crews, in order to determine whether the pilots may have been under any undue physical or emotional stress.

Accordingly, several weeks after the oil company's jet was lost, an NTSB agent had come up from Washington to ask me whether Bobby had ever had a problem with drugs or alcohol, or if I thought he had been having an affair, had gambling debts, suffered from mental illness, etc.

Biting my tongue in order to keep from screaming at the cold, bureaucratic insensitivity of the questions, I had somehow managed to remain dry-eyed throughout the distressing interview.

But even as I calmly denied that some unsavory secret might have caused his jet to crash into the sea I was uncomfortably aware of how little I really knew about Bobby's life before we met.

Miss Practical had snidely asked, "Before you met? You

don't know that much about him now." That's ridiculous, I countered, I know everything about him.

But as the hours passed and the investigator asked questions like, When was he to arrive wherever he was going? I didn't know. Which hotel? I didn't know. I realized then that while he had given me his cell phone number I had no other way to contact him. When was he due back? All he'd said was a week or two and that he was going to the South Pacific. I had no idea what he did or where he went when we were not together.

I rationalized that it was because I never talked about work so he didn't, either. But the seeds of doubt had been planted.

After the man from the NTSB had gone away I had tried to put the unsettling incident behind me. Now the same agency had called me again, this time with an urgent summons.

Dan was silent as we reached the top of the curving interstate ramp and accelerated into a line of swiftly moving morning traffic. "Even with the rain we should be there in a couple of hours," he advised. "Maybe you should close your eyes and try to get a little rest. There's a button on the side of the seat if you want it to recline."

"I don't think I can sleep," I said, lifting a Styrofoam cup from a holder between the seats and sipping bitter 7-Eleven coffee. "I can't tell you how much I appreciate this, Dan. But I feel terrible about ruining your whole day . . ."

He waved off my apology without taking his eyes from the road. "I'm just damn glad you called me," he said. "You shouldn't have to go through something like this alone."

I leaned back with my coffee, trying not to think too much about what awaited me at the end of our journey, and grateful for Dan's strong, reassuring presence at my side.

I closed my eyes and leaned back against the butter-soft tan leather of the headrest, relaxing slightly in the warmth from the heater vents.

Occasionally during the two-hour drive I stole glances at Dan's strong, assured profile behind the wheel, thankful, too, that he was not peppering me with more questions, but seemed content to leave me alone to prepare myself for what was sure to be a soul-wrenching experience.

Chapter 18

The motionless body lying beneath the sheets in the stark, dimly lit confines of a fourth-floor Boston Medical Center ICU suite might already have been dead. Except for a flashing monitor screen above the bed that registered a faint but steady heartbeat, there was no sign of life.

I stood for several moments looking down at the familiar face, now drained of all expression, its skin as ashen and lifeless as that of a corpse. When finally I worked up the courage to move closer and reach out for him I was shocked to find his hand warm to the touch.

Grasping the hand softly—as if by exerting too much pressure I might somehow further compound his grievous injuries—I whispered his name.

"Damon, can you hear me?"

There was no faint fluttering of the eyelids, no weak but unmistakable squeezing of my hand to show that he had heard and recognized my voice, or any similar reaction, such as television has conditioned us to expect in the third acts of weepy medical dramas.

Damon St. Claire lay deathly still in his maze of electronic probes and plastic tubes, looking for all the world like a small, badly broken doll.

I stayed there, holding his hand, for the five minutes

ICU allotted visitors. Then I stepped outside and crossed a sterile corridor to the adjacent waiting area. Dan was standing inside, conversing with an attractive blonde female dressed in wrinkled surgical greens. They both turned as I came into the room and the woman extended her hand to me.

"I'm Alice Cahill, Mr. St. Claire's attending physician," she said. "I'm so glad they finally managed to locate you."

I let her shake my hand, not quite sure where to begin. "What happened?" I asked. "The NTSB simply told me that Damon had been in a plane crash and asked if he had any next of kin—which, aside from an invalid mother in a New Orleans nursing home, he doesn't. They gave me the address of the hospital and said I should come right away."

Alice Cahill looked annoyed. "Leave it to the feds to handle things with tact and discretion," she snorted angrily. Then she gently took my arm and propelled me toward the door. "I'm off duty until this evening," she said. "Let's all go downstairs to the cafeteria and get some breakfast. And I'll tell you everything I know about the crash and your friend's prognosis."

As we passed by the ICU corridor I looked through a window. Damon had not moved a muscle. "He is going to be all right," I said hopefully.

"Over breakfast," Alice answered. "It's a long story and I haven't eaten since last night." She gave me an appraising once-over. "And from the looks of you, I'd say that a little nourishment wouldn't do you any harm, either."

Five minutes later I sat gazing down at the plate of scrambled eggs that Dan had insisted on getting for me from the cafeteria line, as Alice Cahill began to explain about Damon. "Three days ago an evening commuter flight from New York to Newport crashed into Narragansett Bay . . ."

"The night of the big storm," I interrupted, recalling the TV news story about a plane crash that I'd turned off on my second night back in Freedman's Cove.

Alice nodded. "The commuter pilot reported he was experiencing heavy icing and severe turbulence just before he went into the bay," she confirmed. "The Coast Guard began an immediate search and initially reported no survivors. All seventeen crew and passengers aboard the flight were presumed dead."

A weary smile touched the corners of the doctor's full lips. "But miracles sometimes do happen. And your friend upstairs in ICU," she said, raising her gentle eyes toward the ceiling, "is one very tough customer. After floating around all night in a life jacket he was picked up by a fishing boat more than eleven hours after the crash. The Coast Guard flew him directly here by helicopter because Boston Med has the best facilities in the region for treating cases of advanced hypothermia."

She paused to take a sip of orange juice and nibbled at her toast. "I was on duty when they first brought him in. He had the usual assortment of broken bones and internal injuries that we expect to see in plane-crash victims, and he was in the final stages of hypothermia. Actually, when he arrived here his core body temperature was down to around eighty degrees and his heart had stopped during the helicopter ride."

Alice shook her head in wonderment. "That we were able to get his heart going again was nothing short of a miracle all by itself. Anyway," she continued after a moment, "we immediately went to work warming him up—thankfully we have the latest equipment here, which allows us to actually remove and reheat the patient's blood, otherwise he wouldn't have survived. Fortunately, the procedure worked like a charm and his temperature stabilized. So next we took him into surgery and attended to the more serious internal injuries, primarily a ruptured spleen and a punctured lung. He's also suffering from the effects of a severe concussion to the brain."

"You also mentioned broken bones," I said, "but he doesn't seem to be wearing any casts or anything."

The doctor paused and looked directly into my eyes. "His fractures are simply immobilized at the moment," she said frankly. "We'll do further surgery to permanently repair that damage . . . if he makes it through this present stage."

"What are Damon's chances of pulling through . . . this stage?" I persisted.

The soft-spoken surgeon exchanged a worried glance with Dan, who reached over and took my hand. "It's really much too soon to say," she answered. "Your friend is incredibly strong, but he's been through an awful lot. Now it's up to his body to heal the worst of the trauma. As often happens in such cases, especially after a severe concussion, he's withdrawn into coma. Hopefully, he'll come out of it within the next twenty-four hours."

I could feel the all-too-familiar sting of tears welling up in the corners of my eyes. And I was struck by a sudden horrible thought. "The brain injury. If he lives, he won't be . . . mentally impaired?"

I tried to push away a nightmare image of sweet, brilliant Damon propped up in a hospital bed somewhere gazing out a window, his sparkling brown eyes devoid of all comprehension and intelligence.

For the first time since we'd met, Alice Cahill actually smiled at me. "You mean will he have any permanent brain damage? No, I don't think so," she replied. "Hell, I'm sorry. I should have mentioned that right away. Your friend . . . Damon . . . actually regained consciousness for a short time after we reestablished his body temperature. He and I held a brief but coherent conversation." The smile broadened. "He was naturally quite confused and it was a very strange conversation." She laughed and said, "But basically coherent all the same."

"Thank God for that," I breathed. "What did he say?"

Alice grinned. "Well, after I told him where he was and explained that he'd be staying with us a while, he looked around the ICU and said if I expected him to stay I might add some drapes and a few throw pillows. He also suggested I get a more flattering haircut and consider wearing a little makeup."

"That's definitely the Damon I know and love." I giggled, nearly giddy with relief.

Alice's expression turned serious again. "He was also asking for you," she said. "I assume you know he was on his way to see you when his plane crashed."

I stared at her in amazement. Because, in my agitated state, until that very moment I hadn't given any serious thought to the reason Damon had been on a commuter flight bound for Newport, Rhode Island, especially since he detested flying.

"Did Damon say why he was coming to see me?" I asked, remembering with chagrin our last agitated telephone conversation and the way I had screamed at him over the cell phone. Though I had been almost certain then that he had not heard my final stupid accusation about his having always hated Bobby, I must have been wrong.

The doctor shook her head. "He didn't give any reason," she answered. "He just kept repeating that it was extremely important that he see you right away. Then he lost consciousness again before I could get any information on next of kin. So I listed you on the admission forms as the person to be contacted."

I felt my tears returning. The only explanation I could think of was that Damon must have decided he had to come and personally put things right between us, face-to-face. "We had argued," I whispered. "If it hadn't been for the terrible things I said to him, he would never have gotten on that airplane."

Dan's hand was squeezing my shoulder. "Sue, you don't really know why he was on that plane," he said. "You can't blame yourself for what happened."

"Take a look around you," Alice interjected. She made a broad gesture, indicating the dozens of somber visitors and staff members sitting at tables scattered around the huge hospital cafeteria. "You can see a thousand tragedies a day in this or any other big-city trauma center. That's just life, Susan." She smiled. "It's a risky business, living."

Chapter 19

"What would you like to do now?" Dan gave me a long questioning look. We were sitting in the Mercedes and a fine freezing drizzle had started to fall. I noticed that the moisture was forming glaring halos around the orange security lights that were coming on around the hospital parking lot.

Dan had waited for most of the day while I had gone in to be with Damon for the allowed ICU visiting periods of five minutes out of every hour. I had spent those brief intervals holding Damon's hand and talking to him, willing him to wake up. But nothing had changed.

Around noon I suddenly remembered that our Manhattan office had been unattended since Damon had left New York on his fateful flight, so I called in to check voice mail. After jotting down a dozen calls to be returned, I changed the outgoing message, explaining that there had been a medical emergency and that I would get back to everyone as soon as possible.

Then I returned my attention to Damon. In between my brief ICU visits, Dan had brought me coffee and listened quietly while I talked, mostly about my best friend and the unique relationship that he and I shared.

We stayed on at the hospital until Alice Cahill came

back on duty at six and threw us out. "There is absolutely nothing you can do here except make yourself sick," she warned me. "If your friend pulls through this ordeal he's going to need you. So go back home and get some rest. That's an order. I promise I'll phone you the minute there's any change whatsoever in his condition."

"Sue?" Dan was patiently waiting for me to answer his question. I had been gazing transfixed through the misted windshield at the floodlit façade of the medical center, praying for a miracle. "I really don't want to go back to Freedman's Cove. At least not right now," I said at last. "It's much too far away . . . in case something changes."

"Can I make a practical suggestion, then?"

I turned and looked at him, reading the weariness in his eyes. "I'm sorry," I said, taking his hand, "you must be positively exhausted and I've taken up your whole day." I scanned the darkness beyond the security lights, looking for a lighted Holiday Inn sign. "There's supposed to be a motel around here somewhere," I said. "Maybe we should try to find it. Then you can drop me off and get back home to your work."

"My work wasn't exactly what I was thinking about." Dan gave my hand a reassuring squeeze. "I think you need some support right now, and my schedule is whatever I make it. I'm here for as long as you want me."

"Thanks." I leaned over and kissed his cheek.

"Anyway," he continued, "Running Freedan Studios involves a lot of travel for our executives and we also entertain visiting buyers here in Boston. So the company maintains a couple of rooms at the Hyatt Regency out near Logan Airport. It's only fifteen minutes from the medical center. I seldom use the place myself, but we can go out there and stay, if you'd like."

I shook my head in wonder. "You are full of surprises," I said.

"Of course," Dan hurried to assure me, "if you'd feel more comfortable by yourself I can put the place at your disposal and arrange for a car and driver to ferry you back and forth to the hospital—"

I reached out and placed my fingers over his lips. "Please, don't say another word," I whispered. "Just start the engine and drive."

He obeyed, twisting the ignition key, slipping the car into gear and pulling out of the lot.

"What I really want more than anything right now is a long, hot bath," I mused when we were on the road. "I feel like all my joints are creaking and I'm chilled to the bone from the air-conditioning in that ICU. It's a wonder everyone in there doesn't have hypothermia. I hope they have really hot water at the Hyatt."

He laughed. "Scalding," he said.

"Then maybe we can get some actual food, too," I said, feeling my stomach rumble. "Preferably something that hasn't been petrifying on a cafeteria steam table for the past twelve hours."

"I recommend calling room service in your bathrobe," Dan advised. "And maybe we'll get a basin of hot water to soak your feet in, so you won't get chilled again."

"Sounds heavenly," I sighed.

There was a long silence as Dan guided the car onto the beltway leading to the airport.

"Alice talked to you while I was in with Damon the first time," I said in a small voice. "Tell me the truth, Dan, do you really think she believes he'll come out of this?"

Dan thought about my question for several seconds. "I believe if anyone can pull Damon through, Alice is the one," he finally answered. He smiled and reached over to touch my hand. "She told me she felt Damon had been sent to her in order to see if she was really as good as she thought she was."

I nodded approvingly. "I like that," I said. "I like that a lot."

Freedan Studios' "couple of rooms" at the Hyatt turned out to be one of four VIP suites in the penthouse. The Freedan suite consisted of two very large bedrooms, each with its own bath, separated by a vast living room that came complete with a conference table, fax, computer with broadband Internet, wet bar and too many other amenities to mention. The entire suite was furnished in good late-18th-century English antiques in the Japanese style, and the exquisite silk- and rice-paper-covered walls were hung with Dan's original paintings.

He had called ahead from the car, so we were met and escorted upstairs by no less a personage than the Hyatt's manager, who had informed us that the chef in the four-star restaurant was awaiting our room service dinner order.

"Okay," I said when the manager, who'd seemed not at all surprised by my handsome friend's arrival with a bedraggled me in tow, had departed, "I'm impressed."

"Good," Dan replied slyly. "I was wondering what it would take to affect a jaded New York sophisticate like you."

Despite the grim circumstances of our being together I felt better than I had all day. By now I was totally at ease with Dan. And it felt perfectly natural to flop onto his richly brocaded sofa and wearily kick off my shoes. "No wonder poor Debbie Carver—excuse me, Olson—looks so wistful when she talks about the thing she used to have for you," I teased, looking around the palatial suite.

Dan went to the bar and rummaged in the refrigerator for a beer. He popped the top and took a long swallow straight from the can. "You never told me you'd been talking to Debbie," he accused. "Would you like something to drink?"

I asked for white wine. "Oh, yes, Debbie and I had a fascinating chat the other day," I allowed as he found a small bottle of Fumé and poured a glassful.

He brought me the wine and dropped into a soft chair facing me. "Interesting," he said seriously. "Did she tell you that I offered her a job with my company a few years ago?"

I looked up in surprise, for I really had just been joking with him. "And she turned you down?" I asked.

He took another sip of his beer. "Debbie said that if she went to work for me everyone in town would figure we were having an affair. And, of course, they would have done exactly that. But, considering what the town had already thought about both of us in the past, I asked her what difference it would make. Know what her answer was?"

I shook my head.

"She said she wouldn't mind the talk if it was true," Dan said. "But since it wasn't, she'd never have any love life at all if she took the job. 'So, thanks, old pal, but no thanks.'"

I smiled. "I'm beginning to understand why you liked Debbie so much," I said, sipping my wine.

"Like," he corrected. "I still do and I always will. She's a wonderful person."

"So what about your current love life?" I probed curiously. "After all, you're rich, famous and good-looking. Where's the jealous girlfriend who should be calling up here about now to find out who the strange lady is in your hotel room?"

Dan shrugged. "Don't have one, jealous or otherwise." He grinned. "At least not at the present time." He cast me a meaningful look.

Ignoring the look, I took another sip of wine and got unsteadily to my feet, suddenly aware that I was treading on dangerous ground. Thankfully, though, I still had enough sense to realize that the small amount of alcohol I had consumed on an empty stomach was going straight to my head . . . and out my mouth.

"I think I'd better go take that bath before I get myself in trouble." I looked questioningly at the two bedroom doors on opposite sides of the big room.

Dan stood and pointed with a gallant flourish to the nearest door. "Milady's boudoir is right through there," he said. "Sing out if you need anything. While you're soaking, I'll call downstairs and order our dinner. What would you like?"

"You're doing just fine so far," I replied with a smile. "Why don't you order for both of us?"

"Done," he said.

I hesitated in the doorway, all the fatigue and anguish of the past twelve hours suddenly seeming to come back heavily to rest on my shoulders. "Dan," I said softly, "thank you again, for everything."

He winked at me and leaned over to plant a brotherly kiss on my forehead. "My pleasure," he said. "And I really do hope that Damon pulls through this crisis." He smiled. "From what you've told me about him, he seems like a person I'd really like to know."

I went into the bedroom and closed the door.

The bathroom light was on and I stepped inside to discover that it was just as large and luxurious as the rest of the suite, with azure marble flooring, a huge, comfortable tub and a vanity stocked with expensive shampoos, conditioners and bath oils. Arrayed on the countertop beside the built-in hair dryer was a complete set of toilet articles, including a new toothbrush, comb, shower cap and the like.

I started the water running and snatched a thick terry robe embroidered with the hotel logo from a hook by the door, then returned to the bedroom. Peeling off my rumpled clothes, I opened a closet in search of hangers.

Inside were a half dozen articles of feminine apparel, all bearing exclusive designer labels. "Whoops!" I muttered aloud. "Who's been sleeping in my bed?"

I frowned and lifted a delicate black cocktail dress from the rack, wondering cattily who it belonged to. She had great taste and was a size six, whoever she was. A Freedan Studios executive? Heather, the mysterious New York art agent to whom Dan credited his amazing success? It was impossible to tell, for he had said earlier that any number of his people used the suite.

Deciding that it was really none of my business, I carefully replaced the exquisite garment on the rack and hung my own clothes at the opposite end of the closet. But as I walked back to the bathroom I felt just the slightest tinge of annoyance at having to share the space with a stranger's clothing.

"Now you're being ridiculous!" I told my haggard reflection in the bathroom mirror. "Anyway, this is certainly neither the time nor the place to start having possessive thoughts about Dan Freedman."

"I'm not so sure about that," the little voice in my head that is my romantic self replied. "Surely you've noticed that Dan's interest in you transcends his being the nicest, most considerate guy you have ever met in your life."

"Don't give me that crap!" I snorted, lowering myself by slow degrees into the scalding water. "Bobby was by far the nicest guy I ever met."

I closed my eyes and let the heat envelop me. "Besides," I murmured, "I'm not ready for anything like love yet. In fact, I don't know if I'll ever be ready for it again . . . Love hurts too much."

The little voices inside wisely remained silent.

"Anyway, I've got to think about Damon now," I added in a louder voice, just in case she was still listening.

"Dan's right here with you for Damon," Little Miss Practical unexpectedly chided. "Think about that, smart-ass."

"Oh, shut up," I snapped, tired of the blasphemous thoughts she was planting in my brain.

"What do you think Bobby would have done in this situation?" she goaded. "He never even liked Damon."

"Bobby would have been here for me," I snapped back.

"Like he was there when Aunt Ellen died?"

I tried to push her away by concentrating on good thoughts of Bobby. It troubled me to discover that I could not instantly conjure up a clear picture of his face. And I could hear her laughing at me from some dark corner of my mind.

"Dammit! Now look what you've done," I hissed. "Go away and leave me alone."

Little Miss Practical fell silent again. Slipping deeper into the tub I closed my eyes and reminded myself to call the hospital to check on Damon as soon as I was through.

Chapter 20

Dinner was a quiet, low-key affair.

After I'd soaked the deep chill out of my bones I wandered out to the living room in my robe, attracted by the delicious smells wafting under the bedroom door. The plum-colored satin drapes covering the floor-to-ceiling windows at the end of the suite had been opened, exposing a breathtaking nighttime panorama of the rain-swept city a few miles away across the bay.

"I hope you're hungry." Dan stepped out of the other bedroom and escorted me to a small table draped in snowy linen and set with sparkling crystal and silver.

"Mmmm," I replied, allowing him to seat me and place a napkin in my lap.

"Excellent," he said. "My name is Dan and I will be your waiter this evening." He smoothly turned to open a small metal cabinet on wheels and produced a crisp salad garnished with tiny bay shrimp. "Freshly ground pepper?" he asked, holding up a big wooden grinder.

"Thank you." I laughed as he dusted my salad with a showy flick of his wrist, then filled a crystal goblet with a clear Johannesburg Riesling.

"Don't tell me," I said, tasting the wine and licking my lips to show I approved, "before you discovered your artistic talent you used to be head waiter at the Four Seasons."

"Not exactly," he admitted reluctantly, "but when I was in the marines I once spent an entire month mopping floors in the mess hall."

"Aha!" I exclaimed. "I knew you'd picked up that high-toned panache somewhere."

We both laughed and he got his own salad from the cabinet and touched his wineglass to mine.

"Here's to Damon!" Dan proposed.

My smile disappeared and I abruptly set down my glass on the table. "Oh, God," I moaned. "Damon! I meant to phone the hospital . . ."

I started to rise but Dan reached across the table and restrained me. "I called and spoke to Alice five minutes ago," he informed me. "There's been no change in his condition since you last checked. But the hotel switchboard has orders to put through calls from the hospital, no matter what time they come in."

"I'm sorry," I apologized, staring down at my lovely salad. My appetite was suddenly gone.

"Sue, you have to eat," Dan firmly insisted.

"I know," I replied miserably. "It just doesn't seem as if I should be enjoying it so."

He gave me an appraising look. "I wonder what Damon would have to say about that remark," he speculated.

I thought that over for a moment. "Damon?" I found myself smiling again. "My God, Damon is so completely irreverent, he'd probably say something like, 'Girl, if you're not gonna eat those darlin' little pink shrimp, then for the Lord's sake give them to me.'"

"I sort of guessed it would be something like that," said Dan. He raised his glass again. "Here's to Damon. May he soon be with us to help with the shrimp."

"To Damon!" There were tears in my eyes as I raised my glass and clinked it against Dan's. "God bless him."

As it turned out the meal Dan had ordered was just right for stressed-out stomachs. Following our salads we shared a delicate, light-as-air soufflé laced with tender slices of mushroom and succulent bits of chicken. Dessert was a simple lime sorbet.

As we ate, we spoke quietly and hopefully of Alice Cahill's skills and Damon's tenacious fight to live. And before long I found myself telling a funny story about an elderly New York society matron who was convinced that Damon was the reincarnation of a dashing English lord who had escorted her to her 1935 debutante ball. By the time I had finished the story we were both laughing again. And I really did feel much better.

We called the hospital right after dinner. Alice was not available to come to the phone, but the ICU duty nurse informed us that Damon's condition remained essentially unchanged.

Later, we sat together on a sofa in the semidarkness and watched the cold rain falling on Boston. The imminent possibility that I might lose Damon this night weighed heavily on my mind. And our conversation soon shifted to our views on eternity, as we both speculated about what might await us beyond this Earthly life.

From my experience with the ghost of Aimee Marks, I confided in Dan, I felt assured that Damon's spirit would go on, even if he lost his fragile hold on life. And I admitted to him that having encountered my ancestor's gentle spirit was also helping me come to terms with Bobby's death.

"Would you like to tell me about Bobby now?" Dan's arm was resting lightly on my shoulder and his features were masked by the dim light.

I squirmed uncomfortably and tucked my legs up under

me on the sofa. "I already told you about Bobby," I said evasively.

"No, Sue. You only told me how he died and how distraught you were over losing him," Dan challenged. "I'd like to know the kinds of things about Bobby that I learned from you about Damon today. What kind of person he was. The little things he did and said that made you love him so desperately."

"Dan, please don't," I begged. "Not now."

"Why?" he demanded. "Why not now?"

"This is a difficult time for me," I replied.

"I know it is," he said. "It's difficult for me, too. But I didn't choose the time, Sue. Nobody did. You just stepped into my life out of nowhere. Neither of us planned it, and I certainly wasn't ready for it, either." He exhaled loudly, obviously frustrated over the emotions he was experiencing. "But here we are," he concluded.

"Yes," I agreed. "Here we are." I thought I understood what he was feeling. For the same sense of frustration had been nagging at me since the day we'd first met out on the island. Then I'd been plunged into a quagmire of unreasonable guilt over having simply enjoyed our conversation together. Somehow it didn't seem fair that I felt so guilty just for living.

"Why do you want to know those things about Bobby now?" I asked, which was my way of dodging questions for which I feared I would have no ready answers.

"Because," Dan said softly, "I'm falling in love with you. And I don't know how to compete with a dead lover who can never be anything but young and strong and perfect in your mind."

His reply hit me hard, because Laura had said nearly the same thing when she had counseled me about the special difficulty of recovering from the loss of a loved one who vanishes without a trace, like Bobby did. And for once I believed she had been absolutely right on target. Because whenever I thought about Bobby, my thoughts—and dreams—invariably centered on the good things we had shared. Never on the darker moments of our relationship.

"Bobby was hardly perfect." I said it cautiously, the well-intentioned words sounding cold and faithless in my ears. "Wonderful, but not perfect," I amended. "I don't think anybody is perfect."

A clear image of Bobby suddenly popped into my mind, and an invisible wall came tumbling down. "Bobby was headstrong and reckless," I continued truthfully. "And he used to do little things that annoyed the hell out of me, like leaving his dirty clothes on the bathroom floor, or forgetting his keys and then calling to demand that I come home and let him into the apartment."

Dan was looking at me, his expression unreadable in the darkness. I swallowed hard and kept talking, knowing that this was important, but not exactly sure why. "He was strangely secretive, too, often refusing to tell me where he was going or when he would be returning. There were many times when I spent weeks on end, lonely and terrified," I confessed, the emotion gradually rising in my voice, "not knowing where he was or what kind of risks he was taking flying his goddamn airplanes . . . I was always terrified that he was going to kill himself in them."

I paused to catch my breath, surprised at the vehemence of my outburst.

"Then he did kill himself flying," Dan said flatly. "And I think that beneath your grief you're really very angry about that, Sue."

"No!" I shook my head emphatically, knowing even as I denied it that there was a measure of truth in Dan's harsh appraisal. "I mean, maybe I am angry," I stammered. "But

I'm angry with myself, because it was my fault that Bobby was flying that particular airplane. Don't you see? I forced him into it . . ." I could feel my voice beginning to quaver, on the verge of sobbing.

"Sue, nobody forces someone like Bobby Hayward to do anything they don't want to do," Dan countered emphatically. "He was doing exactly what he wanted to do and he kept on doing it, even though he knew it bothered you—the long absences, the worry . . ." Dan stopped himself in midsentence and I could see that he was afraid he had gone much too far.

"I'm sorry," he apologized. "That was out of line."

"No!" I shook my head. Because what Dan had said was true. "Living with Bobby was like living in a vacuum," I continued. "He'd be gone for days or weeks at a time and despite my work and my friends, my life always seemed to grind to a halt without him. I'd be completely miserable and empty, just waiting for his call. Then, suddenly, he'd come back home again and for a few days or a week it was like Christmas and the Fourth of July all rolled into one. Then the cycle would start all over again. The strain was almost intolerable."

I gazed out the window toward the city and the distant medical center. "Damon always said he could never understand why I put up with it," I murmured.

"You obviously loved him very deeply." It was a flat statement.

"Yes," I whispered sadly, "probably more than he loved me, maybe even more than I should have . . ." I paused and took a deep breath to steady myself. "But I guess that doesn't matter when you're so much in love with someone."

Dan stroked my hair. "No," he agreed. "It doesn't." He leaned closer, until I could feel the warmth of his breath against my ear. "And because of the way you lost Bobby," he continued, "you feel like you're betraying him by even considering the possibility of becoming involved with someone else now."

I reached up and with a trembling hand touched Dan's cheek. "I can't be coy about this," I said. "I'm strongly attracted to you. I even think . . . I could very easily be in love with you, Dan. But I just have yet to fully come to terms with the fact that Bobby is truly gone."

He lowered his head and gently kissed my fingers. "It's okay," he assured me. "Take all the time you need, Sue. I'll be here when you're ready."

We sat there on the sofa for a while longer, not speaking, but simply watching the rain and reveling in being close to one another. As I snuggled in the crook of Dan's arm, feeling the warmth and strength of his body next to mine, I knew that something extraordinary had just happened. A bond had been forged that did not require either of us to say another word.

We finally said good night, planning to be up early. I wanted to go to the hospital first thing, to be with Damon. Then, later, I would need to return to the hotel and begin calling our clients, who would be clamoring to know exactly what had happened.

Later, alone and naked beneath the cool sheets of the king-sized hotel bed, I tossed restlessly for a long time before falling into a deep and dreamless sleep.

It seemed as though I had barely closed my eyes when I felt a weight pressing down on the mattress beside me and heard a low masculine voice in my ear.

"Sue?"

I opened my eyes to see him half-kneeling over me, his hard, muscular body sharply outlined in the fall of light through the open door.

With that peculiar sense of disorientation that comes from awakening in a strange place, for a moment I was not quite certain where I was, or who was leaning over me. I saw that he was clad only in black briefs. The tattoos on his upper arms were black in the feeble light.

"Dan," I gasped. "What in the world . . . ?"

"It's the hospital," he said, his voice still husky with sleep. "They want us to get over there right away."

"Oh, my God!" I exclaimed, leaping out of bed. "Damon. He's not . . . ?"

Dan shook his head. "No, he's still alive. But they wouldn't give me any further information," he said, gazing openly at my nakedness.

I looked down at myself, dimly aware that I had let the sheet slip away and I was completely exposed to him. But strangely, I thought, I was not at all bothered by Dan's frank gaze. Naked I walked deliberately across the room and put on my underwear. "Please, let's hurry," I said as I opened the closet to get my clothes.

Dan simply nodded and left the room. As I pulled my dress on over my head I could hear him phoning the hotel garage, ordering someone to have the Mercedes brought up immediately.

Chapter 21

Damon was propped in a half-sitting position as I rushed into his ICU cubicle. He was sipping water through a pink plastic straw from a cup held by a pretty nurse's aide and blinking owlishly at Alice Cahill, who was probing his chest with a forefinger.

"Ow!" he complained, looking over her shoulder and frantically waving a stubby hand at me. "Sue, darling, puh-lease get this awful woman off of me," he demanded.

"Damon, you're awake!" I shrieked with relief.

Alice straightened and grimaced at me.

"Awake and uncooperative," she grunted, though it was plain to see that she was immensely pleased with herself. She pocketed her stethoscope and stepped away from the bed so I could throw my arms around Damon's neck.

"Christ," I sobbed into his ear, "I thought you were going to die on me, too." I pulled away after a long interval and grinned down at him through my tears. "You look like hell." I sniffed.

Damon gave me one of his patented rueful looks. "I feel like Death eating crackers," he moaned, struggling to raise himself higher on the pillows so he could glare directly at Alice and the nurses. "When they're not draining off the last of my blood these philistines insist on sticking their damned freezing probes into every orifice in my body."

Unimpressed by his rhetoric, Alice sternly wagged her finger at him. "Do not even attempt to sit up any higher than you are right now, mister, or I will have you tied to that bed," she warned. "For your information, you have several broken bones in your right leg that are just itching to slice through those fat-lined little arteries of yours. And if that happens, I guarantee you'll find out what real bleeding is all about."

"See what I've been putting up with?" Damon whined, wriggling around to look at me.

"You stop being such a wise-ass and listen to Dr. Cahill," I ordered. "Because whether you know it or not if it wasn't for her I'd be planning your damn funeral right now." I pointed a trembling finger at Alice. "This dear lady has just hauled your sorry, sarcastic butt back from death's door," I informed him. "And I do mean literally."

Damon immediately stopped struggling and the frown vanished from his round baby face. "She did?" he gasped, rolling his eyes onto Alice and fixing her with an awestruck gaze. "Please forgive me, Doctor," he begged. "You are undoubtedly an absolute angel of mercy and I am a miserable and undeserving wretch."

Alice winked at me, then she and the aide withdrew. "Five minutes," she whispered as she brushed past. "He's not out of the woods yet by a long shot."

"So," I said, dropping into a chair and grasping Damon's hand. "Do you remember what happened?"

Instead of answering me immediately, Damon closed his eyes. A beatific expression spread over his shiny countenance, almost as if he was reliving a beautiful dream. "Oh, God, Sue, the light," he sighed. "I remember mostly that there was a dazzling golden light . . . the beauty of it was . . . indescribable."

I sat there transfixed by the sudden blissful transformation that had come over him, not certain whether to interrupt or not. Because, in asking what he remembered, I had only meant, of course, the details of the horrible plane crash and his nightlong ordeal in the frigid waters of Narragansett Bay.

But Damon was obviously remembering something else altogether.

His eyes remained tightly shut. Then, without warning, his placid expression turned fearful. "Sue," he called out, squeezing my hand with such painful intensity that I actually feared he might crush it. "Sue, girl?"

I placed my other hand on top of his, gently prying his rigid fingers away. "Damon, I'm right here," I assured him. "You're safe now, but you were in a plane crash. Do you remember that?"

Damon's wide brown eyes suddenly popped open. "The plane? Oh, God, how could I forget that damned little piss-ant commuter airplane?" he replied in genuine annoyance. "Remind me never to get on another one of those sons of bitches again . . ." Then his lower lip began to tremble like a child's, just before it cries. "Oh, Jesus, Sue," he moaned, "I remember everything now. I was so scared . . ."

"I can't even imagine what it must have been like for you," I empathized. "It must have been dreadful, lost in the sea like that . . ."

Damon shook his head impatiently. "I wasn't talking about the damned airplane crash," he interrupted. Then the panic took hold of him again and his words were spilling out in a jumbled torrent. "Sweet Christ, Sue, I have got to tell you . . . I saw him glaring at me. Looking like a damned evil spirit . . ."

Damon was painfully squeezing my hand again. His eyes had taken on a wild, hunted look and he was struggling to get up.

"It's okay now," I crooned, terrified that he was going to seriously hurt himself. I looked frantically toward the ICU windows in hopes of attracting the attention of Alice or one of the nurses. "It's all over," I told Damon. "You're safe. Please be still."

"Sue." Damon was gasping for breath, his face contorting exactly like the face I had seen in my dream of two nights earlier. "I have to tell you first . . ."

"Hush," I whispered. "Please, Damon, just lie still and don't try to talk. We'll talk later, after you've rested . . ."

"Bobby!" he gurgled, throwing his chubby legs over the side of the bed and strangling on his own saliva. "I saw Bobby," he gasped. "You've got to listen, Sue!"

"What in the name of God did he mean?" I asked the unanswerable question for the tenth time. My hands were trembling so badly I was having trouble lifting the Styrofoam cup of cafeteria coffee to my lips. A moment after Damon made his incredible pronouncement, Alice and two nurses had rushed into his ICU suite and wrestled him back into bed. I had been literally pushed out the door by an arriving orderly as a needle was slipped into Damon's naked thigh and his frantic, high-pitched voice faded to a weeping, incoherent babble.

Dan sat across the Formica-topped table, watching me with worried eyes and obviously trying to think of something to say that would not increase my level of agitation. "I don't know," he said helplessly. "Are you sure you heard him right? I mean, you did say he got pretty irrational in there."

"Bobby," I slowly repeated, trying to keep my voice absolutely calm. "Damon said he saw Bobby." I sipped the hot, bitter coffee, searing my tongue. "What does that mean, Dan?"

Dan's eyes left mine and I could see the relief in them as Alice entered the cafeteria and crossed to where we were sitting. I noticed that there was a long scratch across her cheek as she slumped heavily into a chair beside mine and gratefully accepted the cup of coffee that Dan had already bought for her.

"Sorry about what happened up there," she said after she had taken a cautious swallow of the steaming liquid. "He obviously wasn't ready to see anyone yet."

"Is he . . . ?" I searched for the proper words to frame my question about Damon's condition.

"Sleeping like a baby," she replied before I could get my thoughts together. "Mostly because I popped him with a good, strong dose of Valium and put him on 100 percent oxygen. In his weakened state, the combination hit him like an elephant tranquilizer."

Alice hesitated, and I could tell she was silently reviewing the wisdom of her summary decision to render Damon unconscious again so soon after his miraculous emergence from the coma. "Normally the last thing you want to do in a situation like this is depress the patient's system with drugs," she explained. "But the alternative was risking some severe secondary injury while he was thrashing around."

She reached over and patted one of my shaking hands. "Don't worry. His vitals are still strong and I think he'll be okay after he sleeps it off."

"Thank God," I breathed.

"So," she continued, gazing at me with her cool green eyes, "exactly what happened in that room before I came in and found you trying to keep your little pal from jumping out of bed?"

I stared at my hands and shook my head helplessly.

"When Sue asked Damon if he remembered anything about the crash," Dan answered for me, "he suddenly became extremely agitated and told her that he had seen her dead fiancé. He seemed to be positively terrified."

"Just before that, he was talking about a very bright light," I interjected. "But that part seemed to have been a good experience for him."

I took another sip of my only slightly cooled coffee and thought for a moment. "At first I assumed he was remembering having seen the lights of the boats and rescue helicopters searching for survivors."

Alice Cahill leaned back in her chair and looked into her coffee cup. "I don't think that was what he was remembering at all," she said slowly. "I've seen this kind of thing before." She paused and tested the dark liquid with the tip of her finger. "Do you remember my telling you that Damon's heart had stopped when he first arrived here at the med center?"

I nodded.

"Well, I'm not sure exactly how long he'd been gone—clinically dead, as we call it—before the rescue chopper got him here," the worried doctor continued. "It might only have been a minute or two . . . But it could have been a lot longer. The Coast Guard paramedics were having trouble with their monitoring equipment that morning. So we can't know for certain. Damon might well have been technically dead—his brain deprived of oxygen—for as long as ten minutes . . ."

"Ten minutes?" Disbelief registered in my voice. "But you said he didn't have any brain damage—"

Alice raised her hand, cutting me off. "He doesn't," she assured me. "One of the happier side effects of hypothermia is that extreme cold preserves brain cells that would normally die within a few minutes without oxygen. Except for the concussion, there's absolutely nothing wrong with Damon's brain.

"However," she continued, lowering her voice and glancing furtively around the nearly deserted cafeteria, "there is a fairly common . . . delusion that may explain the bright light and his belief that he met with someone who is no longer living . . ."

I managed a stupid look. "I guess I really don't understand," I confessed.

Dan, who had been listening quietly, suddenly spoke up. "I think what Alice is trying to say is that Damon may have had a near-death experience," he said. "I've read a little on the subject. Essentially, it's a set of memories that are often claimed by people who have been clinically dead for short periods of time. Afterwards, they recall having left their bodies and being drawn upward toward a bright light."

He looked over at Alice, who was nodding encouragingly, obviously relieved at having a layman describe the highly controversial near-death phenomenon for her.

I frowned, vaguely recalling that I, too, had heard something about near death. In the first weeks following Bobby's disappearance my attention had been grabbed by a thumbs-down *Times* book review on the subject. "I saw a review of a book written by an accident victim who claimed she left her body to go to some sort of heavenly light," I said, remembering that the reviewer had flatly dismissed the author's claims as syrupy pop mysticism and unworthy of serious consideration. "But what does that have to do with Bobby?"

"Those who reach the center of this very beautiful light," Dan continued, "frequently report having met people there that they know have died previously, especially friends or relatives." Dan shot Alice a piercing glance. "Though thousands of people have reported them, the implied spiritual nature of near-death experiences is not accepted, however, by medicine or science," he concluded.

"My God, why not?" I breathed, looking at the silent physician beside me and thinking about my own recent experiences with the ghost of Aimee Marks.

Alice sighed and regarded the two of us like slightly backward children. "Admittedly, such stories are pretty common," she replied. "But there is absolutely no proof that anything really happens, outside the dying patient's own imagination."

"In other words, Doctor," Dan responded with a touch of sarcasm in his voice, "if you can't prove it, then it must not exist."

Alice accorded him a tolerant smile that made it clear she'd encountered similar remarks from the misinformed in the past. "Well, that's scientific method for you, Dan," she shot back. "You can't prove what can't be proven. On the other hand," she conceded with a shrug, "who am I to say there's no heavenly light where dear friends and loved ones are waiting to greet us when we die?"

Then she turned to me. "Whether the so-called near-death experience is real or imagined is really immaterial, Sue. Because it definitely does happen, and it could explain why Damon thinks he saw your fiancé."

"I suppose," I reluctantly conceded, "except for the fact that when Bobby was alive he and Damon could barely tolerate one another."

"Oh!" Alice laughed. "Well, I can't say I ever heard anyone claim they were drawn up into an ethereal light and found their annoying next-door neighbor waiting for them there."

"And why was Damon so frightened, anyway?" I wanted to know. "True, he and Bobby never got along, but it was never anything more serious than the two of them avoiding one another. Damon certainly wasn't afraid of him."

I could see that Dan was anxious to express another

opinion. But he ended the discussion by saying, "Well, I guess we'll all just have to wait for Damon to wake up and solve the mystery for us."

"When can I see him again?" I asked Alice.

The doctor averted her eyes and frowned into her coffee cup. "I expect him to sleep for quite some time," she said, swirling the dark liquid round and round the plastic rim.

She looked up at me again. "However, Sue, I don't want you sitting there at Damon's side when he comes around the next time."

"Why not?" I demanded. "Damon is my dearest friend. You were the one who said he wanted me to be here."

Alice nodded patiently. "I know I did, my dear," she admitted. "But I'm beginning to think that your devotion to him might actually be at the heart of the problem right now. Because seeing you obviously placed a great emotional strain on Damon, perhaps because you two had argued just before his accident and he was feeling guilty."

Alice paused for a moment to sip her coffee. "He may also be feeling guilty over his dislike of Bobby, now that Bobby's gone. Anyway, Damon is still obviously quite disoriented and I'm afraid that seeing you was just more than he could handle."

"I see," I murmured, hurt by the implication that the mere sight of me could have triggered my friend's emotional crisis.

Alice suddenly reached out and put her arms around me. "I want you to trust me on this, Sue," she said gently. "Let's give Damon a few days to adjust to being back among the living before we risk upsetting him again for any reason."

"If you really think that's best," I very reluctantly agreed, pulling free of her embrace. "Of course, I only want him to get better."

I swiped at a tear forming in the corner of my eye. "But you must know that I love him like a brother."

"I know you do," Alice whispered. "I will personally call you every day to tell you how he's doing. And I promise that you can come back the minute I think he's strong enough. Okay?"

"Okay," I murmured.

"But first I've got to dispel this dangerous delusion of his," she said worriedly.

"If it really is a delusion," I murmured resentfully.

"Go home," she ordered. "I'll call you."

Chapter 22

Life seldom wraps things up in tidy packages with neat endings, happy or otherwise. I know that sounds like another one of those insipid truisms that I'm convinced Laura makes up just to kill time during her twice-weekly sessions at Elizabeth Arden. So laugh if you must, but that particular piece of homespun philosophy happens to be one that I concocted all by myself.

First Bobby had disappeared without a trace, leaving me hopelessly suspended between the unbearable extremes of bitter grief and unreasonable hope. Then Dan Freedman had suddenly exploded into the shambles of my life and, within days, claimed to be falling in love with me, a painful situation for us both that, under any other circumstances, I could have found deliciously reciprocal.

Now, in the midst of that already impossibly emotional tangle of guilt and self-recrimination, Damon, dear, sweet Damon, had nearly died in a plane crash and was lying doped up in a Boston hospital room, terrified out of his poor battered skull by an otherworldly encounter with my dead lover.

The situation was beyond all rational analysis or explanation. But because of it, sick with worry, half in love and steeped in my own guilt, I felt as though I was literally coming apart at the seams.

If there was any solace at all to be drawn from the confused emotional triangle in which I now found myself trapped it was only my slowly growing conviction that I probably wasn't crazy after all. Or at least no crazier than poor Damon, who thought he'd taken a meeting with Bobby at the Pearly gates, or Dan, who actually believed that Damon had seen Bobby in Heaven, and, bless him, who had also believed me when I said that I'd seen the ghost of Aimee Marks.

When the bizarre becomes commonplace it's time to stop dwelling on the absolute strangeness of life and get on with living it, otherwise you'll probably never sleep again.

No. Laura didn't make up that one, either. It was simply how I decided I would have to personally cope if I was going to avoid a future filled with rubber rooms and heavy trancs. In effect, I had made up my mind to stop questioning *what* was happening all around me and try instead to figure out *why* it was happening.

First and foremost I wanted to know why Damon had encountered such a seemingly frightening visage of Bobby during those lost moments as he hovered between life and death. Because I was thoroughly convinced that what Damon had experienced when his heart had stopped and his vital signs flat-lined was no delusion but an actual event.

And, no matter what Alice Cahill thought, I also knew that when Damon again regained consciousness his physical wounds could not really begin healing until his terrifying otherworldly experience could somehow be explained.

Since I was temporarily powerless to do anything else for Damon I decided to find that explanation for him. And I was convinced that the best place to start was right back in Freedman's Cove, where I happened to have a unique source that just might have some of the answers I so desperately needed.

Who could better explain the odd circumstances of Damon's near-death experience than Aimee Marks? I truly believed that Aimee was real. And, further, I believed that she had attempted to communicate with me, on the night I had awakened to find her sitting beside my bed, easing me out of my own terrible dream of Bobby.

Perhaps, I thought, it would be possible for me to expand that first halting communication into a dialogue with Aimee's gentle spirit.

Though I did not share these thoughts with Dan—mostly because I was afraid he would try to prevent me from exposing myself to any further emotional shocks—they were the ones running through my mind as he and I drove back to Freedman's Cove late on the afternoon of the day Damon first awakened from his coma.

After leaving the hospital we had returned to the Hyatt, where, after a few hours of rest, I had spent the remainder of the day phoning friends and clients in New York, to explain why St. Claire & Marks would be closed for an indefinite period of time.

Fortunately, Damon's name had finally been released to the press the previous evening. So a fairly large news report about the lone survivor of the Narragansett Bay commuter-plane crash had already appeared in the Manhattan morning papers, greatly easing the difficulty of my explanations.

Of course, everyone with whom I spoke had expressed nothing but concern for Damon's condition. And our largest clients had all assured me that St. Claire & Marks would remain on retainers until we were back in operation again.

Still, I was genuinely worried about the survival of our business, and wondering how I could possibly manage without my brilliant partner. I am enough of a realist to know that events move with blinding speed in the high-stakes world of antiques. And the fact that Damon and I were out of action would not stop the next big auction from going ahead without us.

As it turned out I need not have worried. For when I finally got around to calling Sir Edward North at Christie's, the scholarly old curator who'd started Damon and me in the business staggered me by announcing that he was taking a long-overdue holiday from his duties at the auction house. Until Damon and I were back on our feet, Sir Edward informed me, he was applying for a temporary position as St. Claire & Marks's chief appraiser.

I was so relieved and grateful that I blubbered my thanks into the phone for five minutes before Sir Edward managed to convince me that he was actually looking forward to abandoning his stuffy uptown offices and getting "back into the trenches again." Brushing aside my tearful professions of gratitude, the old darling had gruffly ordered me off the line, after making me promise to fax him a list of our clients, so he could begin calling to advise them of the new arrangement.

Chapter 23

Aunt Ellen's grand old Victorian house loomed cold and forbidding in the heavy mist that was rolling in from the sea as Dan pulled his Mercedes into the drive behind my Volvo late that evening.

During the long drive down from Boston we had spoken little of the day's startling events, content in the warm confines of the Mercedes merely to be together, listening to music and the rhythmic sweep of the wipers across the windshield. Now Dan switched off the engine and looked across at me.

"Do you feel like going out somewhere for dinner, or have you had enough of my company for one day?" he asked.

"Neither," I smiled. "Why don't you come in and build a nice crackling fire while I fix us something to eat? I warn you it won't be up to the standards of the Hyatt's four-star chef, though."

Dan laughed, nobly protesting that too much haute cuisine got on his nerves, anyway. So we went inside, debating the relative merits of frozen fettuccini Alfredo versus tuna salad—the only two dishes I could put together in a reasonably short time. We settled on the pasta and I went off to the kitchen while Dan headed for the parlor to see about the fire.

Though the rest of the house had been kept reasonably warm by the central heating, which I had left on while I was away, the kitchen was icy as a tomb when I stepped inside and flipped the light switch.

I stood there for a moment, puzzled and shivering in the unexpected cold as I surveyed the half-filled coffee cup on the counter beside the uneaten slab of burnt toast that I'd abandoned two days earlier.

Only slowly did I realize that the door leading out onto the sunporch behind the house was standing open to the frigid night air.

Frowning, I walked over to the door and peered out into the dark backyard. The overhanging branches of the huge oak loomed eerily through the thickening mist as the lighthouse beacon swept across the empty yard. I quickly closed and locked the door and turned back to the brightly lighted kitchen, shaking my head at my own carelessness in forgetting to lock up and wondering gloomily how much heating oil from the newly filled tank had been consumed while I was away.

By the time dinner was ready the kitchen had warmed up and I'd put the incident with the open door to the back of my mind. Later, sitting in the fire-lit parlor, Dan and I ate our fettuccini and sipped cheap red wine from the grocery store while I carefully directed the conversation to the weather and other mundane subjects.

"So," he suddenly said, after we'd cleared away the dinner things and were looking at each other over mugs of steaming coffee, "where do we go from here?"

"Please, Dan," I groaned, certain he was again bringing up the troubling matter of our deepening mutual attraction for one another. "I thought you were going to let me off without any tough questions tonight."

Dan's intense green eyes refused to release their hold on

mine. "If I learned one thing in the marines, it was never to retreat in the face of a difficult situation," he said. "I watched you pondering Damon's situation all the way down from Boston tonight . . ."

Surprised by the subject, I stammered out a reply. "I was . . . just listening to the music—"

Dan shook his head to stop me. "You and I are too much alike for me to buy that, Sue," he interrupted. "The minute you meekly agreed to come back here and leave Damon at the mercy of Alice Cahill's hard-nosed psychiatric mumbo jumbo I knew you were up to something. What is it?"

I sighed, secretly relieved at not having to address the emotionally confusing issue of our relationship, but dismayed at how easily Dan had seen through my carefully composed acceptance of the good doctor's orders.

"Don't get me wrong," I began, "Alice is obviously an extraordinary physician, and I think her intentions toward Damon are basically good—"

Dan finished the thought for me. "But her diagnosis of him as being delusional is totally off base."

I nodded emphatically. "It was maddening listening to her," I ranted. "There she was, rattling on and on about the need for scientific evidence and hard proof, when the only *evidence* that anyone has about near-death experiences is what people like Damon have reported."

Dan smiled ruefully. "Otherwise sane, rational people," he continued, "whose sworn testimony in a court of law would be plenty good enough to sentence an accused criminal to prison."

"Or death row," I added somberly.

"I guess you know you haven't got a chance of changing Alice's mind about anything," he said.

"Oh, to hell with Alice," I snorted. "It's Damon I'm

worried about. I want to know what really happened to him while he was technically dead—"

"And you think maybe Aimee Marks can tell you," Dan interrupted.

Surprised that he had figured out my scheme, I meekly replied, "Yes. I do."

Dan smiled. "And if she can't?"

I shrugged. "Then she can't. At the very least, if I can establish some level of communication with her I might be able to help free her spirit from this house and Maidenstone Island." I hesitated. "I think that something is holding her here."

Dan raised his eyebrows questioningly.

"Well, isn't that what's supposed to happen to ghosts?" I asked defensively. "Don't they become trapped and unable to go on?"

"I don't know what happens to ghosts," Dan said quietly. "And neither do you, Sue. But I do know that meddling with such things could be extraordinarily dangerous to someone . . ." His voice trailed off and he bit his lip.

"To someone in my fragile mental state?" I demanded. "Is that what you were going to say, Dan?"

"Dammit, Sue, that's not fair!" He was on his feet, pacing back and forth in front of the fire. He turned and pointed a trembling finger at me. "I'm in love with you and I don't want to see you hurt anymore," he declared.

Suddenly I was standing and his lips were on mine, his strong hands caressing my buttocks, our bodies pressed so close together that I genuinely ached with longing for him. Pushing myself away a few inches in order to look up into his burning eyes, I said, "I want to let it happen. Truly I do . . . But attempting to contact Aimee is something I have to do . . . for Damon."

And although I didn't say it, another thought leaped

into my mind at that moment: Because if Aimee Marks could explain what had happened to Damon, perhaps she could also tell me what might have become of Bobby. If I only knew that he was at peace now . . . Then maybe, I thought, I could put away my guilt and grief and Dan and I might have a real chance together.

Still in his embrace I closed my eyes, reveling in the feel of his hands on me.

". . . going to stay here, then. I refuse to let you go through this by yourself."

I opened my eyes and looked up, realizing that Dan was talking to me again. I shook my head and placed my fingertips gently over his lips.

"No," I whispered, my voice barely audible above the fiery crackle of the logs in the fireplace. "I *have* to do this all by myself."

Dan reluctantly nodded. Then a broad grin creased his tanned features.

"What?" I asked. He didn't reply immediately, but continued grinning so I shook him. "What?" I demanded again.

"I was just trying to picture what Alice's reaction would be if she could hear this remarkable conversation we're having."

Suddenly I found myself laughing. "I'm sure she'd order up a couple of straightjackets," I said, wiggling my behind pleasurably in his grip. "Do you think it's possible that we've both gone completely insane?"

"I guess anything's possible." He grinned. "I know I'm absolutely crazy about you."

Dan kissed me again and I kissed him back, hard, fighting the urge to drag him off to the nearest bedroom.

To my great surprise, no mournful image of Bobby filled my mind until minutes after the long kiss was at last done and I had somehow forced myself to push Dan out of Aunt

Ellen's big, lonely house and locked the front door behind him.

I suspect that Laura would have interpreted that first guilt-free kiss as a sign that I was making major progress in managing my grief.

Chapter 24

Weariness hit me like a felled tree as I locked the door and slumped onto the pine deacon's bench in the foyer to catch my breath. "I love him," whispered the small romantic voice inside my head.

"Maybe," countered Miss Practical. "But since you haven't slept for, what—twenty hours?—you're hardly in a position to be making judgment calls."

"Will you two just shut the hell up and let me think?" I grumped.

"How about a nice, hot, lavender-scented bath?" suggested Little Miss Romantic. "That always calms you down."

"Good idea," Miss Practical snottily piped up. "And while you're at it, your legs could use a good going over with a razor. You've got more stubble down there than a corral full of cactus."

Ignoring them both, and too tired even to bathe at the end of this bizarre and exhausting day, I climbed upstairs to my room, tossed my limp clothes in a heap on the floor and crawled into bed.

"What about Aimee?" asked Miss Romantic, her voice tinged with anticipation.

"There's no sense in my trying to contact Aimee tonight,"

I yawned as my head sank into the softness of the down pillows. "I'd better wait until I have all of my faculties about me."

"Oh, hell, it looks like we're in for a very long haul, then," Miss Practical sniped as I fell abruptly into a deep and exhausted sleep.

At some point, hours later, I thought I heard the sound of distant bells ringing.

Wedding bells, I murmured with a smile.

"I can't wait any longer, Sue, honey. I need you so badly. I want things to be like they were."

"Mmmm." I sighed and arched my back like a sleeping cat that is being scratched in just the right spot.

I was sleeping on my side, my bottom tucked comfortably into the crook of a warm stomach. The familiar sandpaper roughness of a light masculine beard brushed pleasantly against my bare shoulder, hard-wiring the tingling sensation between my thighs to reality. Moaning with anticipation I pressed backward against the taut, unyielding core of my fantasy lover.

God, I thought sleepily, but I was having the most beautiful dream of my life. In the space of a few more seconds, I knew, a gentle hand would tenderly cup my breast and I would languidly turn to face my lover. Then . . .

"Oh, God, Susie . . . You don't know how long I've dreamed of being with you like this again." The masculine voice, vaguely familiar, but breathlessly low and rasping, purred in my ear. "I've wanted you, fantasized about you . . ."

Susie? No one had called me Susie since high school.

Suddenly the expected hand slid around my rib cage, eager and grasping, but cold and not at all gentle. Rough fingers found my nipple. Squeezed. Hard. Much too hard.

I opened my eyes in sudden panic, squinting through the darkness at the glowing numerals of the bedside clock. 1:28 AM.

No dream, this.

Real, screamed my panicked mind.

This was really happening!

Rough hands were pulling at me now. I craned my neck around in fright and dimly saw the outline of a man's face, its features masked in inky shadow. Then his hard hands were turning me, as I had myself planned to turn in my interrupted reverie. Pulling me close to the stubbled chin, the stiff, ironlike hardness below.

"What are you doing?" I squealed. A stale, nauseating odor assaulted my nostrils as hot, wet lips engulfed my mouth, forcing me to silence.

"Wake up, you moron," yelled the dual voices in my head, for once in total agreement with one another. "Wake up, for God's sake! You're about to be raped!"

The thought jerked me rudely into full consciousness and I screamed at my assailant. "Let me go, you bastard!"

The unseen face retreated from mine, even as the strong hands grasped my hips, dragging me closer to his thrusting pelvis.

"No, Sue! Wait!" he protested. "Just want to hold you close to me . . ."

I gagged as the stale odor on his breath hit me again full force and I recognized the smell for what it was.

Scotch.

In that same instant, the lighthouse beacon flooded the room with hard white illumination and I found myself staring into the familiar puffy features of my attacker.

"You!" I screeched, going for his piggish, red-rimmed eyes with my fingernails and bringing my knee up solidly into his crotch.

Tom Barnwell moaned in agony and half-crawled, half-fell out of the bed. "Sue," he gasped. "It was just a little joke . . ."

I switched on the bedside lamp and grabbed for the only heavy object in sight, the antique telephone I'd found in the attic and had the phone company wire in a few days earlier. Jerking the clunky receiver off its cradle, I held it up like a club.

"Get out of my house!" I screamed, raising the blunt instrument threateningly over my head.

Tom stood shakily, backing away toward the bedroom door while fumbling to fasten the belt on his wrinkled khaki slacks. "I honestly didn't mean any harm, Sue," he said with a sickly smile that I suppose was meant to set me at ease regarding his true motive.

Frightened and enraged, I was having none of it. For, despite the premature flab showing around his waist and neck, at nearly six feet two inches tall, Tom Barnwell was still a big and powerful man. He easily outweighed me by a hundred pounds and I wasn't in the mood to take any chances on his intentions.

"Get out of here," I said evenly, forcing my voice into a lower register. "Now, Tom."

He took another halting step toward me. "If you'll just let me explain," he said, advancing.

I raised the antique phone higher. "Tom, if you don't get out of here right now you can explain it to the police," I said. "The only reason I'm not already dialing 911 is that it would kill your father to have you arrested for attempted rape and trespassing."

Tom's florid face went pasty white, but he held his ground. "Trespassing?" he gasped. "Sue, you gave me the keys to this house. I'm your rental agent and property manager. Remember?"

"Right now you're nothing but a goddamned criminal!" I shouted.

Tom wagged his head violently from side to side, his pouchy jowls flapping like a bad caricature of Richard Nixon. "Look, I'll admit that climbing into bed with you was a stupid stunt," he blustered. "And I apologize . . ."

I couldn't prevent myself from screaming at him. "I don't want your damn apology! I just want you out of my house!" I reached over and fumbled with the old-fashioned telephone dial on the nightstand. "I mean it."

"Okay, okay!" He raised his hands palms upward and backed slowly toward the door. "But I did not break into your house, Sue," he persisted. "As a matter of fact, I drove by earlier today to see if you needed anything. I thought it was strange that your Volvo was here but you weren't. So tonight, on my way home from Krabb's, I swung by again, just to make sure you were okay—"

"I am dialing the police in exactly fifteen seconds," I threatened.

"Listen. I'm sure I saw somebody prowling around the back of the house," he continued, speeding up his delivery but still not leaving. "I rang the bell and when you didn't answer I let myself in with my key . . ."

I stuck my finger in the 9 hole on the rotary dial and spun it. The old mechanical steel wheel clacked noisily on its springs.

"When I peeked into your room and saw you sleeping, all I could think about was that night we spent together on Dad's boat." Tom's face was ashen and the words were spilling out at a rapid-fire clip as he raced to finish his alibi. "You looked just like you did then, all curled up on your side," he said. "I remembered how I crawled into bed beside you, to wake you up . . ."

A wan little smile curled the corners of his wet mouth.

"You told me that night that you loved being awakened that way . . . I've never forgotten that, or the way we felt about one another, Susie—"

I cut him off by dialing another number. The 1.

He fell silent and reached up to brush a fleck of spittle from his chin, then touched his forehead. Big, greasy beads of perspiration were sliding into rivulets of blood seeping from the two deep scratches I'd inflicted when I went for his eyes in the dark. He winced in pain, finally convinced by the sight of his own blood that I was deadly serious about calling the police.

"I'm sorry I scared you," he muttered, looking down at his scarlet fingertips. "I guess I must have had a few too many down at Krabb's."

Sensing that whatever he had intended when he had crawled into my bed had indeed been inspired by too much scotch, I slowly and deliberately replaced the phone in its cradle. Then I folded my arms across my chest and stared at the doleful, paunchy man cowering before me.

"Time for a reality check, Tom," I snapped nastily. "That great romantic evening on your father's boat consisted of exactly fifteen minutes of clumsy groping, followed by not more than three minutes of very painful intercourse. I was seventeen at the time and we were both extremely drunk. Afterwards, as I recall, I passed out cold and you only woke me up because you were terrified that your father was going to catch us."

I paused to let the harsh facts behind his carefully nurtured memory sink in. "On the very rare occasions that I think of that night on the boat at all," I continued after several seconds of strained silence, "I remember mostly the fact that I spent the next three days throwing up."

I could see that I had his full attention now. He stared shamefaced at the floor as I went on. "You were, in other words, a horrible lay," I said with all the meanness I was feeling. "Hell, Tom, it's a wonder that I didn't give up men entirely because of you."

Tom Barnwell stood there in my bedroom, looking completely defeated and shifting uneasily from side to side, like a sailor trying to regain his land legs after a long, rough sea voyage.

"Except for the memory of that dismal night, there is not now, nor will there ever be anything between us," I continued, the cold fury I felt at his presumption in assuming that he could just climb into my bed was dripping from each carefully pronounced syllable of every word. "And if you are not gone from here in the next minute, or if you ever dare to mention that disgusting incident to me again, I will gleefully call the police and tell them that you broke into my house tonight and assaulted me in my bed. Do I make myself crystal clear, Tom?"

"Assaulted you? But I didn't—"

I cut off his feeble protest with a wave of my hand. "You're not listening to me, Tom!" I shouted. "I know you didn't rape me tonight. And maybe, as you claim, you weren't even planning on it. But I'll tell the police that you did, anyway."

Tom Barnwell's slack mouth fell open, exposing a set of expensively bonded white teeth. "Jesus, Susie," he whined, "you can't go around making groundless accusations!" He shook his head in disbelief. "A thing like that would destroy me in this town," he said. "I can't believe you'd deliberately lie about something so serious."

I pointed a trembling finger at him. "Just try me, Tom," I hissed, looking pointedly at the bedside clock. "Half of your minute is already gone, by the way."

Looking as if he was about to be struck by a cobra, Tom Barnwell backed out of my bedroom without another word. A moment later, I heard his stumbling footsteps trampling down the stairs.

I ran to the bedroom door and shouted after him. "And leave my keys in the hall on your way out, you bastard! You're fired! And stop calling me Susie!"

Still shaking with rage I pulled on a robe and ran downstairs the moment I heard the front door slam behind him. I found Tom's set of keys on the foyer floor and scooped them up. Depositing the keys in the pocket of my robe, I locked the door securely. Then I spent the next fifteen minutes prowling the house, checking all of the windows and doors.

In the kitchen I went directly to the back door to be sure it was double latched. And though I did not for a minute believe Tom's feeble story of having spotted a prowler, I peered out into the backyard through the glass. Out in the darkness thick tendrils of fog swirled around the oak tree, creating the impression of shadowy figures gliding through the gray haze shrouding the yard.

A sudden shuddering chill ran through my body and I retreated to the center of the brightly lighted kitchen and put the teakettle on the stove. The newly installed portable phone on the marble countertop was inches from my hand. I had only to dial Dan's number. He had told me that he was staying in his parents' old house down by the wharf, so I knew he could be with me in ten minutes or less.

I reached for the phone, then stopped myself, unwilling to play the helpless, hysterical woman before Dan Freedman. After all, I reassured myself, I was perfectly all right. Tom Barnwell had fled like a scalded cat and was not likely to come back tonight, or ever again, for that matter.

And, despite the darkness of the night and the eerie effects of the fog, there was certainly no mysterious prowler lurking beneath the branches of the ancient oak in my backyard.

The kettle shrieked and I made the tea, hunching over the kitchen counter with my hands wrapped tightly around the comforting mug for warmth. At least, I thought, the mystery of the open kitchen door had been solved. Tom Barnwell must have indeed come by during the afternoon and let himself into the house, though I still didn't quite understand why he had left the back door open. Perhaps, I speculated, he had done it deliberately, hoping to add credence to his prowler story when he returned late at night, bent possibly on demonstrating some phony macho heroics before hopping into bed with grateful little me.

I didn't know, and at that point I really didn't care, what had motivated Tom Barnwell to do the things he had done. I only knew that he wasn't going to get another chance on my account.

I scribbled a note to myself on the pad beside the phone—a reminder to have all the locks in the house changed the next day, just in case Tom had a duplicate set of keys. Then, with the entire unpleasant incident resolved in my mind, I trudged upstairs to bed for the second time that night.

Chapter 25

Freezing!

I was floating in total darkness, my arms and legs numb with cold. The numbness was a small mercy because the parts of my body that I could still feel were striped with jagged bands of fiery pain. The stink of raw jet fuel burned in my throat and around my neck the stiff, uncomfortable embrace of an inflated life vest was holding me atop the icy surface of a storm-whipped sea, prolonging my agony by managing to keep my chin just above the level of the deep black water in which I was immersed.

I turned my head weakly, straining to see something—anything—in the pitch-black void.

But there was nothing there.

"Help! Somebody help me . . ." My feeble cry was lost in the raging howl of the stormy sea that surrounded me on every side. "What is happening?" I screamed into the night. "Please, God, what is happening to me?"

The sudden memory seared my brain. I had been on an airplane—a commuter flight from New York. One moment I had been seated beside a window, trying to blot out the effects of the turbulent air that was bouncing the plane around by pretending to do some work on my laptop and sipping a cocktail from a plastic airline glass.

Then, without warning, the woman beside me started screaming. I had looked up in annoyance, prepared to patiently explain to her that as violent as it might seem, turbulence in flight—bumps in the road, Bobby used to call it—was routine and nothing to scream about.

Before I could speak, though, the plane had nosed down sharply and smashed into the sea. Then the cabin lights had abruptly gone out and the freezing black water was pouring in through a shattered window.

I didn't remember getting out of the plane. But I calculated that I must have been in the water for some time in order for my limbs to have lost all sensation.

How long could a person survive in the icy waters of the Atlantic Ocean? Not very long. I knew that much. If I wasn't rescued very, very soon, I realized, my life was going to end.

Thrust helplessly to the top of a huge wave, I opened my mouth and screamed as loud as I could. And, to my utter astonishment, a beam of brilliant white light shot out of the darkness and pinned me like a butterfly in a child's science project.

With preternatural calm I gazed into the dazzling glare. For I could no longer feel my body, and I was certain that I had just died. But strangely I was not bothered by that grim realization.

Because there really was a light, just as Damon had claimed. And now I was going to experience at firsthand whatever lay at the far end of that dazzling cone of celestial illumination.

The core of the light came closer and closer, half-blinding me with its brilliance. And over the fury of the storm, I heard the growing sounds of a laboring engine and human voices shouting orders.

I was being rescued.

The white hull of a boat appeared out of the gloom, and

I could see the powerful marine spotlight mounted on its bow, the figure of a tall man standing on the deck. I squinted up into the glare and called out again. The boat's engine stopped as the man on deck came to the rail and peered down into the sea.

My sluggishly pumping heart thudded to a stop within my frozen breast. Because, looking down at me from above, was Bobby. He was wearing his battered old navy flight jacket and he smiled his gorgeous movie-star smile, regarding me with a wink of one crystalline blue eye, as if to say, "Sweet Sue, what kind of a fine mess have you gotten yourself into now?"

My frail voice breaking with joy, I screamed his name. Tiny shards of ice crackled in my hair as I somehow managed to raise my leaden arms to him.

But instead of reaching out for me Bobby merely continued to lean comfortably on the rail, gazing down at my struggles the way one might observe an interesting exhibit in an aquarium.

I floated helplessly a dozen feet below in the Arctic waters, weeping frozen tears and pleading with him to save me as the gleaming hull of the boat slid past and was swallowed up by the night.

"Bobby, come back!" I cried over the howl of the surging sea. "Don't leave me here alone!"

I woke up shivering.

Across the room the sheer lace curtains were billowing in the cold wind. I ran to my open window and slammed it shut, then stood there staring out into the fog, trying to make sense of the dream.

The lighthouse beacon swept silently over the yard, momentarily illuminating a familiar figure in a battered navy flight jacket.

He was standing on the front walk, looking up at me.

"Bobby!" His name stuck in my throat as the yard was plunged once more into darkness. I stood there motionless until the light made its full circuit and again flared across the property.

Restless eddies of gray fog swirled among the shadows of the empty walk.

Even in my dreams and imaginings, as in life, I sorrowfully concluded, Bobby was telling me with finality that he was truly gone.

Chapter 26

"So, tonight's the night?"

Dan was gazing at me from the opposite side of an intimate window table draped in pink linen and set with a single glowing candle that cast soft highlights on the graceful silver place settings. Beyond our window the lights of Newport alternately glimmered and faded through a veil of hard, pelting rain.

"Tonight?" I replied absently, intent on gawking around the richly paneled interior of the elegant seaside restaurant. Flames crackling merrily in a massive fireplace of native stone provided most of the ambient light in the room and showed off a stunning collection of 18th-century English sideboards and wine cupboards that might once have graced the great hall of some nobleman's country manor.

"The furnishings in this place are absolutely exquisite," I whispered across the table. "I'm almost positive the divan in the ladies' room is authentic Empire."

Dan frowned at me. "I wouldn't doubt it," he said, casting a disdainful glance around the richly appointed room. "The Greystone Club was built in the late 1800s by a couple of Newport's original robber barons who needed someplace to drink after a hard day of yachting. And I don't recall having heard that they ever spared any expense when it came to indulging their private pastimes."

He gave me an impatient little smile. "However, I was referring to your planned encounter with Aimee Marks. You did tell me you were going to give it a try tonight?"

"I'm sorry," I said, returning my attention to Dan and noting with relief the amused sparkle in his eyes. "I guess you can take the girl away from the antiques but you can't take the antiques out of the girl."

We both laughed as a wine steward in a snowy-white jacket glided unbidden to the table and silently refreshed our glasses of chilled Riesling.

In truth, I was enjoying our candlelight supper and not particularly anxious at that moment to discuss what now seemed like an increasingly ludicrous plan to lure Aimee Marks back to my room for a conversation. After my disturbing encounters of the previous night with Tom Barnwell in the flesh and then with Bobby—encounters I had deliberately not mentioned to Dan—I was in a mood to relax and shake off my gloomy feelings.

I desperately needed a few pleasant hours before I attempted to contact Aimee Marks. And, until now, my day had not been a particularly pleasant one.

Following my emotionally charged dreams of the night before I had awakened late to the sound of rain falling on the roof of my turret bedroom.

After calling the hospital in Boston and learning that Damon's medical condition remained virtually unchanged, I had spent three frustrating hours locating a locksmith who was willing to come out in the rain to change all the locks in the house. Then, while the grumbling locksmith worked, I had spent the rest of the day compiling and faxing St. Claire & Marks's client list to Sir Edward in Manhattan, along with detailed notes on all of our current projects and each client's special quirks and needs.

By the time I had finished the faxes and paid the locksmith his outrageous fee it had been time to phone the hospital again. Dan had arrived while I was speaking with Alice Cahill, who had taken my call personally and was providing me with a dispassionate inventory of Damon's vitals and clinical test results, but no new information.

"I'm hoping he'll pull out of this within the next twenty-four hours," she had concluded. "In fact, I'm certain he will."

Twenty-four hours.

That was how much time I had to contact Aimee, though my confidence that I would really be able to do so, much less learn anything of significance about Damon's near-death experience, was slipping. But if I was going to have any answers for Damon when he again regained consciousness, I needed to get them tonight.

I had told that much to Dan.

He, in turn, had pointed out that Aimee Marks had never put in an appearance before midnight, and suggested that we drive down to Newport for dinner at the exclusive Greystone Club, once the private preserve of Newport gentry but now open to anyone with the not inconsiderable price of a gourmet dinner.

I had assumed he had brought me out to relax.

So here we were, having a lovely, relaxing dinner in this beautiful and historic old restaurant. And Dan was sitting across the table, his handsome features made even more handsome by the soft glow of candlelight, waiting for me to spill my Master Plan for spirit contact.

The only trouble was, I didn't have a Master Plan. In fact, I didn't have any plan at all, beyond going to bed as usual and lighting my blue fairy lamp, with the fervent hope that Aimee Marks's ghost would obligingly put in another appearance and fill me in on the mysteries of the afterlife.

But for reasons that should be fairly obvious I really didn't feel like admitting that to Dan. And, as I said before, I particularly didn't feel like discussing gloomy and disturbing matters in general.

So I pretended that I either hadn't heard or hadn't understood Dan's previous question. Instead, I picked up the Greystone's big wine-colored, velvet-encased menu—no prices inside, so you knew they had to be atrocious enough to destroy your appetite—and ordered with abandon.

Across the table, my good-humored host simply smiled and shook his head, as if to say, *"Okay, the ball's in your court for now. Run with it."*

"Class! Now that is what I call class. How can you not fall in love with this man?" whispered Miss Romance.

"It doesn't hurt that he's also filthy rich and beautiful," Miss Practical chimed in. "You're finally free of Bobby now. So when are you going to break down and sleep with this guy, you moron?"

"I think I'll have the Maryland Crab Cakes for an appetizer, then the Tournedos of Beef and the Fresh Asparagus Tips," I cheerfully announced, shutting them both up.

Somewhere in the back of my mind I had a quick vision of Laura politely applauding my cleverness in having avoided unpleasant subjects.

Dan politely waited until after dessert—truly marvelous little blackberry tarts drenched in a sinfully rich crème brulee sauce—to burst my bubble.

"I suppose you've been wondering why I chose this particular restaurant," he began as I scraped the last remnants of the delicious cream from my plate.

"Well," I said, licking my lips and taking a sip of coffee, "I must admit the Greystone does seem to go against your alleged aversion to fine dining."

Dan nodded. "It's way too pretentious for my tastes,"

he said, looking around, "even if the chef does happen to be particularly good."

"Well, I suppose you can't have everything." I grinned happily, suppressing the urge to burp.

"I had another reason entirely for bringing you here tonight," he said, "besides the food."

I looked at him in surprise, unable to imagine what he was getting at. "Okay, I give up," I said. "What was the reason?"

Dan folded his napkin and pushed his chair back from the table. "Follow me," he said, pulling out my chair and waiting for me to get up.

I frowned at his theatrics, but did as he asked, following him through the dining room and into an intimate, dimly lit bar just off the lobby.

With the exception of a smiling bartender who rushed down from the far end of his gleaming mahogany domain to take our order, the little room was deserted. After liqueurs—Cognac for Dan, a small Amaretto for me—had been placed before us, the barkeep discreetly returned to his station, leaving us alone.

"Well, what do you think?" Dan asked, raising his glass to indicate our new surroundings.

I briefly scanned the darkly paneled room, which was decorated primarily with gleaming silver regatta trophies and faded photos of Whitneys and Vanderbilts in silly formal yachting attire. "A little too clubby for my tastes," I remarked. "We should have ordered our drinks at the table and continued enjoying the view of rain on the harbor."

Dan smiled mysteriously. "Perhaps you'd like to take a closer look before rendering a final decision," he suggested, pointing to the center of the wall directly in front of us. I followed his gaze to the only nonnautical decoration in the whole place, the obligatory old-fashioned barroom painting of a reclining, rosy-cheeked nude that was hanging in a massive gilt frame above the ornately mirrored back bar.

"Charming," I said and laughed, turning back to him after a cursory glance. "I think there must have been some kind of law around the turn of the century that required every saloon, no matter how ritzy, to have one of those awful paintings over the bar."

Dan continued to regard the picture. "Take a very close look," he insisted.

Rolling my eyes in exasperation, I humored him by looking up at the clichéd painting again. Unimaginative though it was, the artist had certainly known his business, because he had perfectly captured the delicate beauty of his subject. The raven-haired model lay on a red velvet sofa, both arms gracefully raised over her head, resting on the edge of the sofa, the obligatory fringed shawl positioned modestly so as not to expose too much. Her dark, liquid eyes stared brazenly out into the room, inviting the admiring looks of anyone who cared to study her slender limbs and full, soft breasts . . .

It took a full minute for me to realize what I was seeing.

"Oh, my God!" My voice dropped to a hushed whisper.

"Your ancestor, Miss Aimee Marks," Dan said quietly.

"Oh, my God," I repeated, taking a too-large swallow of my Amaretto and nearly choking on the sweet liqueur. "How in the world did you discover this?"

Dan smiled. "I thought at the time that there was something familiar about the face of the girl in that old photo you showed me," he replied. "At first I thought it was just her resemblance to you. But I come here from time to time, with clients, so it was just a matter of time before I connected Aimee with this painting."

"It's amazing," I breathed, standing to get a better look at the scandalous picture. "She really was beautiful, wasn't she?"

Dan glanced up at the painting and nodded. "Very beautiful and, I suspect, set up to be in a whole lot of trouble at home if her family ever found out about this." He gave me a meaningful look. "And, considering what we know about Aimee Marks now, it appears that they probably did find out."

"Oh, Christ!" I whispered.

"The artist was a rather notorious womanizer named Ned Bingham," Dan continued, consulting a small notebook that he'd dug from his pocket. "I did a little research with a local art dealer I know," he said, "and learned that Bingham came up here from New York in the summer of 1909 to work on a couple of commissioned family portraits for an industrialist named Howard Chase. Bingham was a first-rate portraitist and a minor celebrity of sorts at the time, and during his stay in Newport he was probably wined and dined by several social-climbing families in Freedman's Cove."

"That must be how he met Aimee," I breathed.

Dan nodded. "So it would seem," he agreed. "Though I wasn't able to learn a whole lot more about Ned Bingham, he was evidently very good-looking and was rumored to have seduced more than one otherwise respectable young woman by flattering them into taking off their clothes in order to be immortalized on canvas."

"I had an instructor in art school who used the same technique," I mused, gazing up at the nude behind the bar. "But seducing Aimee Marks and then selling her portrait to a private men's club here in Newport, where it was almost guaranteed to be seen by someone who knew the family are two very different things," I marveled. "Ned Bingham must have been a real bastard to do that."

Dan shrugged. "Maybe. But I suspect the painting showing up here at the Greystone Club was purely accidental," he said. "One thing I was able to learn about Bingham was that he had an agent who sold his noncommissioned works through a small gallery in New York. My dealer friend thinks it's more likely that somebody from the Greystone Club just saw the painting and liked it, having no idea at the time that the model was local talent."

I shook my head. "He still sounds like a first-class schmuck to me," I murmured.

Dan and I arrived back at my house a little before ten and I invited him in. After surreptitiously checking the kitchen door to be sure there had been no more uninvited guests in my absence I made coffee and carried it back into the parlor.

We chatted for a while about Aimee Marks and Ned Bingham, then lapsed into silence. There seemed little point in discussing her tragic story further. For a long time we sat silently in near darkness before the fire, sipping our coffee and listening to the sounds of the rising wind and rain and the distant booming of the surf.

And then, effortlessly and without a word passing between us, we were holding one another and kissing.

Our kiss lasted for a very long time, growing deeper and more passionate with each passing moment. When finally it ended, we were half-reclining on the big, comfortable sofa.

I sat up, panting, and looked longingly into Dan's green eyes. They were locked on mine, awaiting some signal from me. Then his lips parted slightly and he moved them close to my ear. "If you want to stop, this would be the perfect time," he whispered in a voice husky with desire.

I remained silent for several seconds, waiting for the guilt that I had for so long carried with me like a cross to well up and pull me back from the brink.

But though my head was filled with a dizzying emotional tempest every bit as powerful as the storm that was raging outside, no reproachful visions of Bobby arose to temper my urgent need, and I no longer felt his watchful presence hovering over me.

I was truly convinced then that all my dreams of Bobby turning away from me and leaving—dreams I had initially interpreted as betrayals of the love we two had shared—really were signs that he had passed on into eternity, leaving me to begin my life anew.

Dan was still waiting for my answer, his patience and love for me shining like rare emeralds in his eyes. And as I gazed into those loving eyes my body felt light as a feather and only my clothes seemed heavy and suffocating in the shimmering heat radiating from the blazing logs on the hearth.

I was struck by the sudden realization that I was at last free to follow my own desire.

"No . . . I . . . don't want to stop," I breathed, pulling Dan's face to mine and engaging him in another long, breathless kiss that ended with the two of us lying together full length on the sofa.

He rose above me and looked down with concern. "I meant it when I said I was prepared to wait," he began.

I responded by reaching up and slowly unbuttoning his shirt. As I slipped my hands inside the warm fabric and ran them over the warm hard contours of his chest I grew blissfully aware that my own clothes were gently falling away from my overheated skin.

"No, my love," I pleaded, burying my face in the soft, damp hollow of his neck and brazenly raising my hips to expedite the silken whisper of panties sliding down my thighs, "don't wait an instant longer."

No words are adequate to describe the torrent of feelings that went coursing through my soul from the sheer physical bliss of our lovemaking that night. All I knew as I strained to make my body one with Dan's was that this was good and natural and right.

And, while a part of me would forever remain devoted to Bobby's memory, I could discern no trace of conflict or betrayal in my newly discovered love for Dan Freedman.

For Bobby and Dan were as different from one another as the desert is from the sea, and the love I felt for each of them, for Bobby's wild and untamed spirit, for Dan's quiet, unwavering devotion, had at long last made one complete person of me.

Yes, I would go on living, I told myself, just as I would have wanted Bobby to have done in my place. Just as I was sure he wanted me to.

Chapter 27

It was well past midnight when Dan and I stood beneath the crystal chandelier in the foyer and kissed for the last time that night.

"Sure you don't want me to stay?" he asked as the old house creaked beneath the assault of the rising wind. "They say this latest storm is supposed to get worse. It'll probably last through the whole weekend."

"Tomorrow," I said seriously. I raised my eyes to the ceiling. "Tonight there's still the matter of Aimee Marks to be attended to. And if there's even a slight chance that I can actually contact her I feel like I have to do it before Damon wakes up."

"Well, you've got a creaky old house and a dark and stormy night," he smiled. "The perfect stage setting for a ghostly encounter." Dan's smile faded and he asked with genuine concern. "Aren't you just a little bit afraid?"

"No," I said, shaking my head. "I get no feelings of that sort at all from Aimee, just an overwhelming sense of a great sadness in her. If I'm afraid of anything it's only that I may not be able to get her to show herself again."

Dan raised his eyebrows questioningly.

"Aimee only came to me before when I was desperately unhappy myself," I explained, taking both his hands in mine and squeezing them hard. "But now I can't really say that anymore."

Dan leaned over and kissed my forehead. "Tomorrow it is, then," he said, reaching for the doorknob. The smile reappeared on his lips. "I'm bringing my toothbrush."

I laughed. "It's a date."

He pulled open the front door, admitting a violent blast of freezing rain and windblown leaves.

"Cripes!" he exclaimed, pulling up his jacket collar and stepping out into the insufficient shelter of the broad porch. "Looks like we're in for a real squall," he yelled over the thunder of the surf pounding the nearby beach.

The beacon from the Maidenstone Light swept past at that moment. With a born seafarer's critical eye, Dan followed its path out over the white-capped waters of the harbor. Medium-sized waves were crashing onto the beach just behind the house. "You keep a close eye on that tide," he warned. "Call me immediately if the water starts rising. After all the trouble I've been through, I don't want you getting washed out to sea on me."

"Aye, aye, Captain!" I shouted back to make myself heard. "Now get out of here before we both catch pneumonia."

He delivered a quick peck to my cheek. "I hope you can actually learn something that will help Damon," he said seriously. Then, without another word he trotted down the steps into the slanting rain, splashed across the puddles on the front lawn and dived into his Mercedes.

I stood on the porch, watching until he started the engine and drove away into the storm. "Good night, my love," I called as his taillights dwindled to crimson sparks and vanished in the night.

A dense curtain of wind-driven rain marched across the street, swept up under the porch roof and drenched me where I stood. Gasping for breath beneath the unexpected deluge, I had just turned to rush for the front door when I had the eerie sensation that someone was watching me.

Despite the cold water soaking my hair and clothes I stopped where I was and slowly turned back to face the deserted landscape. A forked bolt of lightning streaked across the leaden sky out over the harbor, lighting up the street of stately old Victorians like a gigantic photographer's flashbulb. I strained to detect any sign of my unseen watcher, but except for the wildly gyrating trees I saw no living thing.

"Aimee?" I raised my voice hopefully against the din of the storm. "Aimee, are you there?"

There was no reply but the howling of the wind in the eaves.

"Go to sleep. She is definitely not coming tonight." Miss Practical was sniping again, breaking my concentration on the flickering blue light of the fairy lamp playing across my ceiling.

"Shut up!" I ordered, forcing my eyes to remain open. I had been lying on my back staring up at the ceiling for nearly half an hour without any discernible result. And had it not been for the violently battering wind that lashed the turret room and rattled the windowpanes in their frames, I would already have drifted off to sleep and sweet dreams of making love with Dan.

"You're a lucky, lucky girl," purred Miss Romantic, who had obviously been reading my thoughts. "Believe me, you're not going to have any bad dreams tonight."

"And no ghostly visitors, either," Miss Practical yawned. "So why not be a pal and put out the lamp so we can all get a little rest."

Her yawn was infectious and I couldn't immediately

think of a snappy reply. So instead I remained silent, willing her to go away.

Of course, I fell promptly to sleep.

The fairy lamp had burned itself out and the glowing numerals on the bedside clock were reading 3:22 AM when a particularly fierce blast of wind jarred the entire house. I sat up sleepily and heard the explosive crack of a tree limb falling on the lawn. My eyes darted to the windows and I saw the lace curtains floating above the floor.

And then I saw her.

She was standing in the shadows beside the wardrobe, half-concealed among many layered folds of flowing lace. Her face was turned away from me and one hand was holding aside the filmy fabric of the curtain as she stared out through the rain-streaked glass, precisely as she had done on that first night.

I watched Aimee Marks's ethereal form for several seconds, hardly daring to believe she was really there, afraid to speak for fear that she would simply vanish, as she had done before.

But she remained where she was, unmoving, her gaze fixed on some indefinable target in the storm.

Pulling myself slowly upright, I finally worked up the courage to speak her name. "Aimee?" I called, my voice tremulous with excitement.

At first she did not move, and I was certain she had not heard me. For the wind was moaning loudly through the eaves and dead branches were clattering against the sides of the house with a fearful racket.

"Aimee?" I asked again, my voice a little stronger this time. "Do you hear me?"

Slowly she turned and stared across the darkened room. A slight frown creased her lovely features and she cocked her head to one side, as if she was not quite sure she had heard a voice.

"I'm right here," I said, reaching over to switch on a small reading lamp. "Here in the bed."

To my great relief the ghostly spectre did not disappear in the modest fall of yellow light that scattered through the room. Instead, she looked directly at me with a surprised expression.

"Do you see me?" she whispered in a voice as soft and melodic as chimes in the wind.

I nodded dumbly.

"And hear me when I speak?"

My head bobbed up and down again. "Yes," I croaked, certain that my heart would burst if it beat any faster. "I can see you and hear you perfectly well. In fact, I've been waiting since your last visit, hoping you'd come back again."

Aimee was still staring at me in disbelief. "I wasn't really sure anyone could see me anymore," she said in a small, regretful voice. She let go of the filmy curtain and took a silent step closer to the bed. "You never seemed to see me when you were a child."

Feeling curiously light-headed, I tore my eyes from her and watched the yards of transparent lace at the window flutter slowly and gracefully to the floor. "No, but the curtains . . . When I was a little girl," I began, overwhelmed by the sudden return of a long-forgotten childhood memory, "I thought the fairies flew up from the garden to make my curtains float like that."

Aimee's sad, beautiful eyes followed my gaze to the softly sinking curtain. When she turned back to me traces of a smile played at the corners of her full, sensuous lips.

"Yes, I remember how that sometimes made you smile,"

she whispered. "There were times when I was certain you were watching me as I came to the window."

I shook my head in amazement. "My God, you were here all of that time?" I suddenly flushed bright red, remembering a couple of things that I had done in this room, especially during my period as a rebellious teenager.

Aimee smiled modestly. "Oh, I always tried to respect your privacy," she said. "Often, when you were . . . growing up, I did not come at all."

"Thank you," I breathed. I opened my mouth to say something else, then thought better of it and fell silent. Aimee arched her dark eyebrows questioningly.

"I-I'm sorry," I stammered. "I just remembered that I'm sitting here having a conversation with a . . . ghost. And it occurred to me that I should probably be petrified."

"Oh, but I could never, ever harm you," she cried, looking stricken. "Even if I knew how."

I raised my hands to show her that I wasn't afraid, even though I noticed that they were trembling violently. "I didn't mean I was afraid of you," I assured her. "It's just that I've never actually spoken with a gh—"

The smile brightened her lovely features again. "Ghost is a good word," she said, "Or spirit, if you prefer." Aimee paused and thought for a moment. "When you were a small child I often came to this room to watch over you. You always seemed to be such a sad and lonely little thing."

I sat up and sniffled. "I cried for my mother a lot," I said, remembering the anguish of those early years.

Aimee nodded. "It broke my heart to hear you sobbing into your pillow at night. Sometimes I would sit beside your bed and whisper nursery rhymes to you, or tell you fantastical stories of voyages to faraway places . . ."

I felt as if my heart was going to stop. "But those were

always my favorite dreams," I gasped. "Dreams of a great sailing ship that carried me off to Africa and the Indies."

Aimee smiled, pleased that I had remembered.

I suddenly heard myself laughing hysterically. She looked at me with renewed concern. "I thought I had such a wonderful imagination when I was a child," I explained, shaking my head. "I always wondered what had happened to it after I grew up."

"Please, I didn't mean to upset you—" she began, her shadowy image beginning to waver ever so slightly.

"No," I interrupted. "Please, don't go. My God, this is so fantastic . . ." I narrowed my eyes. "Are you sure I'm not just imagining you?"

Aimee's laughter tinkled through the small room like the sound of fairy bells on the summer wind. "No," she said, looking down at her insubstantial form. "I'm really here . . . at least as much as is left of me is here."

"Incredible!" I sighed and fell back onto the pillows, exhausted. A thousand questions raced through my mind. I suddenly remembered Damon and Bobby and all the carefully rehearsed things that I had planned to ask her about them. I sat upright against my pillows, trying to compose myself.

"Why are you here, Aimee?" I whispered. "I mean, aren't people supposed to pass on, or cross over, or something, after . . . ?"

"After they die, do you mean?"

I nodded.

"Yes," she said without hesitation. "When it is time, everyone goes on."

"And you?"

A shadow clouded her lovely features. "I'm not sure," she whispered, sounding miserable and confused. "I'm . . . waiting."

"Is that why you come here to look out the window?" I asked. "Are you waiting for someone?"

"I . . . I don't know," Aimee replied softly.

Again I felt the pall of unbearable sadness surrounding her. And suddenly I was once more immersed in my own profound melancholy of the past several months. My throat grew tight and I felt tears beginning to stream down my cheeks as I thought of Damon, and of those I had recently lost, of Bobby and Aunt Ellen.

"I'm so sorry," Aimee whispered, her slight form shimmering and fading like smoke in the wind. "I should not have come and upset you so."

"No," I begged her. "Please stay, Aimee. I desperately need your help."

Her image seemed to grow stronger once more and her eyes widened in surprise. "Me? But I am only a spirit. I can do nothing anymore."

My head bobbed up and down eagerly. "Yes, you can," I said. "I need to know what it's like, being a spirit. You can tell me. Exactly what happens after someone dies?"

Aimee's face fell and she again looked stricken. "It is . . . difficult to explain," she whispered, turning back toward the window. "I can't really remember very much . . . You feel utterly lost . . . and terribly alone."

"Oh," I said, suddenly at a loss for something to say. For her voice had been filled with anguish as she had uttered those last words. And I felt sure that I was on the verge of losing her again.

"Can you recall anything at all?" I asked softly. "Perhaps if you remember what happened to you, you can leave this place and go on."

She was staring out the window now, gazing into the rainy night. "I can't . . ." she murmured.

"Please try," I urged. "You died so young. Surely you remember that much."

The lighthouse beacon flashed, the beam of strong light passing eerily through her body and illuminating the room behind her. "I fell from the top of the lighthouse," she said, turning back to face me as the room went dark once more. "As I fell I was certain there would be pain . . . But there was only the falling and then . . ." She looked down at herself again. "Then I was like this."

"How did it happen?" I asked.

"There was a man," she began, turning back to the window and the distant tower on Maidenstone Island. And I had the feeling that she was speaking not to me but to someone else in some other time.

"He was a very handsome and charming man . . . a gifted artist." Her voice caught and I heard her stifle a small sob. "He loved me dearly, and I him."

"Ned," I said quietly, working to suppress the undercurrent of anger in my voice. "His name was Ned Bingham."

Aimee whirled about and stared at me.

"How could you know that?" she asked, her tone filled with despair. "Our love was a secret. Our secret." She wrung her pale hands in despair. "Father would have killed my dear Ned if he'd suspected," she moaned.

"But your father did know, Aimee," I said as gently as I could. "He went down to New York and brought you back home. Back here, to this house. Surely you must remember that." Something told me it would not be a good idea to mention the painting in the Greystone Club, so I shut up.

Aimee thought for several moments, then she slowly sank to her knees, her lovely head bowed onto her chest. Her smooth back was wracked with deep, shuddering sobs and I longed to be able to take her into my arms and hold her.

"Oh, God," she wailed. "Father! I remember it all now. That wicked man told him everything. That horrible man with his horrible, obscene letters—"

"Amos," I said. "Amos Carter, the lighthouse keeper."

Aimee slowly raised her head and gazed into my eyes, her beautiful face a mask of profound grief. "Amos," she whispered, as if repeating a name from a frightening Gothic horror story. "That wicked, evil man." She shook her head in disbelief. "Amos tried to lure me into his house on Maidenstone," she whispered. "Tried to put his dirty hands on my bosoms . . ." She paused, struggling to cope with the foul memory of Amos Carter. "He said he would tell Father about Ned and me, said he'd make me sorry if I didn't do what he wanted."

I was momentarily speechless. For though I had suspected Amos Carter of the worst kind of lechery, the despicable lighthouse keeper's blatant attempt to trade his silence for Aimee's sexual favors was a revelation that even I had not anticipated.

"Why, that dirty son of a bitch!" I finally hissed.

Aimee seemed to recoil in shock from the sound of my voice. And it took me a moment to understand that Victorian sensibilities would have prevented a young woman of her class from ever expressing herself in such crude language.

"I'm sorry," I apologized. "I know women didn't talk like that when you were . . . in your time."

"Nevertheless, it's true," she whispered after a further moment of painful reflection. "Amos Carter was exactly what you said, and worse. He was a terrible, terrible man."

Her head fell back onto her chest and she sobbed as

though her heart were breaking. "He made everything that had been so sweet and beautiful between Ned and me seem filthy and degraded," she said and then wept.

Aimee's stricken eyes were filled with girlish innocence as she raised them to mine. "Ned and I were going to marry," she said. "He had pledged himself to me. I only left him and returned home after Father threatened to have my love thrown into prison."

She shook her head in despair. "Father refused to understand that Ned painted me as the great Renaissance masters painted, with purity and reverence . . ."

I did not trust myself to reply to that. For I realized then that Aimee must be blissfully unaware that her painting had ended up hanging behind the bar at the Greystone, there to be leered at by generations of rich old men. Evidently she had not lived long enough to discover that Ned Bingham had been every bit as big a bastard as the despicable Amos Carter.

"The night you fell," I began, confident now that I finally had the full picture, and determined to guide the subject back to the circumstances of her death. "Am I correct in supposing that Amos Carter lured you up into the lighthouse with some new threat? And that he pushed you off when you refused to submit to his advances?"

Aimee's dark eyes widened in astonishment and she shook her head emphatically. "Oh, no," she exclaimed. "That's not what happened at all."

Her voice suddenly caught and she turned to gaze out through the window at the ghostly white outline of the old stone tower on the nearby island.

"If that had been what happened . . ." She sighed as if she devoutly wished it was true. "If Amos Carter had murdered me, then I could have gone straight to the loving arms of those waiting for me in the heavenly Light."

Aimee was rocking back and forth on her knees in profound sadness, causing her raven tresses to scatter over the pale ivory of her shoulders.

"If only that awful man had killed me," she moaned, her words directed not to me this time, but to whatever cruel fate held her trapped in perpetual limbo, "then I would long ago have passed over to the glories of the other side."

I stared at her as an explosive, cracking noise outside signaled the loss of another tree limb in the yard.

Chapter 28

Following a few hours of troubled sleep I had anxiously phoned Dan shortly after dawn. He had driven over and picked me up for an early breakfast. Now we were sitting in a window booth at Krabb's, overlooking the choppy waters of the harbor.

Dan was positively thunderstruck.

"You're saying that Amos Carter was innocent? That Aimee Marks actually did commit suicide by jumping from the lighthouse tower . . ."

I held up my hands to stop him. "I said no such thing! And even though Amos Carter didn't murder Aimee Marks he can hardly be considered innocent," I retorted angrily. "In fact, if there really is a Hell, I sincerely hope that evil—" I paused to regain my composure. "I just hope he is slowly roasting in it this very second."

Taking a deep breath and forcing a calmer tone into my voice, I continued. "Aimee's death was far more complex than a simple suicide. You just didn't let me finish."

Dan threw up his hands and leaned back against the hideous pink vinyl of the restaurant booth. "I'm sorry," he said, genuinely puzzled. "But if Amos didn't kill Aimee and she didn't kill herself, then who did?"

Before I could answer him a tired-looking waitress appeared at our table with two mugs of steaming black coffee and pulled out a pad to take our orders.

I felt Dan's eyes worriedly scrutinizing my haggard features and rain-soaked hair as I ordered toast and poached eggs. He ordered his scrambled, with bacon, and the waitress departed. When she had gone, he leaned closer, anxiously awaiting my explanation.

I looked around the nearly deserted restaurant to be certain that nobody was eavesdropping on our bizarre conversation. "Ned Bingham murdered Aimee Marks," I said. "But the poor thing doesn't even know it."

Dan couldn't have looked more confused. He dumped a packet of sweetener into his coffee mug and waited for me to continue.

"Aimee's father went to New York and broke into Bingham's little love nest, threatening to have the jerk arrested for alienation of affection and seduction with promise to marry . . ." I began.

Dan's brow wrinkled into a frown. "Arrested for what?" he spluttered in disbelief. "She was twenty-five years old, hardly a child."

I shook my head. "It may seem unbelievable now," I said, "but in 1910, Victorian thinking remained firmly rooted in society and the law. Women hadn't yet been given the vote and were still essentially treated as property. Accordingly, an unmarried female was considered to be the ward of her father until she was turned over to the care of a proper husband."

I paused to let that information sink in before continuing. "The bottom line is that either of those seemingly silly charges I mentioned—even discounting the far more serious offense of unlawful intercourse—could land a man like Ned Bingham in seriously deep ka-ka. I'm talking prison time."

Dan took a gulp of the scalding coffee and the hint of a smile creased his features.

"What?" I snapped peevishly.

"Oh, nothing." He grinned. "I was just wondering how many years I would have gotten for what went on in your parlor last night."

"Very amusing," I said, scowling. "Do you want to hear the rest of this or not?"

He looked suitably chastised and nodded. "Please do continue," he urged. "I find it absolutely fascinating."

I sighed, reached for a container of low-fat milk and stirred some into my coffee. "Anyway," I went on, "in order to protect Bingham, Aimee returned to Freedman's Cove and became a virtual prisoner in her room. Because, no matter how much the family might have blamed Ned Bingham for what had happened, Aimee had been his willing accomplice. So, until they could pack her off on a long European tour or some similar diversion that would get her out of town for a while, they were afraid to let her out in public, where, thanks to Amos Carter, people would be sure to gossip about her . . . and the family."

"It all sounds terribly Victorian," Dan remarked.

I nodded. "Depressingly so," I agreed. "But similar things frequently happened to 'good' families in that era. But if they had enough money, which Aimee's family did, the wilted flower could generally be married off to a suitable man in another city and the scandal would eventually be forgotten. Or at least it would never be spoken of in polite society." I paused for a sip of my own coffee. "So that was the plan."

"But something went wrong," Dan said, finally coming up to speed. He thoughtfully stirred his coffee. "Like Aimee discovering that she was pregnant."

I rewarded him with a small smile. "Very good," I said.

"Although the term Aimee used was 'with child.' And that presented the poor woman with an entirely new dilemma. Because she couldn't even imagine what her father would do to Ned Bingham if he found out."

"More likely than not, there would have been a formal shotgun wedding," Dan cynically interjected.

I nodded impatiently. "You may be right. But you must remember that Aimee had heard her father issuing death threats against her lover and promising him prison time, just for having slept with her. So she had no reason to imagine that the old man would suddenly welcome the creep as his son-in-law."

"I think I see where all of this is going," Dan said. "Aimee didn't tell her family about her, *ahem*, condition . . ."

He paused as the waitress returned with plates of eggs, toast and a platter of crisp bacon.

"Of course she didn't tell them," I replied impatiently when the waitress had finished and gone away again. "She was absolutely terrified."

Dan snagged a piece of bacon. "But she did tell Ned Bingham," he guessed, "who, being disinterested in giving up his mad Bohemian lifestyle, obligingly took the next train north and killed her."

He popped the piece of bacon into his mouth and waited for me to confirm his conclusion.

I shook my head. "Wrong again," I said, deliberately pausing to butter my toast.

"You're punishing me now," he complained.

"No," I said, enjoying the suspense of making him wait. "I'm just trying to show you the folly of leaping to one false conclusion after another."

"I won't say another word," he promised.

I gave him a jaundiced look as I bit into the corner of my toast and thoroughly chewed the morsel.

"But you were at least partly right," I finally conceded, "in that Aimee did write to Ned Bingham, describing her plight and beseeching him to come secretly to Freedman's Cove to take her away and marry her, just as he'd promised."

Dan skeptically raised his eyebrows. "The girl was not exactly a rocket scientist, was she?"

"That's unfair," I snapped, waving my toast for emphasis. "Like most young women of her time, Aimee Marks had been deliberately kept ignorant of the most basic facts of life. As a result, she had absolutely no experience of what love was supposed to be, other than what she'd absorbed from silly Victorian romance novels, where lovers sent one another flowery notes and ladies swooned at the thought of a bare ankle. She'd never even seen a naked man before Ned Bingham blew into Freedman's Cove and bowled her over."

I slowly let the anger drain out of my voice. "By our standards, Aimee Marks was nothing more than a sheltered, provincial child who fell hopelessly in love with this charming jerk. She wholeheartedly believed every word Ned Bingham ever uttered to her."

"But he didn't kill her?"

I shook my head. "No! The miserable son of a bitch did something far, far worse than that."

Dan remained silent while I took another sip of my coffee, followed by a deep breath.

"After he received her letter, Ned Bingham got a message to Aimee. He said that he would indeed come in secret for her, by boat. He named a night when the moon would be dark and the tide low, and instructed her to wait for him out on Maidenstone Island. After Amos Carter had retired that night, which he always did by midnight, Aimee was to climb to the top of the lighthouse tower and watch the sea from the balcony for Ned's signal. If she signaled back to him that the coast was clear, he would sail in and pick her up."

"Well, old Ned certainly wasn't taking any chances on running into her old man," Dan observed.

"That's what convinced Aimee to do as Ned instructed," I told him. "To her it seemed a perfectly logical and wildly romantic way to begin an elopement. On the appointed night, Aimee went out to Maidenstone Island and climbed to the top of the lighthouse to watch for Ned's signal. But when she got there, Ned was already waiting for her."

"Uh-oh," Dan muttered.

"Ned appeared to be distraught," I continued, ignoring the interruption. "He told Aimee he'd just learned that her father had already filed charges against him and that he was a ruined man. Henceforth, no self-respecting millionaire would allow him into his home to paint portraits of his wife and daughters, et cetera."

Dan interrupted again, waving his hand to get my attention. "May I assume that Bingham's entire story was a big fat lie?" he impatiently queried.

I nodded. "I think we can safely assume that," I said, "considering what good old Ned did next."

Dan leaned forward. "Go ahead," he urged.

"Well," I continued, "after Ned informed Aimee of his own ruination, and reminded her that she was a fallen woman—by Edwardian standards, anyway—he suggested a solution to their joint problem. It was exactly the kind of solution the cunning bastard knew would fit perfectly into one of Aimee's flowery romantic novels."

Dan raised his eyebrows.

"Because he loved her so much and could not bear to see her suffer the indignities that her pregnancy and his disgrace were sure to bring," I said, my voice filled with loathing, "Ned Bingham proposed a suicide pact."

"Oh, hell!" Dan exclaimed.

"He and Aimee would share one last kiss, then step out onto the balcony of the Maidenstone Light and leap to their deaths on the rocks a hundred feet below."

"Sweet, Jesus!"

"And," I went on, "being a perfect gentleman, Ned said he would allow Aimee to jump first. So that, in the extremely unlikely event that she somehow survived the fall, he would be available to gallantly go down and deliver a coup de grace, before climbing back up and offing himself."

Dan looked like he was going to be ill. "So Aimee jumped," he said.

I nodded. "It would have been a simple matter for Ned to remain hidden in the lighthouse until Amos Carter came out and discovered Aimee's body. Afterwards, Ned must have sneaked down from the tower, gone to the boat he had hidden among the rocks and sailed away into the night."

"Having just committed the perfect crime," Dan whispered in awe.

"Perfect except for one small detail," I said.

Dan looked at me, puzzled.

"Aimee's ghost," I said. "She's trapped eternally somewhere between Aunt Ellen's and the lighthouse, still waiting for Ned Bingham, to join her."

"Good Lord, you mean you didn't tell her the truth?"

I wearily shook my head. "Tell her that the only man she had ever loved betrayed her, in return for her having made the greatest sacrifice that any human can make?"

I lowered my voice and swiped an angry tear from my cheek. "How could I tell her a horrible thing like that, Dan?"

He reached across the table to touch my hand. "I see what you mean," he said.

I wiped my nose on my napkin and looked up to see his green eyes filled with concern. "Your breakfast is getting cold," he said.

"But don't you want to hear what else Aimee told me?" I asked.

"Later," he said, "after you've eaten something and calmed down a little." He pointed to the food on my plate. "Now eat!"

"Yes, sir," I meekly replied.

Chapter 29

Reeling from too much of Krabb's high-cholesterol cuisine and their even higher octane caffeine, we left the restaurant twenty minutes later.

While we had been inside, the gray sky had ominously turned the color of overripe plums. Now the wind was picking up in short, brutal gusts and there were whitecaps speckling the protected waters of the harbor.

"No doubt about it," Dan observed as we huddled in the shelter of Krabb's recessed doorway. He sniffed the freshening wind like one of the old-timers who'd spent a lifetime at sea and now whiled away their days telling stories while they fished from the end of the wharf. "The weather forecasters were dead-on accurate for a change," he announced. "I'd say we're in for one big mother of a blow by nightfall."

I squinted up at the sky. "Isn't that what we had last night?" I queried, noticing as I said it that new lines of dirty-looking clouds seemed to be lowering nearly to the level of the sea, and that the usual mob of screeching gulls was curiously absent from the area around the wharf. "The wind was so strong that it broke several limbs off my trees."

"Last night was nothing compared to what's coming,"

Dan grimly predicted. He pulled up the collar of his blue denim jacket and hurried me across the rain-wet parking lot to the Mercedes.

"The good news," he said, "is that it's a perfect day to huddle up in front of a good fire." Dan smiled and touched my hair as we ducked into the soft, leather-lined cocoon of the car interior. "So I suggest we go straight back to your place and camp out in front of the fireplace while the storm blows through."

"Sounds great." I grinned, leaning over to give him a quick kiss. "But before we get started on the huddling we'd better pick up some fresh groceries, unless you'd prefer canned chili and spam for lunch, dinner and tomorrow morning's breakfast."

He returned a tender, lingering kiss. "'Drink to me only with thine eyes' and I'll not ask for wine," he whispered, pulling away and starting the engine.

"Good thing, I'm all out of wine, too," I said, laughing. "So get thee to the nearest supermarket, lover."

Dan groaned and slowly eased the big car out of Krabb's parking lot. "Your wish is my command," he said. "And on the way you can finish telling me about the rest of your visit with Aimee."

As we cautiously drove to the Food Mart, our tires splashing through the deserted streets of Freedman's Cove, I tried to explain to Dan what the tragic ghost of my ancestor had said happened to her, following the actual moment of her death.

"Dan, it was so eerie," I began, shivering involuntarily at the still-fresh memory of Aimee's haunting recitation of the night before. "Eerie and disturbing," I emphasized. "Because Aimee's description of being drawn upward toward a beautiful golden light was almost precisely the same as Damon's so-called 'delusional' near-death experience."

Dan kept his eyes on the road, expertly swerving to avoid a fallen metal sign. When the Mercedes was again gliding smoothly along the partially flooded street he turned and frowned at me. "Well, that's good, isn't it?" he asked. "I mean, it supports Damon's story of a supernatural encounter during those lost minutes when he was technically not living."

I slowly nodded, invigorated despite my weariness by the bizarre story that I was about to relate, and anxious to hear his opinion.

"That much of what Aimee told me is good," I haltingly agreed. "Just like Damon, she described entering a brilliant shaft of radiance. And there, waiting for her just beyond the dazzling light source, she could clearly see the figures of her long-dead grandparents and a beloved cousin who had drowned when she and Aimee were both twelve years old.

They were all waiting for her in the Light, their arms extended in welcome, ready to enfold her . . ."

I paused to dig a tissue from my purse, and wiped my nose again, then nervously crumpled the sheet in my hand. "But before she could cross over to embrace her loved ones," I said, "Aimee realized that Ned wasn't with her. She turned away from the Light to look for him, and felt herself being pulled back down to Maidenstone Island."

I looked at my hand, pale as death in the pallid light filtering through the windshield, and clenched my fist more tightly around the tissue, reducing it to a tiny ball. "Aimee's spirit has been trapped here ever since, still waiting for Ned Bingham," I said. "She's free to move only between the lighthouse and her old bedroom in my aunt's house."

Dan tore his eyes from the road just long enough to shoot me a quick sidelong glance.

I sniffled noisily before continuing. "And what makes it

so terrible for her," I said, "is that she's seen that golden Light, Dan. She knows it's there, waiting . . ."

Dan frowned. "You couldn't convince her to go back to the Light again?"

"Not without Ned Bingham." I sighed in frustration. "You see, Aimee thinks her lover got lost somehow when they . . . she . . . jumped, and that he's just a heartbeat behind her. So her spirit wanders endlessly, waiting and searching for him."

Dan thoughtfully chewed his lower lip for a moment. "If you told her the truth, about Bingham," he suggested, "perhaps it would set her free."

I shook my head dubiously. "I don't think she would believe me," I replied, remembering how recently I had myself been convinced that Bobby could not possibly have died on me, despite an overwhelming volume of hard evidence to the contrary.

"No," I said. "I think that hearing the truth about Ned Bingham would simply drive Aimee farther away from reality, and the Light."

The glowing red sign atop the Food Mart's flat roof appeared through the steamy windshield. Dan did not speak again until we had pulled into the crowded parking lot and found a space between a new Explorer and a rusting Chevy pickup.

"And what about Damon?" he asked, switching off the engine and turning to face me, as though he'd been reading my next thought. "Could Aimee explain why your friend had such an unpleasant and frightening encounter with Bobby in the Light?"

I shook my head helplessly. "That was the most disturbing thing about our conversation," I answered. "Aimee didn't really seem to understand what I was trying to ask her when I brought up the subject of Damon's near-death experience."

I turned to look out through the mud-splattered side window, recalling the unfortunate phantom's unexpected reaction to my question about Damon's terrifying encounter with Bobby.

Dan tapped his fingertips softly on the steering wheel as he awaited my reply. "Sue, what did she say?" he finally prodded, with just a tiny note of impatience in his voice.

"She laughed at me," I haltingly replied, my eyes fixed on the ominous, lowering sky over the Atlantic.

"She laughed?"

I slowly nodded without looking at him. "Aimee insisted that nothing like what Damon reported could ever happen in the Light," I muttered, my voice barely audible in the stillness of the car. "She told me that the Light illuminates a place of supreme peace and goodness," I continued, listening uneasily to the flat, dull sound of my own words. "It is the portal of entry to the Other Side. A neutral place of welcoming and joy, where all Earthly pain is forgotten."

I suddenly turned and looked at Dan. "She laughed at my question and told me that Damon could not possibly have met Bobby in the Light," I whispered. "Not unless they had been the dearest and most devoted of friends in life."

I lowered my eyes to the clenched, bloodless fist in my lap, feeling the tiny ball of the tissue compressing further within my palm. "But, as I've told you, Damon and Bobby were never friends," I said. "They didn't even like one another. So what can that mean?"

Dan's brow furrowed and he thought about my question. Suddenly, the worry lines vanished and a broad grin creased his features. "Obviously it doesn't mean a damn thing, Sue," he said, reaching over to pry open my clenched fingers. He took the crumpled tissue from my hand, unfolded it and dabbed at my wet cheek. "Except that Alice Cahill may have been partly right after all."

I stared at him, uncomprehending.

"Don't you get it?" Dan laughed. "Damon's near-death experience in the Light and some bad dream or feeling about Bobby that he'd had, either before or afterwards, simply got tangled up together in his memory."

"Oh," I said, not entirely convinced of his logic.

"Look," Dan said more gently, "let's cut Damon a little slack here. We have to remember that the guy miraculously survived a devastating plane crash. Then he spent a whole night bobbing around in near-freezing seawater before finally lapsing into a coma."

Dan threw up his hands at the sheer impossibility of Damon's being alive at all, much less having returned from his ordeal with 100 percent perfect recall. "Given the same situation," he proposed, "I suspect that you or I might have suffered a minor hallucination or two ourselves, don't you?"

I nodded, mentally reliving those last insane weeks in New York, when I had gone out each day fully expecting to run into Bobby on every street corner, certain I'd even caught fleeting glimpses of him.

I looked up at Dan again. He was still talking, his deep voice turned soft and persuasive. "Haven't you ever had a dream that seemed so vivid you had to force yourself to separate it from reality?" he asked.

The image of Bobby placidly smiling down at me while I pleaded to be saved from an icy death in my dream of two nights before flashed into my mind.

"Yes," I said, suddenly feeling much better than I had seconds earlier, and managing to smile. "I guess I have at that," I confessed. "Of course you're right. That must be what happened to Damon."

Dan rewarded me with a triumphant kiss and opened the door, admitting a blast of Arctic air into the car. "Good," he said. "And, as for Aimee, we won't forget about her now that we understand what's keeping her here. We'll do some serious research into trapped spirits. Maybe we can find some nontraumatic method of pointing her back toward the Light."

"Oh, Dan, it would be wonderful if we could help her," I said, loving him all the more for his concern over my poor lost ancestor.

"We'll do our best for her," he promised. "Now, let's go into that store and grab a few supplies so we can hurry back over to your place and settle down in front of a big, roaring fire."

"Right," I happily agreed. "And while you're building that big, roaring fire and, by the way, planning what you're going to prepare for our dinner tonight, I'm going to take a long, scalding bath."

Taking my hand he pulled me out into the cold. We scampered like a pair of carefree kids into the crowded store, where everybody in Freedman's Cove seemed to have gathered to stock up on batteries and bottled water.

We staggered back outside almost an hour later, our arms filled with bags containing everything we thought we could conceivably need or want to make it through the worst of the storm and the several meals we planned to share.

In the interim, the wind from the intensifying storm had increased dramatically from seaward. It tugged stubbornly at our coattails, blew its icy breath down our collars and tried to jerk the bags of groceries from our arms as we hurriedly ran across the parking lot and dumped everything into the trunk of the Mercedes.

"I really don't like the looks of that sky," Dan grumbled

when we were once again safe inside the car. He squinted out at the low, ragged clouds scudding over the rooftops. "Maybe we ought to consider driving inland a few miles and finding a motel."

"What? And give up our roaring fire?" I exclaimed. "Not on your life, buster."

"That's what I'm worried about," he said only half-jokingly. "Your house is awfully close to the water, Sue. And my folks' old place by the wharf is no better."

"Well, I don't know about your house, Dan Freedman," I challenged, "but mine has stood right where it is, through hurricanes and blizzards, for over one hundred and twenty-five years. One more little storm certainly isn't going to blow it away.

"Besides . . ." I pouted, moving closer to him and boldly tucking a hand between his thighs. "I really wanted you to see my new Jacuzzi tub and my great, big, warm captain's bed." I slid my hand just a little higher up his thigh.

Defeated, Dan laughed and started the engine. "Is this what the Mafia calls an offer you can't refuse?" he asked as we drove back onto the street.

"Everyone has told me you are a very smart man," I growled in my best Brando-as-the-Godfather tone.

"Your house it is, then." Dan's grin widened.

"Since you have agreed to do me this small favor, I am in your debt," I whispered, squeezing him very gently with the naughty hand.

"I'll collect in a little while." Dan chuckled before carefully extricating the roving hand from its snug hideaway and dropping it back into my lap. "Meanwhile, I think you'd better let me concentrate on driving us there, or we'll end up in a ditch."

"Very well," I smiled. "But we must very soon go to the mattresses."

"I don't believe this!" I heard Miss Romantic's astonished voice cheering me on from somewhere far in the back of my head. "Oh, Sue, I'm so happy. I never would have believed you had it in you to get your way by deliberately seducing him."

Miss Practical chimed in with a wicked little laugh. "If she keeps this up, that's not all she's going to have in her," she sarcastically observed.

"Go away, both of you!" I ordered.

Chapter 30

Sometimes even the best ideas turn out in retrospect not to have been so hot.

More of my very own homespun philosophy.

Standing out in the cold, gusting wind in the Food Mart parking lot, the prospect of a long, luxurious soak in the green Jacuzzi tub had seemed utterly delicious.

But the moment I slipped into the seductively scented waters I knew I had made a big mistake. Because, in my exhausted condition, the lethal combination of searing heat, soothing bubbles and lavender all came together like a giant velvet fist, slamming down to remind me that I had not slept more than three hours out of the last twenty-four.

Weakly clawing my way out of the tub like a drowning kitten, I barely managed to wrap a robe around myself and run a comb through my damp hair before my knees turned to Jell-O. I called out to Dan as the room started spinning around me. And the next thing I knew, he was effortlessly lifting me off the bathroom floor and cradling me in his strong arms.

"Sorry," I murmured sleepily. "I'll be okay in just a minute."

"I think that's highly doubtful." He smiled. "I'm taking you straight up to your bed to let you sleep it off."

"Don't you dare!" I shook my head drunkenly. "I wanna have slow, meaningful sex with you."

Dan lowered his head and gently pressed his lips to mine. "You will, my love," he whispered. "After you've rested."

"Okay," I readily agreed, burrowing my chin into the warm hollow of his neck. "But I wanna rest downstairs by the fire, where you'll be close. And don't forget about the lovemaking, later."

"No," he promised, carrying my limp body out of the steamy bathroom. "I won't forget."

Covered by a warm afghan I'd crocheted for Aunt Ellen when I was a teenager, I dozed comfortably on the parlor sofa until late that afternoon, opening my eyes from time to time to gaze into the crackling fire and marvel at the sheer violence of the newly arrived storm that was buffeting the house.

The first time I awoke, Dan was on the phone, straining to hear over the crackling line. He hung up and came over to tuck the throw under my chin. "I finally managed to get a call through to the hospital in Boston," he said. "Damon's condition is about the same, but Alice promised to call if there are any new developments."

He saw the pain in my eyes and gently stroked my hair. "He's going to be okay, Sue. Alice is sure of it."

I closed my eyes and went back to sleep.

The next time I awoke, Dan was sitting in a chair across from me. His bare feet were propped on the ottoman and he was drinking beer from a can and watching a televised CNN weather report with the sound turned down. I favored him with a goofy smile and drifted off again.

When finally I had slept enough I opened my eyes to discover that the room was bathed in candlelight and the TV screen was dark. Dan stepped in carrying a flashlight and gave me a reassuring wink. "Power went out about half an hour ago," he explained over the roar of the wind in the eaves. "I'm starting our dinner and keeping an eye on the beach from the kitchen window. It hasn't come up very much, so it looks like we'll be okay here after all."

He looked toward the sea and his brow furrowed with concern. "I am a bit concerned about the lighthouse museum, though. I wish I'd thought to move all the records up into the attic. If the tide starts to come up much above normal, I may run out there."

I nodded my understanding and started to rise, prepared to tell him that I'd help.

"Stay!" he ordered. "I probably won't need to go out, anyway. And you need to sleep. I'll call you when dinner's ready."

Far too comfortable to argue with him, I obediently snuggled down under the warm throw and slipped back into another welcoming slumber. It was so nice for a change, I thought, not to be having disturbing dreams.

"Sue, wake up!"

The voice seemed to be coming from a great distance. I opened my eyes and looked up at the dark figure silhouetted against the glow of the dying fire.

"Dan?" I struggled to sit up and looked around the darkened room. "What time is it?"

A match flared, illuminating his chiseled features. He touched the flame to a candle in one of Aunt Ellen's old Georgian silver holders and set it on the coffee table. "Nearly ten," he said, glancing down at the steel diver's watch on his wrist.

"Ten at night!" I abruptly sat up and swung my legs off the sofa. "You let me sleep away the entire day?"

"You needed it," he said unapologetically, then turned away and busied himself arranging new logs atop the embers of the old fire.

I shook my head and ran my fingers through my tangled hair. "I'm furious with you," I spluttered without any real conviction, because I actually felt wonderfully rested for the first time in days.

Dan turned back to me and grinned. "Now why did I know in advance that you were going to say some bitchy thing like that?"

"God, I must look like hell," I said, ignoring the sarcasm.

He regarded me critically for a few seconds in the flickering light flaring from the fresh flames in the fireplace. "Yes," he agreed, "you do look absolutely terrible. Maybe you should take another ten-hour nap."

I stood and aimed a punch at his midsection. He caught my wrist in flight and held me off at arm's length. "Temper, temper!" he teased.

"You promised me a wonderful romantic dinner and incredible lovemaking," I accused.

Dan grinned. "Let it never be said that Dan Freedman doesn't keep his promises." He smiled, pulling me closer and slipping his hand into the front of my loose robe. "Which would you like first, the main course or dessert!"

Snuggling close to the tingling warmth of his hand on my breast, I looked up into his sparkling green eyes with feigned innocence. "Why don't we start with a little appetizer, then work our way up to the main course?" I suggested, letting my robe slip to the floor and reaching for his belt buckle.

Within moments we both stood naked, our lips and our bodies welded together in the dancing ruby light of the fire.

All around us windows rattled and the timbers of the old house groaned and creaked under the punishing assault of wind and rain as, oblivious to the worst that nature could deliver, we kissed with deepening passion.

Then, somehow, the soft throw from the sofa was

spread on the carpet and we sank slowly to our knees in perfect unison.

I threw my head back joyfully as Dan's lips moved to my neck, my breasts, then ever downward . . . to the very core of my being with sweet, fiery kisses.

The unspent fury of the crashing waves on the shore behind the house was nothing to the soaring crescendo of my desire as I fell back onto the velvety softness of the throw and urged my new lover to make of us one single, magical being.

I don't know how long we remained together like that—an hour, two hours, more—for time had ceased to have any meaning, except as measured by the flaring and gradual decline of the firelight on our skin, the urgent rising and honeyed ebbing of our unleashed passions, the whispered vows and tender oaths we swore to one another.

At last we could do no more and lay cradled softly in one another's arms, all passion completely spent. Only then did I dare to smile and make a little joke.

"We really should try doing this in a bed sometime." I giggled. "I hear it's quite comfortable."

"A bed?" Dan managed to look astonished. "Now there's an original idea. I'd thought we'd work our way up to that, after we'd done the kitchen table and the bathroom."

I kissed him tenderly and got to my knees, peering into the shadows for some sign of my robe. I found it in a heap beneath the sofa and got to my feet, untangling it. "Speaking of bathrooms," I said, "I'm going upstairs to visit mine now, and maybe I'll even put on some clothes."

Dan propped himself up on one elbow, watching appreciatively as I wrapped the robe around my body. "Okay," he said, "but I can't promise that I'll let you keep them on for very long. I like you much better stark naked."

"I'll be happy to get stark naked anytime you say," I said and laughed. I stepped over him and put my hands on my hips. "In the meantime," I reminded him, "didn't I once hear you mention something about dinner? My stomach is beginning to rumble."

"Oh, yeah, dinner. Let me get right on that," he replied, not moving.

"I'm going up now," I said, moving toward the stairs. "And there'd better be some serious cooking going on by the time I get back."

"Nag, nag, nag!" Dan laughed and rolled over, searching for his clothes.

I stopped at the foot of the stairs and turned to watch him for a moment. The Maidenstone Light suddenly flashed past a window across the room. I automatically raised my eyes to the sudden burst of illumination filling the room . . . and froze. My mouth dropped open and, as the window went dark again, I stood there gaping at it.

Dan gave me a puzzled look. "Sue, what's the matter?"

Tearing my eyes from the window, I looked down at him and then shook my head. "Nothing, the, uh, lighthouse beacon . . ." I stammered. "It startled me."

He laughed. "I was going to say you looked like you'd just seen a ghost, but in this house that would probably be a mistake." He found his shirt and pulled it over his head. "You'd better get moving if you want some dinner," he said.

I nodded dumbly and made my way slowly upstairs with the disconcerting feeling that cold, calculating eyes were boring into my back. For, in the brief instant that the lighthouse beacon had filled the room, I had seen a face pressed up against the streaming window, a face rendered unrecognizable by slashing rain and stark shadows. A face, I realized with growing horror, that might well have been watching Dan and me for minutes, or hours.

Or, perhaps it had been only my overactive imagination at work . . .

Or . . . Tom Barnwell had returned!

The realization that the prowler at the window must have been Tom—who had already broken into my house twice in the same week—back for one more shot at getting me into bed, filled me with a stomach-churning sense of disgust, tempered only by my relief that it was only him and not some deranged serial killer.

Because Tom Barnwell, low and despicable though he might be, was also a devout coward. And, having been spotted by me at the window, he would by now be high-tailing it back to whatever bar he had come from.

My disgust quickly turning to outrage, I paused halfway up the stairs, tempted to retrace my steps and tell Dan what I had just seen. Then common sense took over and I continued on up to the bathroom. Because I knew that if I said anything to Dan, the sweet memory of our extraordinary lovemaking that night would be forever soiled. And, too, I feared the consequences of my big, muscular ex-marine's anger, should he insist on going after the pathetic, slightly flabby Peeping Tom, as I knew he surely would. Dan, I was genuinely afraid, might actually kill the bastard.

So I went into the bathroom and closed the door, silently vowing to say nothing about the incident to Dan, but grimly determined to deal with Tom Barnwell later, in my own special way.

Chapter 31

With plots of suitable revenge percolating through my mind—Miss Practical suggested calling town constable Harvey Peabody and swearing out a complaint against Tom Barnwell, while Miss Romantic was holding out for challenging him to a duel—my appetite slowly returned. And I decided before leaving the bathroom that I was not going to let the alcoholic creep's pathetic antics ruin my life, or even my night.

In the candlelit parlor Dan and I sat on the hearth and grilled thick New York steaks over the open flames. We had them with green salads garnished with slices of fresh California avocado, dressed with a delicious raspberry vinaigrette—Dan's own secret concoction—and washed down with a good California Pinot Noir.

We were just finishing dinner and debating whether it was really possible, as I steadfastly claimed, to bake apples for dessert in the hot fireplace coals when a high-pitched electronic sound shrilled over the noise of the worsening storm outside.

"The hospital!" The words exploded from Dan's and my lips simultaneously and we leaped to our feet, searching frantically among the dancing shadows for the portable phone he'd brought in from the kitchen. The thing screeched again and Dan located it on an end table beside the chair in which he'd been sitting earlier.

"Hello?" he asked, pressing the phone to his ear.

Dan listened for a few seconds, then shouted back into the handset. "Yes, Alice, I can hear you, but barely . . . Speak louder, please." He covered one ear and strained to hear over the noise of the wind and surf outside and the loud crackling of static on the line.

I was standing anxiously beside him now, watching his face for some indication of what was being said. After a moment, Dan winked at me, repeating Alice Cahill's words for my benefit. "Damon's awake? That's fantastic!" Then he nodded and grinned. "Yes, she's right here!"

Dan handed the phone to me and I put it to my ear, only to be assaulted with a crescendo of electronic noise. The static subsided a bit and I recognized the faint voice on the other end of the connection as that of Dr. Alice Cahill, but her words were being broken up by the interference.

". . . Damon . . his first . . . you . . . so . . . thought . . . right away and get . . ."

"Alice," I shouted, "you're breaking up too badly. Let me call you back."

"Damon says . . ." Alice yelled back, her voice fading away in a fresh burst of static.

"Tell Damon I love him," I hollered. "I'll try to get a better line and call you right back."

Frustrated, I broke the connection and looked at Dan. "Call the long-distance operator," he suggested. "Maybe they can get through."

I dialed long distance. The phone continued to crackle and sputter, though I could faintly hear it ringing on the other end. "What did Alice say?" I asked Dan while I waited for an operator to answer.

"All I really got," he said, "was that Damon is out of the coma again and his vital signs are good."

"Thank God!" I breathed, impatiently pressing my ear closer to the phone. "Come on, dammit!" Far away, a recorded voice finally answered the ringing and informed me that all circuits were temporarily out, due to weather conditions.

"Damn!" I switched off the useless portable phone and dropped it to my side. "What are we supposed to do now?"

"I say we go back up to Boston immediately," Dan replied without hesitation. "It's what we were planning to do, anyway."

Surprised by his answer I let my eyes dart to a window lashed by the driving rain. "Tonight?" I asked.

"The full force of the storm isn't due to hit us until mid-morning tomorrow," he said. "So we might actually have a better chance at getting out of here tonight than we will after daylight." Dan took me into his arms and held me tight. "Don't worry, I'll get you to Damon." He smiled. "I think that for both your sakes, you two need to see one another as soon as possible."

I reached up and kissed him hard, then swiped a tear from the corner of my eye and cleared my throat. "Dan Freedman, has anybody ever told you that you are one hell of a great guy?" I asked.

Dan blushed furiously for the first time since we had met. "Well, I have been told I make a pretty mean salad dressing," he said, shyly casting his eyes down at the floor.

Fifteen minutes later, Dan went outside to the Mercedes and drove away.

Following a brief discussion over the coffee we had not yet gotten around to drinking after dinner, we had come up with a rough plan to expedite our late-night trip to Boston: Dan would go by his place to pick up an overnight bag, then he'd drive out to an all-night truck stop near the interstate to gas up and inquire about road conditions.

Meanwhile, I was to get my own things packed and be ready to go when he returned in about half an hour.

I was upstairs in my room, throwing makeup, underwear and a few similar necessities into an overnight case, when the old-fashioned black telephone on my nightstand rang. Thinking it must be Dan calling with some bit of last-minute information about the trip, I lifted the heavy receiver and said hello.

Free of much of the airborne static that had plagued the portable phone downstairs, the new long-distance connection from Boston came through with surprising clarity on the antique telephone wired into my bedroom wall. So much, I thought, for space-age technology.

"Sue, thank God I got through to you," said a faint but familiar voice.

"Damon, is that really you?" I broke into a delighted grin. "My God, you sound wonderful." Look, I'm throwing some things into a suitcase right now and driving up there tonight."

"Sue, listen very carefully . . ." The pitch of Damon's voice was strangely high, and I was suddenly fearful that all might not be well with him after all.

"Are you okay?" I cautiously queried.

"For God's sake, just shut up and listen to me, please," he snapped, confirming for me that something was definitely wrong.

"Is Dr. Cahill there with you?" I interrupted before he could say more.

Damon's voice dropped to a barely audible whisper. "Don't talk to me about that bitch," he fumed. "I escaped in a wheelchair, broken legs and all, while she wasn't looking. But by this time I have no doubt the good doctor is probably organizing a search party."

There was a brief silence on the line, followed by the

sound of labored breathing. “I don’t think it’ll take them more than a few minutes to find me,” Damon said weakly, “so listen carefully . . .”

“Damon, where are you?” I demanded.

“I don’t know,” he replied, his voice suddenly thick with pain. “In an office somewhere, the maternity department, I think.” Damon uttered an abbreviated version of his trademark idiotic giggle. “I only know that because I can hear the newborns squalling like banshees in the next room.”

“Are you out of your mind?” I screamed at him. “You have been seriously injured, Damon. You are going to hurt yourself. Now get back to your room this second!”

He didn’t answer and again I heard only the rasp of his ragged breathing over the occasional burst of electronic noise on the line.

“Damon? Are you there?”

“I’m still here,” he said wearily. “And I am most assuredly not crazy, Sue. As I have been trying to explain to these hospital Nazis for hours, I saw Bobby . . . But every time I open my mouth to tell someone about it, the bastards jab another needle into my ass. I had to call you . . .”

Forcing a note of calm into my words that I was not really feeling, I said, “Okay, take it easy. I believe you, Damon. You saw Bobby in the Light and he—”

“No!” Damon screeched. “I did not see Bobby in any goddamn Light! That’s what I have been trying to tell these medical morons here. Christ! Why won’t any of you just listen?”

He paused for breath and his voice dropped an octave. “I saw Bobby in Manhattan, Sue. And he was very much alive!”

“What?” I stared at the receiver.

“The day after the break-in,” Damon wheezed, “I went

back to your apartment late that afternoon to finish cleaning up. Bobby was just coming out of your building, wearing that crappy old leather flight jacket of his."

Damon wheezed again and gasped for breath. "The man is not dead, Sue," he insisted. "In fact, I think he's probably the one who broke into your place."

I was shaking my head slowly from side to side in disbelief. "That's not possible," I shrieked, my voice cracking with emotion. "You and Bobby never got along, Damon. We think that you only had a bad dream about him that you confused with—"

"Dream, my shiny black butt!" Damon exploded with maniacal fury. "I saw that bastard Bobby Hayward coming out of your apartment building late Monday afternoon. So don't tell me I was dreaming, dammit!"

"Oh, God!" During the last part of Damon's angry outburst I had dropped onto the bed in shock. Now I was just sitting there, paralyzed.

Because suddenly nothing made any sense. If Bobby was really alive and had been rescued, why hadn't he called me right away? And why hadn't his company called me, or the FAA?

"Sue?" The pain was back in Damon's voice.

"Yes?" I replied dully, after a long pause.

"I think Bobby saw me, too," Damon whispered, slowly emphasizing each word as if it might be his last. "I was sure he started to follow me," he continued. "I jumped into a cab and lost him . . . Then I tried to call your cell phone, but I couldn't get through. So I went straight out to the airport and got onto that damn commuter flight to Hell, to warn you—"

"Warn me!" I ended the astonished exclamation with a short, hysterical laugh. "Warn me of what?"

Damon's voice was rapidly fading now, his breath coming in short, uneven gasps. "Sue, I thought about it the whole time I was waiting to catch my plane," he whispered. "Those times when you thought you saw Bobby during the past few weeks, when you were sure you must be going crazy . . ."

I tried to concentrate on Damon's implausible theory but my head was beginning to spin. If Bobby had been alive all this time, then I . . . I had betrayed his love, with Dan.

"I-I've been unfaithful to him," I stammered. "I didn't have any idea . . ."

Damon swept aside my feeble confession with another angry outburst. "Unfaithful, you? No, Sue, don't you understand what I'm saying?" he croaked in his odd Southern accent.

"All the time you were grieving for him, Bobby was alive. He came back to New York and started watching you, stalking you. You didn't *think* you saw him. You did. You didn't do anything wrong, Sue. That lying bastard betrayed *you*."

"But why?" I wailed, unable to come to terms with what he was saying. "I loved Bobby and he loved me. Why would he do a thing like that to me, Damon? Why?"

Before he could answer me, I heard the sounds of other voices in the background. Then something fell over with a loud clatter and Damon was cursing. His outraged screams faded away as someone else picked up the phone.

"Susan?" I recognized Alice Cahill's firm, no-nonsense tone on the line. "Susan, are you there?"

"Wh-What happened?" I stammered. "Is Damon all right?"

The doctor let out a long, patient sigh. "Yes," she said. "At least he doesn't appear to have done any major damage to himself, thank God. Hang on for just a second . . ."

I heard Alice issuing stern orders to someone, then she came back on the line. "At this moment," she said, "two very large, very gentle orderlies are taking your Mr. St. Claire back to his bed, like a very naughty child."

Alice suddenly sounded very tired. "I was afraid that something like this might happen if Damon spoke with you too soon."

My head felt like it was going to explode and I wasn't sure I understood what she meant. "Do you mean you think Damon's still . . . delusional?" I asked. "I mean, he just told me—"

Alice snorted derisively, cutting me off. "I know exactly what he told you, Susan. God knows I've been listening to it here all evening. Damon is now saying that he saw your dead fiancé alive."

Everything was moving far too fast for me. I was having trouble getting my breath and felt as if I might pass out at any second. "But you don't think Bobby is really . . . alive?"

"No, Susan." Alice's gruff tone had turned gentle, soothing. "I'm afraid that's just your poor, befuddled friend's way of defending his earlier paranoid delusion. Actually, it's relatively common for patients with Damon's condition to change their stories to fit changing circumstances . . ."

"Oh!" I whispered, all my fears and hurts of a moment before draining away to a single, dull ache in my chest. If what Alice was saying was true, then Damon's mind had obviously been seriously affected by his injury, perhaps worse than any of us could have imagined.

The old house creaked and shuddered under a powerful blast of wind. I glanced nervously toward the turret windows, glimpsing the wink of the lighthouse beacon on its endless circuit across the troubled sea.

"I . . . We were going to drive up to Boston tonight," I said.

Alice's reply was immediate and firm. "No!" she insisted. "Please, Susan, don't do that. As you must have realized by now, Damon is still very . . . confused. I've called in an excellent psychiatrist to see him, but it's going to be some time before Damon is going to be ready for visitors."

"A psychiatrist?" I had a sudden mental image of Laura sitting in her Italian leather chair, making glib pronouncements about what was going on inside my head, when she couldn't in her wildest dreams have imagined the things I was actually experiencing. As a result of that experience, psychiatrists rate only slightly higher on my credibility scale than witch doctors and companies that run million-dollar sweepstakes.

Besides, I reasoned, although Damon's story was unbelievable it at least explained why he had been flying up to see me that night.

And *somebody* had broken into my Manhattan apartment and gone through Bobby's things.

"Alice, are you absolutely certain this new story is all in Damon's mind?" I asked suspiciously.

"Absolutely," she replied without hesitation. "I hope I don't have to remind you, Susan," she added, sounding slightly injured by my lack of faith in her judgment, "that I saved the man's life. I assure you that Damon's well-being is my only concern here. You've got to trust me completely on this."

Chapter 32

After hanging up the phone I lay across my bed, trying to rearrange my shattered emotions while I waited for the tightness in my throat to ease.

For a few heart-stopping seconds during poor Damon's paranoid rant I had actually allowed myself to believe that Bobby might still be alive. And with that belief all of the grief and hurt of the previous months had come rushing back once more, an unbearable, rending hurt that had been compounded by the mad accusation that Bobby had somehow lied to me, lied and betrayed our love by deliberately making me suffer.

I derided my own foolishness for having believed for even a second that such a thing was remotely possible. Surely the Bobby I had known and loved and whose memory I would always treasure, no matter how much I now loved another man, could never—would never—have put me through such an agony of despair.

Of course, I told myself, Alice Cahill had to be right. Damon's horrible accident had mentally unbalanced him. And though I still wanted to see my dear, confused friend as soon as possible, and help him in any way I possibly could, I realized that, under the circumstances, attempting to drive to Boston in a major winter storm would be foolhardy.

My thinking thus adjusted, I finally sat up and looked around me, half-hoping that Aimee would show herself, so that I could talk to her.

But my sweet, gentle ghost was nowhere to be seen.

After a few minutes I slowly started taking my things out of the overnight case and replacing them in the dresser.

I decided as I unpacked that Dan and I would spend the rest of the stormy weekend together, just as we had planned. Then, in a day or two, perhaps, I would go up to Boston and meet with Alice Cahill, offering to assist with Damon's recovery in any way that she thought might help.

By the time I heard the front door opening downstairs and felt the accompanying blast of damp, Arctic air that rushed into the house, I had washed my face and combed my hair and was coming down the stairs.

"You're back sooner than I expected," I called, stepping into the fire-lit parlor.

Dan did not reply, and I squinted into the dim light of the room. To my surprise, he was hunched over in the big easy chair, his features obscured in deep shadow.

"God, I'm happy to see you," I exclaimed. "You are not going to believe what I've just been through." I walked directly to the chair and sat on the edge of the padded armrest.

Iron-strong arms encircled my waist and I shivered as I felt the clammy, grave-cold touch of wet leather against my skin.

"I'm happy to see you, too, Sweet Sue," snarled a hoarse, menacing voice, a horrible, chilling voice that I had never again expected to hear in this life.

"Bobby!" His name erupted from my lips in a choked little scream and I attempted to leap to my feet. But the sodden, leather-encased arms held me in their viselike grip like a spider holds a struggling moth.

A terrible face vaguely resembling Bobby's suddenly thrust forward into the light, its icy-blue eyes regarding me without a trace of human love or emotion.

I did not trust myself to speak as I stared at that once-handsome face that now seemed to wear a mask of evil. As terrified as I was, the only thing I could think of was that Damon had been right. Dear, loyal Damon, who at this very moment was being subjected to God-knows-what manner of psychiatric indignities because of me.

"Why, Sue," Bobby growled after what seemed an eternity of stunned silence on my part, "you said you were happy to see me. Change your mind already?"

"I . . . They said you had been . . . killed," I stammered through trembling lips.

Bobby's battered head moved slowly up and down and he stared blankly into the fire. "Yeah," he muttered, his ruined voice filled with bitter irony. "At least that was the general idea."

Suddenly his body was wracked with a violent spasm of coughing. Bobby released me and doubled over, holding his sides. I jumped to my feet and stared down at him, uncertain whether to run for my life or go to his aid.

"You're sick," I said softly, feeling an unexpected wave of pity sweeping over me. For I could see that his blond hair was unkempt and dirty and his clothes, except for the leather flight jacket, were ragged and appeared to be soaked clear through to his feverish, pale skin.

"My God, Bobby, what happened to you?" I breathed.

The coughing attack slowly subsided and Bobby shook his head like a drugged animal and tried unsuccessfully to clear his throat. "Nothing," he said hoarsely. "Nothing and everything." He raised those icy eyes—eyes I had once adored—and smiled a smile that was really more of a grimace. "Got any hot coffee?" he asked. "I damn near froze to death out there, waiting for your new boyfriend to clear out."

At the mention of Dan I glanced fearfully toward the front door. "He'll be back any minute," I warned.

Bobby's crafty, red-rimmed eyes followed my gaze without concern. "Oh, I don't think so," he retorted, unconcerned. A wicked smirk made my stomach turn. "At least not before you and I have had a little talk."

Thanks to Damon's warning and the emotional firestorm I had already survived, my initial shock at seeing Bobby alive was quickly wearing away. Now I felt it being replaced with a terrible, dangerous anger.

"What do you mean, you don't think so?" I demanded. "If you've done anything to Dan . . ." I left the threat hanging in the static-charged air.

"So his name's Dan, huh? Got over me in a hurry," he sneered. "You must really have it bad for old Dan." Bobby suddenly pulled a large military survival knife from his jacket and held it up for me to see.

"Don't you worry about a thing, Sweet Sue." He laughed, seemingly enjoying my terrified reaction to the brutal weapon. "I only made a minor adjustment to the boyfriend's fancy car . . . so far." Bobby's emaciated body was wracked by another intense coughing spasm. "Now, how about that hot coffee?" he demanded between coughs.

I remained where I was, staring at the reflected firelight gleaming wickedly along the razor edge of the huge knife. My mind was rapidly filling with visions of Dan's Mercedes skidding out of control, its brake lines severed. "What kind of adjustment?" I shrieked. "What did you do to his car, Bobby?"

Bobby grinned. "Relax. I just punched a little hole in

the gas tank," he said, "to be sure your pal would run out of juice after a few miles." The grin faded and his tone turned sinister. "I don't want any interruptions while you and I have our reunion."

Unwilling to believe him, and fearful of what he had come all this way to do, I backed warily away. "I'll get the coffee," I murmured.

Considering how sick he looked, Bobby jumped to his feet with surprising agility and roughly grabbed my elbow. "On second thought, I think we'd better go get that java together." He grinned. "I wouldn't want you walking out on me before we have our chat."

"Bobby, why are you doing this?" I pleaded as he roughly shoved me through the darkened house and into the kitchen. "Why?"

"Call it bad breaks," he growled menacingly in my ear. "Just a case of plain-old everyday bad breaks, Sweet Sue."

Bobby sat at the counter in the kitchen, wolfing down the canned soup that he'd made me heat up, and drinking black coffee.

I sat exactly where he'd told me to, directly opposite him, with the big survival knife on the counter between us, scrutinizing his drawn features and his darting, hunted eyes by the light of a flickering candle.

"It was such a sweet deal," he began, wiping soup from his chin with a stained sleeve, "a perfect deal, Sue . . . too perfect." Bobby's blue eyes took on a distant look and he shook his head at the irony of his present degraded condition. "It started with the Gulfstream 550 . . . Of course, that was the prize."

I shook my head, bewildered. "I don't have even the vaguest idea what you're talking about, Bobby. What deal?"

He shot me an annoyed glance. "You remember Al Pearson, don't you?" he abruptly asked.

I nodded. Albert Pearson was the oil company executive who had been lost when Bobby's plane had disappeared over the Indian Ocean in July, the only passenger onboard.

"Okay," Bobby continued, slurping the soup like a starving man. "The whole thing was Pearson's idea. He'd spent years in Asia as the company's front man, and he knew how things work down there. I mean, how things really work, the official bribery, the government corruption, the tie-ins to organized crime . . . all the usual crap that goes into cutting big-time oil deals."

I was staring at him, still trying to reconcile the shifty-eyed human wreck sitting before me with the man I had once loved so desperately. The question of whether I had ever really loved him spun out of control in my brain.

"Oh, my, don't look so shocked," Bobby taunted, reading my expression. "Didn't you know that was how the big, bad world of international business really functions—on bribes and crooked deals?"

"You were telling me about the late Albert Pearson," I replied coldly. "Or is he still alive, too?"

Bobby shook his head and shoved his cup across the counter for more coffee. I grudgingly lifted the pot from its candle-fired warmer, briefly considering whether I could get away with flinging the bubbling hot liquid in his face and bolting for the back door.

"Don't even think about it," he warned, placing his hand menacingly on the black handgrip of the knife. "In response to your question, good old Al Pearson is flat-out dead," he said when the coffeepot was sitting safely back on its stand. "But the whole thing originally started out as his idea. And it was sweet—"

"Yes, you've already established that it was sweet," I said impatiently.

Ignoring the sarcasm Bobby leaned forward until I could smell the flat, foul odor of his breath.

"It was like this," he confided like a bookie with a hot tip. "Al had a friend down in Malaysia, a very rich friend. And this friend was in the market for a long-range corporate jet, a Gulfstream 550, as a matter of fact. So when the company offered me the chance to fly their new one, of course I jumped at it."

Bobby stifled a fresh round of coughing with another gulp of hot coffee. "Now, Al's rich Malaysian friend wasn't so rich that he felt like shelling out 25 or 30 million for a brand-new jet—"

A bitter laugh escaped my lips. "So you and good old Al decided to steal one for him," I interrupted, suddenly understanding everything. "My God, Bobby, was that worth risking your career for? Worth leaving me thinking you were dead?"

For the first time since he'd appeared in my parlor, I thought I detected a faint trace of regret in his eyes. "Oh, Christ, no," he protested, sounding for the tiniest of instants like the other Bobby, the one I thought I knew a lifetime ago. "I never meant to leave you. You don't understand how it was."

"Then make me understand," I spat. "Make me understand what was worth destroying both our lives for, Bobby. Because that's what you've obviously done to yours and very nearly did to mine."

He stared silently at the countertop.

"Make me understand, you bastard!" I yelled.

Bobby's eyes slowly came up to meet my enraged gaze.

"It was supposed to be foolproof," he explained, looking suddenly like a frightened little boy. "Pearson and I had dropped off the other two passengers and were making a long, over-water crossing alone. At a predetermined point in the flight—a spot where the Indian Ocean happens to be more than 20,000 feet deep—I put the Gulfstream into a steep dive and we just dropped off the radar. To anyone tracking us it would have looked exactly like we'd had a major mechanical problem and crashed into the sea.

"Then we flew south at wave-top level for a couple of hundred miles, to a tiny island with an abandoned World War II airstrip. Pearson's friend was waiting for us there with a boat. He had his own flight crew ready to ferry the stolen jet back to Malaysia."

Bobby's eyes grew misty as he recalled the details of the illicit deal. "Before they took off, the Malaysians stripped some identifiable gear from the stolen Gulfstream, gear that would float—a couple of seats, life jackets and so forth—and put it aboard the waiting boat. The boat was supposed to take me and Pearson back out to the general vicinity where we'd disappeared from radar and dump all the stuff in the water, along with a couple of drums of jet fuel. So it would look like there'd been a real crash. So the Malaysians took us back out to sea. And, after they'd dumped all the debris, they inflated the life raft, which had also been taken from the plane, and Pearson and I got into it."

"I'm very impressed," I said sarcastically. "I suppose then you were supposed to activate the raft's emergency radio beacon and wait to be rescued. You and Pearson would come home with a great story and, how much money, Bobby?"

"Three million apiece," he said miserably. "I'd made

arrangements to have mine deposited directly into a series of numbered offshore bank accounts I'd set up a few years ago, for some money I'd made in other deals . . ."

I nodded, not trusting myself to comment. But my mind was racing furiously. So there had been other illegal "deals" before the stolen jet, deals big enough to require secret bank accounts. I winced inwardly as the full realization struck me of how little I had really known about this man I thought I had been in love with.

Bobby was silently observing me, obviously waiting for me to say something. I whistled softly. "Three million tax-free dollars! Not bad," I said, no longer pitying him even a little. "So what went wrong?"

"Those cold-blooded bastards double-crossed us," he whined, anger mixed with disbelief creeping into his tone. "As soon as we were helpless in the life raft, they moved off a little way and machine-gunned us."

Bobby closed his eyes and shuddered, obviously reliving for the umpteenth time the exact moment when they had been betrayed. "Pearson was killed instantly," he said, "three rounds to the head . . . I ducked into the bottom of the raft and only took one hit in the leg. But a stray round shattered a steel first aid kit."

He absently fingered the knife. "That damn first aid box saved my life."

"And then?" I asked, intrigued by Bobby's story, but increasingly wary of his reasons for confessing it to me—*me,* who had thought for months that he was dead.

Bobby slowly shook his head. "Then the dirty sons of bitches just sailed away." He drained the rest of his coffee. "Of course," he continued, "they'd thoughtfully removed the emergency radio from the raft before they put us in the water. And, as it turned out, they'd also taken us a hundred miles in the opposite direction from where the jet had gone off the radar."

"Guaranteeing your silence, if by some miracle you happened to survive," I finished for him.

Bobby nodded and stared back down at the counter. "I dumped Pearson's body over the side and drifted for six days in the sinking raft before a native fishing schooner picked me up. It was another four weeks before the fishermen got back to land. Not that it mattered at that point," he said bitterly. "Between the bullet hole in my leg and what the fishermen would report about where they'd picked me up, if anybody asked, I was a dead man. As dead as Al Pearson. Because there was no way the accidental plane-crash story was ever going to wash in an investigation."

His treacherous story told, Bobby finally looked up and met my frightened, unsympathetic gaze. "So you see, I couldn't call you or come back to you, Sue. Not right away, anyway . . . Hell, it took me another two months just to work my way back to New York on a rat-infested Liberian container ship." He laughed. "I was hired on as the damn dishwasher. Can you imagine me a dishwasher?"

"But, of course, you called me immediately as soon as you got to New York in, when was that, September?" I said viciously.

Bobby shrugged. "Even then I didn't dare contact you. I had no way of knowing if the feds were suspicious about the crash, or whether they were watching you—"

"So you watched me instead, followed me around . . ." My whole body was suddenly trembling. "My God, Bobby, do you realize what kind of living hell you put me through? It was bad enough at first, just thinking you were dead. But then, in those last few weeks, I actually believed I was going insane when I started seeing you on the street, in the subway . . ."

He reached out and tried to take my hand. Angrily I jerked it away and leapt to my feet. "What do you want from me, Bobby?" I screamed. "Why are you here?"

He remained sitting, his coldly calculating blue eyes boring into me. "Whether you believe it or not I'd hoped you might still have . . . some feelings for me," he said after a long silence.

Scalding tears were streaming down my cheeks and my tenuous composure was falling away in pieces. "Yes," I sobbed, "I do have feelings for you, Bobby. I feel disgust and revulsion and loathing for you and what you've done to me, for what you've become . . . I hate your guts, Bobby. Is that what you came all this way to hear?"

Bobby very deliberately picked up the knife on the counter and held it up to regard the candlelight shining along the viciously curved blade. "I sort of figured you'd feel that way," he said, stepping around the counter and placing the needle-sharp point at my throat. "But I had to be absolutely certain." He frowned almost regretfully, tracing the edge of my jawline with the cold steel.

"You and I had something good together, Sue," he murmured softly.

"Lies," I sobbed, straining to pull away from the knife. "It was all lies, Bobby. Even the reason you took the job flying the Gulfstream was a lie. I thought you did it for me . . . for us."

"In a way you could say I did it for us," he responded. "If those bastards hadn't double-crossed me we would have been set for life . . ."

I was much too frightened to laugh at his grotesque suggestion that what he had done was somehow for us. "How, with stolen money?" I taunted.

He suddenly spun me around, stepping deftly behind me so that I could no longer see his face. The knife tip bit sharply into my skin. "I didn't really expect you to understand," he snarled, "which brings me at long last to the real reason for my visit tonight.

"What did you do with my skiing trophy, Sue, the one I got in Aspen?"

Chapter 33

Where reason departs fantasy begins.

I felt as though I had fallen into an insane nightmare, a nightmare comprised of unreasonable fears, impossible to explain. I seemed to hang in space for an eternity, with the deadly tip of the knife biting into the soft skin at the base of my throat, the wavering candlelight casting grotesque shadows onto the walls and ceiling.

But Bobby's free arm encircling my chest like a crushing steel band, his feverish cheek pressed urgently against the back of my neck, the smell of his foul breath reeking in my nostrils, all proved that what was happening was all too real.

He waited in silence for many long seconds, then whispered softly in my ear. "Where is it, Sue? What did you do with my ski trophy?"

"Ski . . . t-trophy?" I repeated the words like a dull student reciting an incomprehensible phrase in a dead language that she is supposed to have translated the night before.

"Yes, dammit! My ski trophy!"

Bobby jerked me around to scream in my face, then shoved me up against the counter, drawing back the knife so I could see the thin trickle of blood—my blood—running down the haft.

I gingerly touched my fingers to my throat, brought them away crimson and stared at them in disbelief. "I . . . I don't understand," I croaked.

"The trophy, Sue! I need my trophy!" Bobby's pallid features were flushed with unnamable fury. "The access numbers for my bank accounts are inside that trophy, you stupid bitch! What did you do with it?"

A hysterical giggle erupted from somewhere deep inside my bleeding throat. "You hid your secret bank account numbers in a ski trophy?"

Bobby's patience was quickly running out. His face went purple with rage as he brought the knife close to my right eye. "Everything but the clothes on my back was supposed to have been lost when the Gulfstream went down," he yelled, moving the blade a millimeter closer to my cornea. "I couldn't carry a list of bank account numbers halfway around the world with me when I might be searched or have to clear customs in some damn Third World country, now could I?"

I shook my head a terrified fraction of an inch.

"There's more than half a million dollars in those accounts from my other deals," Bobby explained. "I put the numbers inside the ski trophy, for safekeeping. But it wasn't in your apartment. Where is it?"

I opened my mouth to speak, then paused and thought about what I was doing. So far I had done nothing but fan the flames of Bobby's growing rage. And if I told him the truth—that for all I knew his precious ski trophy could be buried in a garbage dump somewhere—he would have no reason to leave me alive.

For I had not given him any reason to believe I would do anything but turn him in to the police as quickly as my little fingers could dial 911.

So I started lying.

"I kept the trophy . . . as a memento of our trip," I stammered.

Though it was exactly what he wanted to hear, I could tell he couldn't quite bring himself to believe me. Bobby cocked his head to one side like a deadly raptor about to devour a helpless rabbit.

"Smart girl! Where is it?" he demanded.

I shook my head. "If I tell you, you'll just kill me," I sniffled, not having to fake the note of sheer terror in my quaking voice.

He gently caressed my cheek with the flat of the knife. "I'll kill you if you *don't* tell me," he threatened, but I could tell he really didn't mean it. Because it was clear that Bobby desperately needed that half million dollars to buy himself a new life.

So we stood there, facing off in our deadly game of threat and counterthreat, while the storm outside roared and shook and battered the house.

"How do I know you're not lying?" he finally asked.

"How do I know *you're* not lying, about letting me live if I give you the trophy?" I countered.

"I'll find it anyway."

"You might not."

He stood there thinking and, I noticed, swaying slightly from side to side. I suspected that he was very close to collapsing from whatever sickness he had, and I quickly factored that tiny advantage into the hasty plan I was devising.

"You're not thinking clearly, Bobby," I suddenly blurted out. "Take the knife out of my face and listen to me for a second."

He looked startled. But he slowly lowered the knife to his side. "Don't cross me," he warned. "Because if you do, I will kill you, and your boyfriend and that little faggot Damon."

"They have nothing to do with this," I said.

Bobby shook his head. "Damon saw me in New York."

"Well, Dan didn't see you," I shot back. "And, as for Damon, he's locked up in a mental ward, telling anyone who'll listen to him that he died and met you at the entrance to Heaven."

A slow smile crossed Bobby's haggard features. "No shit?" he asked, seemingly pleased to hear that his nemesis had been officially adjudged crazy. "And what about you, Sweet Sue? What's going to keep you from talking?"

I emitted a long, weary sigh. "I just want to get on with my life, Bobby. Personally, I'd just as soon have you dead, if for no other reason than you made a complete fool of me. Besides," I added convincingly, "if you kill me you're tempting fate. There'll be police and an investigation. Right now, nobody's even looking for you, Bobby. So why don't you just take your damn trophy and go? I've even got five hundred dollars in cash you can have."

I held my breath while he considered my argument. And, to tell the truth, if I had actually been able to hand him the trophy and let him walk out of my life forever I would have happily done so.

Unfortunately, that was not an option.

"Where is it?" he asked.

I knew I had to play this just right, as if I really did have what he wanted, so I pretended to hesitate. "Do we have a deal?" I asked suspiciously.

He nodded. "Deal! You give me the trophy and I'm out of here in thirty seconds."

I picked up the candle, turned and walked briskly out of the kitchen. "It's upstairs," I said. "You can wait down here if you want."

Bobby laughed through another bout of violent coughing and followed me to the stairs. "Fat fucking chance," he said.

I climbed the steps to the darkened second floor with Bobby trailing behind. Glancing over my shoulder, I noted the way he leaned heavily on the banister, pausing at the landing to catch his breath. "Slow down," he wheezed.

"You don't look too good," I said as I reached the end of the pitch-black upstairs hallway. "You really need to see a doctor."

He gestured impatiently with the knife. "Don't get any ideas about how sick I am," he grunted. "I'm more than strong enough to kill you if I have to."

I shrugged and started down the windowless hall toward the short stairway leading up to the turret room. This is going to work, I told myself. It has to work.

I stopped at the end of the passage and held up the candle so he could see the set of steep, narrow stairs leading to my bedroom. "It's right up there."

Bobby glanced up the short stairway and nodded. "Ah, yes, I remember now, the famous turret bedroom I never got to see."

I said nothing, but hurried quickly up the stairs and entered the bedroom. I heard him cursing in the darkness below as he stumbled after me. "Very cute," he said as he walked into the room a moment later.

I looked at him as if I didn't understand what was wrong. "Oh," I said, looking at the candle in my hand, "I didn't mean to leave you alone in the dark."

Ignoring me, he quickly surveyed the small room with its sparse furnishings. "Okay, Sue, I'm completely out of patience. Where's my damn trophy?"

I held up the candle and pointed to the piece of tall Victorian furniture between the windows. "Over there in the wardrobe," I answered. "It's in a cardboard box, along with a few other things of yours that I kept. I'll get it for you . . ."

I started to move toward the wardrobe but, just as I

prayed he would, Bobby grabbed my elbow and moved me aside.

"No!" he snarled. "You stand right where you are and hold the light for me. I'll get the box." His suspicious eyes glittered in the candlelight and he flashed a terrible, menacing smile as he brushed past me. "Just in case you have any little surprises hidden in here," he said, putting his hand on the wardrobe door handle.

I shrugged, pretending indifference. "The box is on the top shelf, at the back," I offered helpfully as he swung open the door and peered into the inky depths of the wardrobe. "I can't see a damn thing, bring that candle over here," he ordered.

I glanced out the nearest window, watching the track of the Maidenstone Light as it swung over the water and across the lawn, painting the wind-blasted trees and stripped shrubbery with light. Bobby turned his head and followed my gaze to the window. "What the hell are you looking at? What's out there?" he asked.

I clapped my free hand over my eyes as the room abruptly filled with brilliant white light.

"Damn!" Bobby threw up a hand—too late to shield his dilated pupils from the dazzling light.

Then the lighthouse beacon was gone.

Blinded by the sudden flare of illumination, Bobby stood momentarily paralyzed. I snuffed out the candle, pitching the bedroom into complete darkness.

His scream of rage echoed through the house as I took to my heels and ran for my life, bounding effortlessly out of the room and down the stairs—plunging into the depths of the pitch-black hallway that I had traversed since childhood.

"I will kill you!" Bobby bellowed, crashing heavily into something on the floor above me. "I will cut out your lying heart, Sue!"

Racing blindly down the main staircase, I ran to the kitchen, pausing only to extinguish the dim flame beneath the coffee warmer. I heard more enraged shouts from upstairs, and the sound of Bobby's heavy footsteps in the hall.

I ran to the back door, then hesitated. My purse lay across the kitchen beside the sink, where I had left it when Dan and I had come in from shopping earlier in the day. And my car keys were in my purse.

"You can't get away, Sue!"

Bobby was at the top of the stairs, seconds away. I peered across the kitchen, trying to pick the outline of my purse from varying shades of shadow.

I heard Bobby's footsteps clumping down the stairs.

There was no more time.

Flinging open the back door, I hurled myself across the sunporch and down the back steps into the freezing teeth of the storm.

Blinking against sheets of rain that stung my skin like needles, I swung my head frantically around, looking for a place to run. Beyond the thick stand of shrubbery at the foot of the yard lay the narrow beach. The shoreline ran down to the Maidenstone Island causeway in one direction, back toward Freedman's Cove in the other. Bobby might not expect me to go that way.

Heedless of the thorns ripping my clothes and tearing at my hands and face, I forced my way through the head-high growth of wild rose and oleander, only to be greeted by an unbelievable sight.

The beach was no longer there. Driven by the approaching center of the storm and a rising tide, crashing white surf was licking at the exposed roots of the bushes. The beach—and the alternate avenue of escape I had counted on—was completely gone, obliterated by the inrushing sea.

"SUSANNN!"

Incredibly, Bobby's hoarse, murderous shout carried over the din of howling wind and booming surf. Though I couldn't see him, I intuitively knew that he was standing on the sunporch behind the house, peering out into the sheeting rain for some sign of me.

Within a minute or two, perhaps less, he would calm down enough to realize that there had to be a flashlight in the house. Then he would easily track me down.

If only I had thought to grab my car keys instead of wasting precious seconds on the damn coffee warmer . . .

"SUSAN, DAMN YOU . . . !"

Shivering with cold and already soaked to the skin I backed painfully out of the brambles and ducked into the shadows to scan the yard for another escape route. As I crouched there, ankle-deep in freezing water, I realized that my ripped hands were already going numb, and I knew I could not survive long without shelter.

I threw myself onto my stomach, splashing into muddy water and clinging to the shadows beneath the rosebushes as the lighthouse beacon swept the yard again. As I lifted my head from the ground, the rear of the carriage house loomed momentarily bright in my vision, its white clapboards shining wetly. Then the yard went dark again.

I got to my feet and dashed to the side of the building, then edged along the wall to the corner nearest the street. My faithful old Volvo sat tantalizingly close in the drive where I had left it, useless without keys. Cursing myself for never getting around to hiding a key in a magnetic box as Damon had repeatedly begged me to do, I pulled the carriage house door open a few inches and slipped into deeper darkness.

Inside the pitch-black building, out of the wind and rain, the temperature was at least thirty degrees warmer. I hovered indecisively by the door, chafing my frozen hands together and peering back up at the big house.

As I had feared, Bobby's rage must have subsided enough for his thinking to clear. Because, as I watched, a bright light flared in the kitchen windows, followed by the steady glow of a candle. Even now, I knew, he would be savagely ripping open doors and cabinets, searching for a flashlight.

I backed farther into the carriage house, feeling around blindly for something I could use as a weapon. The backs of my legs touched something. I turned and extended my hands, touched a smooth, cold surface with my torn and bleeding fingers.

And smiled.

Chapter 34

My already-pounding heart skipped several beats as I ran my fingers over the familiar bullet shape of the Vespa's headlamp. Kneeling quickly beside the bike in the darkness I located the fuel valve by feel and turned it on. Then I stood and grabbed the back of the seat frame, preparing to roll the little moped off its stand.

There was something on the seat. My fingers touched the hard shell of my bike helmet, which was sitting on top of the old ski jacket that I'd worn on my last ride and had meant to take inside to be washed.

Quickly I shrugged my arms into the blessed warmth of the thickly padded jacket and zipped it up to my chin. As I clapped the helmet on my head I went to the door and chanced another look out at the house. Candlelight flickered steadily at the kitchen window.

Praying that my luck would hold and that Bobby would stay inside searching for a flashlight, I shoved the carriage house doors open, climbed onto the moped and pedaled for my life. The cold engine abruptly caught, then just as abruptly sputtered and died.

Heedless of the noise I was making, which I assumed was lost in the roaring gale anyway, I pedaled even harder and twisted the throttle all the way to its stops. The wonderful little motor buzzed to life as I passed the Volvo's back bumper and I accelerated down the driveway.

A sharp right turn onto the street at the end of the drive would take me directly into the heart of Freedman's Cove—and other people—in less than five minutes. If I could make it that far I would be home free. Because Bobby, I was certain, would not dare follow me anyplace where he might be seen.

Raindrops lashed my unprotected face like burning needles, forcing me to squeeze my eyelids into narrow slits. As I approached the front of the house I swiveled my head around, trying to see and half-expecting Bobby to leap down from the front porch.

But there was no one there.

My luck was still holding.

Swinging my face back around into the blinding storm, not yet daring to turn on the headlight, I squinted toward the end of the drive, preparing to make the hard right-hand turn to Freedman's Cove and safety.

Then, out of the rain and darkness a tall figure loomed up directly in front of me.

Bobby!

He stood in the center of the drive, where it met the street. His back was to me and he was looking toward Freedman's Cove, and blocking my way. The hurtling motorbike was almost upon him as he slowly turned, raising the deadly survival knife in one hand and switching on the flashlight in his other.

The glow of the flashlight imparted a demonic look to Bobby's revenge-crazed features and his ruined mouth opened in a strangled scream of rage as he clumsily lunged at me with the knife.

I felt rather than heard the shiny nylon sleeve of my padded ski jacket ripping. Then a fiery streak of pain shot up my right arm from elbow to shoulder. The scream in my throat froze as I threw the Vespa into a sharp left-hand skid that threatened to hurl me onto the pavement at my murderer's feet.

The skidding rear tire struck Bobby's leg a glancing blow, knocking him awkwardly to his knees. For one horrible second our faces were inches apart and his maddened eyes locked with mine. Looking into those cold, cruel eyes was like peering into windows cut directly into the side of Hell. For they promised nothing but suffering and death.

The instant was shattered as the Vespa's fat, knobby tire suddenly caught hold on the slick pavement. Then the motorbike straightened and I was speeding away into the darkness. Away from Bobby Hayward and my own certain death, but also away from Dan and Freedman's Cove and the refuge they promised.

For my encounter with Bobby had forced me to turn left, toward the stone causeway and the beckoning finger of the storm-bound Maidenstone Light.

A few hundred yards from the house, at the point where the stone causeway began, I slowed to a stop and switched the Vespa's headlight on. The powerful beam lanced out ahead of me, revealing a scene nearly as terrifying as the one I had just departed.

The raised causeway leading to Maidenstone Island was just barely visible above the surging sea. And as I stared, a particularly large wave broke against the stones, sending a froth of swirling white water all the way across the narrow road.

I looked behind me, able to make out only the dim outlines of the empty Victorians ranked along the deserted street—the street that was the only route back to Freedman's Cove.

That was the way to safety, and Dan.

But it was also the way back to Bobby and the murderous blade of his razor-sharp knife.

I hesitated for a moment longer, wiping my eyes to clear them of the pelting rain and stinging salt spray. An errant thought nagged at me from the farthest corner of my mind, warning that nothing but danger awaited at the Maidenstone Light. Stay away, something pleaded. Don't go there!

But I had no other choice.

So, gritting my teeth, I revved the Vespa's engine and drove out onto the partially submerged causeway. For there was at least a chance I could make it to the lighthouse and the emergency telephone I remembered having seen up in the beacon tower.

The power of the wind and the sting of driven rain that I had thus far encountered were nothing compared to the elemental forces that smashed into me the second I rode out onto the unprotected causeway. With blood loss and the pain of my injured arm rapidly sapping what little strength I still had, just keeping the moped upright in that howling tempest required all of my effort.

Three times during the crossing, breaking waves smashed over the stones beside the roadway, hiding the pavement beneath swift cross-currents of rushing seawater that tugged and pulled at my wheels and threatened to drown my tiny engine. With the road thus obscured, only the constantly rotating beacon of the lighthouse kept me from losing my way and driving off into the sea.

By the time I finally rode up onto the slightly higher ground of Maidenstone Island my injured arm was sending jolts of pure agony to my brain and I was barely able to force my benumbed hand to maintain its grip on the throttle.

Alarms were going off in my brain. I was dizzy from

loss of blood and my vision was blurring, and I knew that I was dangerously close to losing consciousness.

If I did not get to shelter, and quickly, I realized, I was going to die in the cold.

Urging the Vespa onward, I sped past the darkened lightkeeper's cottage and up the flooded walkway leading to the door at the base of the lighthouse tower.

Its lifesaving work done, the staunch little moped fell onto its side as I stepped off and stumbled to the lighthouse. To my great surprise, the heavy steel door swung open easily at my touch and I gratefully stepped into the dry, dimly lit interior of the lighthouse.

I stood there swaying dizzily, resisting the compelling desire to simply collapse on the black-and-white-tiled floor and rest for just a moment. Behind me, the steel door clanged noisily against its frame, demanding my waning attention.

"Don't go getting stupid on us now," Miss Practical scolded from her hidden nook in my brain. "Close that damn door and lock it. You're doing great so far, but if you managed to find a way to get here, then Bobby might find a way, too."

Nodding dumbly, I forced myself to walk back to the door and with great effort pulled it shut against the screaming wind. "There's no lock on it," I wailed, examining the simple latch that allowed the door to be opened from either side.

From the corner of my eye I glimpsed the ripped, blood-soaked sleeve of my ski jacket. My eyes followed the blood welling out of the ripped nylon to the end of my arm, then to the floor, and I stared in fascination at the sizable crimson pool growing beneath the dripping fingers of my limp right hand.

I screamed and, feeling suddenly faint, slumped to the

tile and sat there rocking slowly back and forth, cradling my bloody, injured arm with my good one. "Dan," I murmured. "I want Dan."

The relative warmth of the room, combined with the soft hum of the independently powered electric motors spinning the huge light high over my head and the distant sounds of the storm were making me incredibly sleepy.

My eyelids fluttered shut as I tried to remember why I had come to this pleasant place.

"Wake up, dammit!"

Miss Practical's shrill voice brought me instantly to my senses and I looked around, trying to decide how long I had been sitting there. Seconds? Minutes? I had no way of knowing.

I knew only that I had to get to the emergency phone in the cupola atop the lighthouse.

Clambering to my feet with the aid of my good arm, I crossed the room to the foot of the winding iron stairway and craned my neck.

Miss Romantic softly urged me up the dizzying flight of steps. "Go on. You can do it, honey."

I placed one foot on the first step, clinging tightly to the cold iron railing with my good hand. "But if I pass out up there, I'll fall," I whimpered, pulling back.

"If Bobby comes, you'll die," Miss Practical reminded me.

So I started to climb.

I don't know how much time passed before I at last reached the circular glass room at the top of that endless flight of stairs. I only know that my progress was agonizingly slow and that I had to stop several times to catch my breath. Once, when I was perhaps two-thirds of the way up, I stumbled and fell, bouncing on my tailbone down five or six sharp-edged metal steps before coming to a dazed and painful halt.

I sat huddled and shivering against the cold stone wall for another long while after the fall, drifting in and out of consciousness and softly weeping as I relived the bizarre chain of circumstances that had brought me to this unthinkable place in my life.

So weak and weary and racked with pain was I that the temptation was great to surrender to sleep and let Bobby come and find me.

In the end, though, it was not thoughts of Bobby's murderous eyes that drove me upward once more, but sweet memories of Dan's tender kisses and the loving care he had bestowed upon me.

Such love can neither be denied nor abandoned.

So I forced myself to get up and go on.

Many minutes later, I stepped into the circular room at the top of the Maidenstone Light.

Unlike the interior of the windowless stone tower below, the cupola was isolated from the full fury of the storm outside by nothing more than panes of glass. It was a frightening, claustrophobic place, a tiny lighted bubble suspended in a measureless black maelstrom of shrieking wind and racing clouds above a heaving, tortured sea.

Several feet above my head, in the center of the room, the massive Victorian brass and crystal mechanism of the beacon turned majestically on its track, its dazzling lifesaving beacon slicing like a laser through the driving rain.

Moving as quickly as I could, I made my way around the wall to the wooden desk beside the antique brass telescope and spotted the black emergency phone that I'd seen on my earlier visit.

I slumped gratefully onto the padded stool beside the desk and stared at the unusual telephone. It had no dial or keypad, only a small placard that read USCG EMERGENCY USE ONLY.

I lifted the heavy handset, praying that it was working.

There was a brief, reassuring buzz of a dial tone, and then a crisp male voice answered with the words, "Coast Guard Rescue Station, Narragansett. Seaman Kowalski speaking, sir."

"Thank God you're there!" I breathed into the mouthpiece.

Coastguardsman Kowalski sounded startled. "Ma'am, this is an emergency military line," he began . . .

"Well, Kowalski," I said a bit indignantly, "I just happen to have an emergency. I am stuck at the top of the Maidenstone Lighthouse and I need to be rescued . . ."

Kowalski hesitated. "Yes, ma'am," he replied after a moment, "I can tell where you are from the line you're calling on. What exactly is the nature of your emergency?" he inquired politely.

I started to tell him that I was being pursued by a knife-wielding madman, but I'd watched enough television to know that would probably only confuse the issue.

After all, I wasn't talking to the police and I didn't want to waste time being transferred to them or anyone else. I just wanted to be rescued—the sooner, the better—and I knew the Coast Guard could do the job. So I said, "I'm alone, injured and bleeding badly and the causeway to the island is impassable."

That was enough for Kowalski, God bless him. "Yes ma'am," he said, "stand by one . . ." I heard him excitedly conversing with somebody else, then he came back on the line. "A rescue helicopter with a paramedic onboard is being dispatched from Quonset Point Naval Air Station. They will be airborne in less than three minutes and should reach your location within fifteen minutes. Can you hold on that long?"

Feeling strangely light-headed, I smiled dopily into the phone. "Oh, yes, Kowalski." I giggled. "I can hold on for fifteen more minutes, twenty even, if I have to. I am a natural-born holder-oner."

"Ma'am?" The young coastguardsman's voice seemed to be coming to me from a great distance. I frowned and pressed the phone more tightly to my ear. "Ma'am," Kowalski sounded concerned, "have you applied direct pressure to the bleeding?"

"Direct pressure?"

"Yes, ma'am. If you press down hard on the place the bleeding is coming from, it will slow down . . . I think you might have lost a lot of blood," he added diplomatically, "because you're beginning to sound very weak."

"Mmmm," I murmured with a drunken nod, "I do feel very weak, now that you mention it. Thank you so much, Kowalski. I'll try that direct pressure."

Carefully balancing the telephone handset as if it was an incredibly heavy weight, I replaced it on its cradle. Then I hefted my bleeding arm up onto the desktop and stared at the bloody mass of nylon and shredded insulation, trying to remember what I was supposed to do.

The black emergency telephone rang.

I stared at it, wondering who on earth would be calling me here at this time of night, especially when I was having so much trouble catching my breath.

The phone rang again.

I slowly lifted a leaden hand to reach for the receiver, intending to firmly but politely tell whoever it was that I did not need any magazine subscriptions this evening, thank you very much.

I saw my hand pause in midair as the whole room started slowly revolving in perfect time with the huge lighthouse beacon.

The phone rang, again and again. Gasping for air, I

stubbornly willed my hand to continue its slow journey toward the irritating instrument.

"Don't answer that, Sue."

I rolled my eyes upward and saw Bobby standing over me, his face deathly pale.

"Kowalski is coming . . . to rescue me in his . . . helicopter," I gasped, no longer afraid.

Bobby coughed and nodded. "Yes, I know," he said. "I heard you talking with him." Then he moved away, out of my field of vision.

I frowned, trying to recall something that I knew about Bobby, something very important. But it was too hard, because I had to keep remembering to breathe. So I sighed deeply and stared down at my bloody arm instead. "God, that really . . . hurts," I moaned, looking around to see where Bobby had gone.

I saw him standing by a small metal-framed door set between two large panes of rain-streaked glass. He opened the door and a blast of icy wind roared into the small room. He briefly stuck his head outside, then beckoned to me.

"What?" I asked. Bobby's lips were forming words that I could not hear above the shrieking wind. Leaving the door standing open, he walked back to my side and bent to shout into my ear.

"The helicopter is here, Sue. It's waiting for you."

I smiled and tried to stand, but my legs felt faraway and oddly disconnected from my body. Bobby obligingly put a hand under my elbow and boosted me to my feet. Then, with his arm around my waist, he slowly walked me to the door.

I squinted out at the narrow catwalk and the howling void that lay beyond. "No!" I whispered, attempting to pull back. "I'm afraid."

Bobby wordlessly pushed me through the door, at the same moment releasing his grip on me. I lurched forward, falling to my knees against the slender safety railing. Far below I saw the familiar outline of my Volvo. Its headlights were burning brightly, illuminating the rows of giant rolling breakers that were thundering onto the black shiny rocks at the base of the lighthouse.

The sight of the car instantly brought me back to my senses. I swiveled my head around just in time to see Bobby advancing on me, his mouth twisted into an evil smile. "It will be much easier for me this way, Sue," he shouted as he grabbed the collar of my jacket and attempted to hoist me over the railing.

The myth about your entire life passing before your eyes in the final moment before death is just that, a myth. At least it was for me.

Because what flashed before my eyes in that moment, as Bobby struggled to tip my helpless body over the edge of the catwalk atop the Maidenstone Light was a crystalline image of Laura in her tastefully decorated Park Avenue office.

Sitting in her Italian leather chair, her long legs enticingly crossed in the direction of a grim-faced investigator, my fashionable shrink was clucking her pretty pink tongue and saying that the suicide of Manhattan antiques appraiser Susan Marks, while surely lamentable, did not surprise her even one little bit.

After all, Laura went on, poor, demented Susan had been acutely depressed, emotionally distraught and had of late been experiencing increasingly vivid hallucinations in which she was always reunited with her dead lover.

I cannot tell you how badly that pissed me off.

Huffing and puffing like an asthmatic in a dust storm, Bobby finally had the upper half of my body bent over the railing. He turned me around to face him, then grabbed hold of my legs and was in the process of tipping me over backward.

"Oh, my God!" I croaked, staring wide-eyed at the incredible sight just beyond his shoulder.

Startled, Bobby looked back and his flushed features turned instantly the color of dead ashes.

For floating above him, her white gown billowing softly about her slender form, was Aimee Marks. Bobby dropped me. I fell heavily onto the catwalk as my gentle spirit opened her mouth and emitted an ear-shattering scream that drove him backward with the force of a sledgehammer blow.

Bobby's icy-blue eyes rolled toward me, pleading for some explanation, as he was catapulted sharply backward and disappeared into the darkness below.

Then Aimee smiled at me and she, too, was gone.

As my eyes fluttered closed Dan's face floated above me. I felt myself smile before everything went black.

Chapter 35

I opened my eyes as a handsome young paramedic deftly slipped a needle into my good arm. He smiled, telling me it wouldn't feel any worse than a bee sting.

I couldn't seem to talk so I didn't tell him that I'm allergic to bee stings. I felt like I was at the bottom of a swirling whirlpool and wondered why I was thinking about bee stings.

My arm felt detached, like it wasn't really connected to my shoulder, but my fingers moved when I wiggled them. Your arm has to be attached to move your fingers, right? So why was it twice its normal size? And white? The idea that I had been wrapped in bandages entered my muddled brain and I heaved a sigh of relief.

Whatever the nice young man had put in the needle was making it difficult for me to keep my eyes open and as I closed them I once again saw Dan's sweet, concerned face. Why was he concerned? I felt fine.

Blessed sleep swept over me as the clattering Coast Guard helicopter lifted off Maidenstone Island.

The hospital room at Boston Medical was cold, stark and quiet. No beeps, clicks and whirrs like the ones that had filled Damon's room.

What day was it? How long had I been here?

My arm was heavy and I could move it only at the shoulder. A plaster splint kept it immobile from above my elbow all the way to my fingertips. Why was it in a cast? Had Bobby broken it?

Bobby! The horror of it all came back to me. My mind reeled at what had happened. I'd been coming to the realization that he hadn't been my knight in shining armor but I never imagined him capable of murder. Thank God for Aimee.

I no longer had anything to fear, but the anger and humiliation of having been so wrong about him made tears well in my eyes. Feeling sorry for myself, I suppose. I really did feel like an idiot.

Miss Romantic reminded me that the same thing had happened to Aimee. "Yeah," I countered, "but she was a sweet, young girl, sheltered and naive, as were all daughters of wealthy Edwardian men." Making it easy for her to be swayed and seduced by a handsome rogue. What was my excuse?

I considered myself an educated businesswoman, to some extent experienced in the ways of the world, yet I had been just as easily duped by a handsome stranger. And like Aimee had been given fair warning by friends—i.e., Damon—but had blithely refused to take heed. Just as Aimee had ignored her parents' warnings. And we'd almost come to the same end.

I sighed, saying again, *Thank God for Aimee.* I only hoped that Bobby's fall over the icy railing of the Maidenstone Lighthouse could take the place of Ned Bingham's aborted plunge and allow Aimee to move on into the Light.

A strange noise made me open my eyes and I tried to sit up but got too dizzy, collapsing back onto the bed. From my slightly elevated position I looked around the room in an effort to discover the source of the noise; that's when I saw Dan asleep in a green vinyl club chair. He looked tired and uncomfortable. The two- or three-day beard told me he'd been waiting for me to wake up. My heart swelled with the love I'd been suppressing, I couldn't help but smile.

I watched him sleep for a while, then called his name. My voice was scratchy and almost a whisper but his eyes popped open and in a single smooth motion he was sitting on the edge of the bed, my hand in his.

"How do you feel?"

"Not too badly, all things considered. How long have I been here?"

"Two days."

I could see he was restraining himself, afraid he might hurt me. I reached up and placed my hand on his cheek, brushing away a tear with my thumb. He couldn't seem to help himself and leaned down, gathering me in his arms. I felt the warmth of his tears on my neck and held him as best I could with my one good arm.

"I was afraid I'd lost you," he sobbed as he released me and sat up.

"You can't get rid of me that easily," I said as chirpily as possible.

His eyes flashed. "It's not funny, Susan, you almost died. The doctors said the cold was the only thing that kept you from bleeding to death." He paused and more quietly added, "On the helicopter it was touch and go."

I was sure that seeing his face had been a delusional vision brought on by my injuries. "You were on the helicopter?"

He dropped his eyes in embarrassment or pain, I couldn't tell. "I carried you down from the lighthouse to the chopper." He almost whispered, "I saw Aimee."

I reached out and took his hand. "It's over now, for Aimee and me."

He looked up and smiled; it was a heartbreaking smile that made the breath in my chest catch. I realized in that instant that I truly loved this man.

Our emotional reunion had drained what little energy I had and after getting multiple assurances that Damon was doing well, since Dan unequivocally refused to take me to him, I fell asleep.

I finally realized that I'd never really loved Bobby at all. As Damon had insisted, I had been in love with the idea of being in love. I had tried desperately to turn it into the real thing but had failed miserably.

Dreaming of Dan, I was glad.

He returned a few hours later, having showered and shaved, his arms filled with flowers, magazines, books and a stuffed pelican. I'd never seen a stuffed pelican before but it was very cute and Dan said it reminded him of home . . . our home. He put the flowers in my water pitcher, the magazines and books on the bedside table, and gave the pelican to me with a kiss. Then he said he had a surprise for me and left.

Within moments he wheeled a chair into the room with a boisterous Damon. Dan had convinced Alice Cahill that a meeting would be good for both of us and promised her faithfully to not let us overdo it.

I burst into tears when I saw my best friend's bruised and battered body, and the look on his face made it clear that I wasn't in much better shape. Dan pushed the wheelchair next to the bed and gave me a quick kiss, then stepped back, allowing Damon and me our time together.

I wanted to jump up and throw my arms around him but got dizzy when I sat up; with all the hardware in his legs he couldn't stand. So we had to content ourselves with holding hands and crying for each other.

When his tears were fianlly dry, Damon admonished, "You just can't do anything the easy way, can you?"

In spite of the pain, I laughed. "I'm not sure you're the one to be throwing stones."

On we went without missing a beat as though the last few days had never happened.

But they had and we all had our stories to tell.

Damon started by relating to us that he'd seen Bobby on the sidewalk in front of my apartment building and although they didn't speak Bobby knew he'd been found out and had bolted. But Damon had seen a look in his eyes that made him afraid for me. He didn't know why but was compelled to get to me when the phone service proved inadequate.

Dan pulled his chair closer to the bed to hear all the sordid details of my own encounter with my vengeful ex-lover. They were both awestruck and fearful for me by turns. Quiet throughout the telling and sorry that they hadn't been there to help me. I guess I was stronger than I'd ever imagined possible.

But now I was anxious to find out why I had seen Dan's face as I drifted in and out of consciousness.

Turned out, he had walked back to my house when his car had run out of gas, thanks to Bobby. He had arrived just as my Volvo was pulling out of the driveway, being driven by a man Dan had never seen. Terrified that I was inside the house lying injured he rushed inside and searched from the kitchen to the attic and back down. Unable to find me he ran back out into the raging storm.

After finding the carriage house open he ran after the Volvo, realizing that I must have left on the moped, and since I hadn't passed him on the street he assumed I'd gone to Maidenstone Island and followed both of us there.

Lashing wind and surf slowed him down as he ran across the causeway leading to the lighthouse. He found the steel door to the tower open and blood pooled in the entry, where I'd stopped to gain my bearings. He ran up the metal stairs unheard through the sound of the wind buffeting the building.

He reached us just as Bobby went over the railing. He saw Aimee as she watched Bobby land on the painted rocks below. She turned and smiled at me and then at Dan, before fading away into the mist that shrouded the lighthouse.

Dan rushed to my side, which was the first time I remember seeing his face and, cradling me against his chest, he carried me down the steep, winding steps to the waiting helicopter.

And now here we all were, weary but alive and well and together.

I was starting to fade and Dan could see it; he stood up, taking my hand and Damon's hand in his own, he smiled. "Okay, you two, that's enough. You both need rest." He leaned down and kissed my forehead, then took hold of Damon's wheelchair.

"I'm taking you back to your room now so you can continue to make life miserable for Alice Cahill."

Damon looked up at Dan and smiled like a cat who had just eaten a canary, then looked at me and in a stage whisper said, "Don't throw this one back, girl. He's a keeper."

Then, as Dan started to pull the chair away, Damon reached out and patted my hand. "I love you, you know."

"The feeling is mutual."

I watched as my men left the room. Sighing, I drifted off to sleep.

Chapter 36

I was grateful for the luxurious comfort of the Mercedes seats. After my confrontation with Bobby and a week in a hospital bed everything ached, not just my arm.

My tearful departure from Damon, who would remain in the hospital for another week or so, had drained a lot of my energy and I laid my head back against the soft leather seat.

Dan had graciously offered the use of the penthouse for my recuperation so I could stay near Damon and as much as I appreciated it, I really wanted to go home. Sleep in my own bed.

The house looked like one of the picture postcards they sell at the shacks along the beach every summer. With the lighthouse behind it, white puffy clouds in the azure sky, it even looked like a Freedan painting. I smiled at the thought.

My trusty Volvo sat in the driveway, no worse for the wear. While I was in the hospital Dan had brought it and the Vespa back from Maidenstone Island and closed up the house. He stopped the Mercedes behind it and looked over at me.

"Well, here we are."

"It feels like it's been months."

Weaker than I realized, I leaned heavily on him as he helped me out of the car.

"My legs feel like Jell-O."

It was all I had to say before he swept me into his arms and carried me toward the house. I'd never felt more safe and secure than at that very moment. With my injured arm in a sling I put my good arm around his neck and held tightly, resting my head on his shoulder. He kissed the top of my head.

You know the old movies where the groom carries his new bride over the threshold? That's how I felt as Dan took me into the house. I giggled.

"What's so funny?"

"Oh, nothing." I sighed.

He smiled at me with the question still in his eyes as he deposited me on the sofa in the parlor.

The first thing he did was start a fire and turn on the heater so the rest of the house would be comfortable soon.

Going out to the car to retrieve our bags Dan left me with the roaring fire melting the cold of that late-October day from my bones.

There was something different about the room but I couldn't quite put my finger on it. Then I noticed it. The painting of Aunt Ellen that I'd hung only a couple weeks before was gone. Replaced by another.

Pointing at the portrait when he came back in I queried, "What's this?"

"Homecoming present."

Aimee seemed to be smiling at us again.

"Thank you, it's wonderful." I paused. "Although I'm not sure a Victorian parlor is the appropriate place for it." I stopped short; it was as though I was channeling Aunt Ellen. Dan and I looked at each other and laughed.

"How did you ever get Greystone to give it up?"

"Trade. Years ago I did a watercolor of the club."

He sat next to me on the edge of the sofa and with a

lecherous grin said the scandalous painting reminded him of me.

"In your dreams, maybe."

"Yes," he said and kissed me. A long, passionate kiss that was so gentle I wasn't sure how it was possible. Warmth spread throughout my body and I longed for him. I pulled away slightly. He sat up suddenly.

"Did I hurt you?"

"No." Looking up at the portrait of my ancestor I demured, "But I was thinking that you might be interested in doing a comparative study."

With a huge grin, "Am I dreaming?"

With a grin of my own, "Maybe."

Dan, once again, held me in his arms and carried me upstairs. I felt like Scarlett O'Hara in *Gone With the Wind*. I sighed, burying my face in his neck.

Unable to be of much help I let Dan gently undress me and then modestly cover me with my light but warm down comforter. He slipped under it next to me and took me in his arms.

There in my captain's bed we made wonderful, unhurried love. Luxuriating in each other and the warm afterglow, I lay with my head on his shoulder, his arms around me, happier than I ever remember being.

Tenderly outlining the curve of my jaw, then with his fingers under my chin he tipped my face up to meet his and kissed my nose. I smiled, snuggling into the warmth of his embrace.

A flock of gulls flew by the window and we watched as a pelican dived into the sea, catching his evening meal.

Looking out over the top of my head Dan said, "I've been thinking that with the lawn going down to the beach in front of the house, it would make a perfect . . ." He paused a moment and I was sure he was going to say painting.

"... location for a summer wedding."

More than a little surprised I looked up at him. "Is that a proposal?"

"Could be. If it was, what would your answer be?"

Without hesitation I almost shouted, "Yes. Yes. Yes."

"Well, then I guess it is."

We kissed, then turned back to watch the sun set outlined by the casement window. The white lace curtains hung still as the sun reached the horizon and cast a wondrous glow on the Maidenstone Lighthouse standing sentinel over our love.

Author's Note

Often I'm asked how I write, what the process is. The truth of the matter is *I* don't write; we did—Michael and I. Here's a secret . . . He did most of the writing.

I lost my husband, Michael, suddenly, unexpectedly, several years ago. My happiest memories are the hours and hours we spent collaborating—whether on the business Kelly (his daughter) and I had, entertaining friends, taking care of family or writing.

Michael was a gifted writer capable of bringing the written word to life in stories like *The Man Who Loved Jane Austen* and *The Maidenstone Lighthouse*.

How these stories came about is the story of our partnership. We'd talk about new ideas . . . What if Mr. Darcy from *Pride and Prejudice* was a twenty-first-century man? What if a New England lighthouse was haunted by a girl thought to have committed suicide, but didn't?

That's how they started. We'd talk things through, then Michael would write. Sometimes I would write something, like interior descriptions or some direction I wanted the story to take, and he would make it better. I would edit and then we would go on to the next project.

Sally Smith O'Rourke was originally chosen as a pen name that incorporated my name, Sally Smith, and Michael's name, F. Michael O'Rourke; as his wife, however, it is my legal name as well. So even the name is a result of our collaboration, the collaboration of our lives.

I like to think that his spirit has been guiding me as I prepared the books alone for publication. It has kept his spirit that much more alive for me and kept his words alive for you to enjoy.